Years ago Asher Winsome almost lost his life in the jaws of a great white shark. It was the scariest moment of his life—until his four-year-old nephew is kidnapped. Called home to be with his family, who see him as the black sheep, Asher must rely on every bit of his courage if he's going to help get his nephew back. But this is not an ordinary kidnapping. And the outcome will leave Asher running for his life.

Former FBI agent Alec Banner buries himself in his work to forget everything that's missing in his life. His job, at a private company run by an old friend, locating missing children can be tough and brutal, but Alec is no stranger to working with the worst of humanity. From the minute he's called to help on the Winsome kidnapping he knows something is different.

Thrown together under such difficult circumstances Asher and Alec are drawn to each other's unrelenting courage even in the face of their fears. But a relationship begun under such impossible stress can't survive. When his job is finished Alec runs from Asher and his growing feelings, but the danger hasn't passed, in fact it has only just begun. And both men will need to be brave if they are to survive.

VALOR

Until You, Book Four

Karrie Roman

A NineStar Press Publication

Published by NineStar Press
P.O. Box 91792,
Albuquerque, New Mexico, 87199 USA.
www.ninestarpress.com

Valor

Copyright © 2019 by Karrie Roman
Cover Art by Natasha Snow Copyright © 2019

Printed in the USA
First Edition
January, 2019

Print ISBN: 978-1-949909-86-9

Also available in eBook, ISBN: 978-1-949909-85-2

Warning: This book contains sexually explicit content, which may only be suitable for mature readers, child abduction, and mentions of pedophilia and past shark attack.

Prologue

JESUS CHRIST, HE couldn't get out of that happy, fucking home quick enough. The fact he'd put a bullet between the eyes of an abusive monster less than twenty-four hours ago wasn't what had Alec Banner's heart aching, his breath stuttering, and his legs itching to run. No, he'd had little trouble doing that.

What had him fleeing from the company of a man he considered his best friend, and three other men who'd become very important to him, had been all the fucking love wafting around the room—infecting everyone but him.

Alec had been friends with Ben Cronin for well over a decade. Though they'd lost contact for a few years, they'd reconnected close to a year ago. These days, he spent plenty of time with Ben. They'd been working together for several months now, locating missing and abducted children. Working at Chasing Hope was grueling, but very rewarding. Alec didn't regret leaving the FBI to join Ben's company at all.

It wasn't Ben he was fleeing, though. Nor was it Ben's partner. Ethan was a fucking dreamboat, but Ben was the lucky asshole who'd snagged his heart. Alec had no problem admitting he had a tiny crush on Ethan. Would it ever cause trouble between him and Ben? Fuck no, because no matter what, there was no way Alec would ever do anything about it. Alec Banner had a lot of faults, but disloyalty wasn't one of them. He'd pine away for Ethan like a miserable bastard until he—hopefully—found a dreamboat of his own to love.

No, despite his messy feelings, the reason Alec was fleeing Ben's brother's house before he completely fucking lost it was because he couldn't stand to see how happy the two couples there were. He'd witnessed the love between Ben and Ethan for months, and despite them going through a really rough time, they'd been going through it together. Alec had seen firsthand what it should be like to have a real partner. Someone to love, to care about. Someone who'd have your back no matter what.

Instead, he was expected to fucking sit back and watch how happy Ben's brother, Cameron, and his lover, Zach, were? He couldn't do it. Selfish maybe, but he was nearly forty years old and he'd had one boyfriend who'd lasted six months and a nine-month relationship with a woman, which had been explosive but ultimately fizzled out because she wouldn't walk down the aisle with him. Her refusal had hurt like hell at the time, but looking back on it, years later, he was so glad Heather had rejected him. He was pretty sure he'd be a divorced father of three by now if she hadn't.

Here was Zach, who was twenty-fucking-two and had found the love of his life in Cameron, and try as he might, Alec couldn't shake the jealousy. He wanted that; he wanted what those men had.

There was only one thing Alec knew of to help when life went to shit, and that was work. He never turned to the bottle or eating his feelings when he was miserable, like some people did. Alec's choice of pick-me-up was to tuck his head down and his ass up and get stuck into as much work as possible.

He pulled out his phone and thumbed through his contacts. Ryan Lowe was near the top of his list. Ryan was the brains and bank behind Chasing Hope, the company Alec worked for locating missing kids. Ryan had told Alec earlier he may have a job for him, and as he hit the call button he hoped to god Ryan did. Alec desperately needed something to keep him busy.

"Alec, how'd it go?" Ryan answered without preamble.

Alec knew Ryan would have heard from Ben or Ethan that they'd rescued Zach from Cameron's crazy ex, but he wasn't exactly sure if they'd have told him how far they'd gone, so he offered only a concise answer. "Good. All done. What else have you got for me?"

"Well, I'm sure we've got a case, but I'm waiting to hear back. I've already got Jacey putting a file together for you. Little boy, four, was taken this morning from his local park. The family is affluent and well-known in their community. The mother is certain there'll be a ransom demand. She wants the cops called, but she's getting pushback from her husband and the in-laws. I think you should head out to them ASAP, see what you think and be ready to act."

His phone beeped as Ryan spoke, likely to signal the arrival of the file from Jacey. She was an absolute genius with technology, and he expected she'd have provided him with information, not only about the immediate family but the extended one, including friends, staff, and coworkers. Knowing Jacey, he'd even get information on the people the parents went to kindergarten with. She'd have dug up whatever dirt there was to find in a short amount of time, and no doubt she'd already be digging through old data to find even more.

"Got it. Where am I headed?"

"Del Mar. Get a flight to San Diego. I'll get a hotel booked for you in Del Mar and text the details."

"On my way."

"Hey...you okay, Alec?"

Ryan was a sweetheart, tender and caring and far too innocent for this line of work. And yet he'd dragged himself into the misery of missing kids because he wanted to help—and found himself in a position where he could. He was one of the good guys, but Alec worried how it would all affect him. Alec had been dealing with scum for years; he knew the horror stories, and he'd hardened his heart to them, but Ryan? Alec worried about him.

"Tired, that's all. I'm fine, Ryan, but thanks for caring."

They exchanged a few niceties regarding Ryan and his partner, Lucas. Alec repeated several more times that he was, in fact, all right, despite the events of the past twenty-four hours, when Ryan asked before hanging up.

Alec made his way to the airport and settled in to wait for his flight. Getting in and out of Cody, Wyoming, wasn't always easy. He didn't mind curling up on one of the uncomfortable chairs common to most airports while he waited, though. He pulled out his tablet and opened the file Jacey had sent him.

The Winsome family of Del Mar wasn't simply affluent, they were filthy fucking rich. The patriarch was one Edmund Winsome, who was a founding partner of one of the biggest law firms in Southern California. Matriarch Phyllis Winsome had brought her family's considerable wealth to the marriage and together they had built a formidable empire for their two sons. From the images Jacey sent, they were an austere-looking couple who screamed wealth from every perfectly coiffed hair on their heads.

Oldest son—and father of the missing boy—Kane Winsome worked for his father's firm. He hadn't quite made partner yet, but from what Alec read, he was well on his way. Alec found the photo Jacey had sent and studied the image of Kane Winsome. He was a younger version of his father.

Light-brown hair was cut to within an inch of its life and was gelled into what was probably the latest style, steel-gray eyes glared at the lens, and thin lips pursed to show their impatience with whomever had taken the photo. Alec tried not to judge a book by its cover, but if he had to, then the title would be *Pride and Prejudice*. A more modern day Fitzwilliam Darcy he couldn't imagine finding.

Kane's wife, Madeline, came from a wealthy family herself, though not on the scale of the Winsome's wealth. She worked as a florist and could not look more opposite to her husband if she tried. She had a mane of flowing, dark, almost black hair that perfectly matched her dark skin. Her eyes were a deep brown but were lit by what Alec suspected was her natural *joie de vivre*. It was hard to tell from a photo, but she looked petite. Alec had no doubt she would be a lioness, though, when it came to her loved ones. While her husband glared and pouted at the camera, Madeline Winsome laughed and flirted with it.

He scrolled to another image—this one of Kane and Madeline together each holding hands with a toddling child he assumed to be the missing Jack. The photo must be at least a year old given that Jack was now four. The family looked—happy. Gone was Kane's stern face, replaced with a beaming smile, his gaze fixed on his son. Madeline looked the same as in the solo photo as she, too, stared at her son. The little boy was adorable. His smile matched his parents' as he seemed to be frozen in an attempt to take an ungainly step. The photo captured more than a simple image of family—it portrayed love, purely and simply.

Alec would read the file more thoroughly on the plane and over the days to come, but for now, he only wanted to get a feel for this family. He couldn't even begin to imagine the hell they must be going through.

Movement around him alerted him to the fact that his flight was boarding. Alec took his place in line, greeting the staff politely as always. He was a firm believer in catching more flies with honey than vinegar, and a pleasant exchange with airline staff had him either sitting in an exit row or with an extra beverage more times than he cared to remember.

He made his way to his seat, delighted to see an almost empty flight. With luck, the two seats beside him would remain vacant so he might be able to get a couple of hours sleep. He settled in and took another look at the files while he waited for takeoff.

Next in the file was the second son, Kane's brother. As Alec skimmed his bio, he realized instantly that Asher Winsome was the black sheep of the family. He too had studied law, as his father and brother had, but Asher's most recent job was listed as marine photographer, location—varied. Interesting.

Alec scrolled to the attached photograph, his eyes popping like some kind of cartoon character. Jesus Christ, he'd never seen anyone more gorgeous. Asher Winsome was drop-dead stunning. The photo wasn't even a good one, so he could only imagine how devastating the man would be in real life. His hair was a few shades darker than his brother's, and he wore it long, just scraping his shoulders. His gray eyes were lighter than Kane's. Alec couldn't wait to see them in person to find out if they were as silver as they appeared in the photo. His smile was crooked and shy; his entire demeanor coy. Alec was insanely jealous of whoever had taken the photo and coaxed that look out of the man.

He knew he'd sat there staring too long when the flight attendant had to actually tap his arm to get him to prepare for takeoff. He shut down his tablet and fastened his seat belt. He leaned his head against the fuselage, letting his eyes drift shut. Glimmering gray eyes and a crooked smile followed him into sleep.

Chapter One

ALEC

Alec Banner stood at the massive oak door, with his ear pressed against the wood, and listened. There was plenty of yelling going on behind it, but the words were muffled. He moved to the glass paneling to the side. It afforded much better acoustics for his eavesdropping on the family.

Tempers were usually frayed in situations where a child was missing, but he'd never encountered the level of rage and viciousness coming from the other side of the front door of the Winsome mansion this early in a child abduction case. Normally, the family members of the missing child initially clung to each other, desperate for some comfort and reprieve from the waking nightmare they were living. The Winsomes, however, sounded as though they were about to tear each other to pieces.

He refrained from knocking even though he was certain the occupants were well aware of his arrival. There were enough cameras around the entrance to the Winsome estate to make it difficult for even the most accomplished cat burglar to sneak through. Instead, he did his best to hear the argument still raging behind closed doors. He couldn't make out much but got the general gist that someone wanted to contact the police and was fighting hard for the call to be made.

Time was coming up on twelve hours since Jack Winsome had been stolen, literally out of the arms of his nanny, at the local park. He'd received a call from Ryan as soon as he'd landed in San Diego, confirming Madeline and Kane wanted him out at the family estate as soon as possible to help them get their son back.

The battle inside wasn't easing up, but Alec had heard enough. Their arguing was wasting time better spent on finding little Jack. He pressed the doorbell and waited. The noise from inside ceased immediately, replaced by quick steps approaching from the other side. When the large door swung open, he stood face-to-face with Kane Winsome.

The photos he'd been sent were all recent, within the last two years, and yet the Kane who stood before him seemed to have aged by at least a decade. His hair was messy, his eyes red-rimmed and swollen, and his skin was pale. In short, Kane looked as though he was a small, shaky step away from the grave.

"Alec Banner?"

Alec put his hand forward and received an extremely weak shake from Kane. The man seemed to be using every bit of energy he had for the sole purpose of keeping on his feet. "Yes. You must be Kane Winsome."

Kane nodded and ushered him in. He quickly glanced around the entryway, taking in as much detail as possible. The ceiling here was two stories, making the second-floor landing easily visible. The staircase was covered in a lush, cream carpet and was met with a complementary cream tiled foyer. Several large pots added a touch of greenery to the otherwise muted color scheme of whites and beiges. To the left, Alec noted a formal room that continued the natural coloring throughout, with cream leather sofas and the same carpet as the staircase. A splash of color was added with a handful of throw pillows and a mosaic-tiled coffee table. To his right, the tiled floor continued into a far less formal-looking living area. Though the colors remained neutral, this room was far more colorful and casual than the formal room.

"Thank you for coming, Mr. Banner. Please follow me," Kane said, leading Alec through to the sitting room. "This is my wife, Madeline."

Madeline Winsome, in contrast to her husband, looked ready to go several rounds with Rocky Balboa. Her hair was wild, and she wore not a scrap of makeup, but the woman looked fierce. She *was* the lioness preparing to protect her cub as he'd imagined.

"Thank god. Alec, let's dispense with niceties. I'm Maddy, and I'll call you Alec. Please tell my in-laws we need to call the police. We've been told not to, but I still think they need to be called. I won't allow anything to jeopardize my son." Maddy finished breathlessly.

Alec was taken aback by mini-tornado Madeline Winsome—and the news they'd heard from the kidnappers. Either Ryan had forgotten to mention that—unlikely—or Ryan hadn't been told. "You've heard from them?"

"Yes. They sent me a text immediately after taking my son. It simply said 'No cops.' So I was okay not calling them at the start, but we haven't heard from the kidnappers since then, and I think it's way past time now to call." Even though she was talking to him, Maddy glared at her father-in-law as she spoke.

"Why didn't you tell Ryan about the text when you called for our services? We have a tech wiz who could have been working on tracing the text for the last several hours." Alec did his best to not sound too accusatory. People in the Winsomes' position did irrational and illogical things all the time; such was the nature of their distress. But, depending on the level of sophistication of the kidnappers, Jacey might have been able to trace them, and this could have all been over by now.

"That was me." Edmund Winsome's voice was as powerful as he'd expect from someone in his position.

Alec turned and shook Edmund's outstretched hand. "Mr. Winsome." He nodded to the man. Meeting people under these circumstances was always difficult. Social niceties such as saying "good to meet you" could hardly be used. Alec preferred to get straight to the point. A no-nonsense approach gave the family confidence and set the tone for how Alec would handle the situation. "Can you tell me why you withheld that information?"

"Let me get one thing straight, Mr. Banner. I don't want the police called. I only allowed Madeline to call you as a concession. The text message was clear and we're more than happy to pay the money. My son and daughter-in-law have wanted them called in since Emily came home battered and hysterical, telling us Jack had been taken. You're only here in deference to my son. But my patience is wearing thin. It's been almost twelve hours, and no further contact has been made."

Alec watched Edmund as he spoke. The man's chest puffed up and his face got redder as he continued. A quick glance also showed the utter disdain with which Maddy viewed her father-in-law's opinion. Frankly, Alec was surprised Maddy hadn't gone ahead and called the cops, regardless of Edmund's wishes.

Phyllis Winsome's hand closed gently over her husband's forearm and squeezed. The man deflated instantly, allowing Alec a glimpse of the pain behind the bluff and bluster. Phyllis looked at him intensely with nothing but judgment in her sharp eyes. Whatever she saw in him, she must obviously approve, because Alec got the feeling, if she didn't, he'd have been shown the door immediately.

"Mr. Banner, thank you for coming. You must forgive us as we are all under a lot of strain right now, and to be honest, not one of us knows how to handle this situation. Your guidance and expertise would be much appreciated." Phyllis Winsome spoke with the barest hint of a leftover Southern accent and with impeccable pronunciation and manners. "Let's all take a seat. Maddy, dear, why don't you go get Emily so Mr. Banner can speak to her?"

Alec followed Phyllis to the sofa, and though she gestured for him to sit, he shook her off and remained standing. If he was going to help little Jack, there could be no more lies and none of the manipulations he suspected this family was so good at.

Maddy left the room immediately after receiving her orders from the matriarch. The men sat as soon as Phyllis took her seat, and Alec was left with the distinct impression this little family was governed with the iron fist of its queen.

Despite the viciousness he'd listened to through the door only moments ago, the family had officially closed ranks. They had all expressed their opinions, but they'd used their public facades with him to do it—the shouting was over for now.

"Before Maddy returns, please tell us, Mr. Banner, is it your recommendation the police are called in?"

"Mother, we agreed—"

"Hush now, Kane. We've all had our say, so it's time to get the opinion of an expert." Phyllis turned her eyes, gray like her son's, to Alec, her gaze piercing with its intensity.

"My recommendation would be to call the police. When the call comes from the kidnappers, it is up to you how you handle it, but the police can be investigating in parallel with whatever you decide to do regarding paying a ransom. I'm sure you've all heard the first twenty-four hours are crucial when somebody goes missing. The unfortunate statistic is that if the missing person isn't located within that time the chances are high they are already dead or long gone and out of reach." Alec looked around. His words were harsh and difficult to hear, but the family needed to know. They'd already lost too much time.

"I want to get Jacey working on the text message Madeline received immediately, regardless of whether or not you call in the police. She's the best at what she does, and the advantage with her is we won't need to wait for warrants or official approval. Our goal is to get Jack back, whatever it takes."

Alec looked up as Maddy approached with a younger woman in tow. The other woman, probably in her early twenties, was extremely petite. Her hair was in disarray as though she'd just woken up. Bruising was coming to life on her face and upper arms. The girl looked terrified.

"I'll get Maddy's phone," Kane offered as he stood and walked out of the room. Maddy and Emily took the seat he'd vacated, with Emily practically curling into the older woman. Whatever had taken place had understandably left Emily shaken.

"Emily, this is Alec Banner. He used to work for the FBI. He's going to help us get Jack back."

Alec kneeled in front of the woman, bringing himself to eye level but keeping a safe distance so he didn't spook her. "Hi, Emily. Do you think you could tell me exactly what happened this morning?"

Her eyes were already glistening with tears, but a look of determination changed her expression. Whatever else she may be, Emily obviously cared about her charge and was going to do what she could to help get him back.

"Um...well, Jack and I walked to the park as usual. We'd been there about half an hour when I noticed two men turn up with no children. It's a children's playground, so I was immediately wary. I kept my eye on them."

"Could you give us a description of them?"

"In general terms, yes, but I never got a clear look at their faces. They had ball caps pulled low. They were both similar height. I'd say maybe a little under six foot. One was solid but not too muscular and the other was on the slender side. The slender one had long, mousy brown hair curling out from under his cap. The other one I think had a buzz cut because I couldn't see any hair poking out. They were both Caucasians. Nothing remarkable about either of them, and they never spoke." Emily looked up at him and waited.

"That's good. Everything helps," he encouraged. She was young but had given an excellent description. "What happened? How did they get Jack?"

"I wasn't comfortable with them there, so I wanted to leave. A few other people had already left, and I didn't want to be there alone with them, so I got Jack and started walking away. I knew...as soon as I heard noise behind me, I knew what was happening. But there were two of them and one grabbed me from behind and threw me to the ground while the other pulled Jack away from me. I ran after them but I couldn't—" Emily wrestled with her tears, and Maddy leaned in to comfort her.

How long would it be before they started blaming Emily? Unfortunately, a natural part of the process, when a child was taken, was to start blaming the person who had been responsible for them at the time it happened.

As he looked around the room, he noticed all eyes were now teary, even stoic Mrs. Winsome. This poor family. No matter how many times he witnessed it, he'd never get used to the pain suffered by people who'd had a child taken.

"Alec, here's Maddy's phone." Kane handed over the latest iPhone and immediately took the seat beside his wife. He comforted her as she continued to try to console Emily. Kane turned and looked at Alec. "Tell us what to do. Whatever you think we should do, we'll do. Whatever it takes."

"Right now I'm going to call Jacey and get her working on the text message. Then we're all going to sit and make a plan—including getting the police involved." Alec didn't wait for an answer as he turned on his heel and left the room, heading for the foyer.

Jacey answered on the second ring in her usual cheery manner. "Hey, Alec, my favorite ex-fed who came to see the light. How can I help?"

"Hey, Jacey. You really should try to cheer up a bit, ya know." Alec winked even though Jacey couldn't see him. She was one of those very rare people who brought out the goofball in him. "I've got Madeline Winsome's phone. She got a text message right after Jack was taken, and we think it could be from the kidnappers. Can you see what you can do?"

"Of course. I need her phone number, phone company she's with, and for you to forward the message to me."

As Alec began giving Jacey the information, the front door opened behind him. Alec turned and was suddenly face-to-face with Asher Winsome. Oh, he'd been so right; Asher's photo hadn't done him justice at all. The man was fucking breathtaking. Alec had fallen in lust at first sight many times, but Jesus Christ, this man was utter perfection.

Asher stood about the same height as his own six-foot-one, but he was a little broader across his chest, which tapered to a narrow waist and sensational-looking legs. His wavy, sun-bleached, brown hair grazed his shoulders, and his jaw was covered in light stubble. His light gray—almost silver—eyes never flinched as he watched Alec watching him. Alec's dick stirred under the delicious scrutiny.

"Hey, you're new," Asher drawled, and Alec's cock hardened even more from the husky tone. *Fuck.* There was nothing but trouble there, but damn if Alec didn't love a bit of mischief.

Chapter Two

ASHER

Well this wasn't exactly what he'd expected when he set foot inside his parents' house for the first time in close to three years. He didn't know who the man was, but god, he wanted to find out all about him. Normally he'd be flirting his pants off by now, but panic for his nephew and his frantic need to find out what the hell was going on was an absolute wet blanket to his libido.

Asher watched as the gorgeous man finished his call, his gaze never leaving Asher, even as Asher continued to stare at the magnificent creature. The man was tall and well-built with long, long legs—a runner's body. His ginger hair was a spiky mess and his cherry-red lips were thin and scarred. The man had beautiful, intelligent hazel eyes. Asher wanted to lean in closer to see all the flecks of color in them. And to top off all the visual pleasure, the man's scent was a heavenly mix of cinnamon and sweat.

When the stranger finished his call, he extended his hand causing Asher to jump at the chance to actually touch him.

"I'm Alec Banner. I've been called in to help find your nephew."

So Alec Banner knew who he was. He'd either done his research, or his parents had mentioned him—and he couldn't imagine them ever doing that. "Asher Winsome. Are you with the police?"

"No. I work for a company called Chasing Hope. We specialize in locating missing children. Your sister-in-law called us."

"How is Maddy?" Out of the whole family, his brother included, Maddy was the only one he really got along well with. She was the only one who ever bothered to try to understand him. His parents had written him off years ago and strangely it hadn't been because of his sexuality. They'd taken the news he was gay with surprising equanimity. It had been his announcement that he was not going to pursue a career in law that had damaged his standing in his parents' eyes.

"She's holding up. She's a fierce lady. Your brother doesn't look too good, though. I'd be more worried about him."

Handsome and straightforward. The more Alec Banner talked, the more Asher was impressed by him. "Do you know anything yet?"

"Why don't you come through and see your family? We were about to start planning our next steps."

"I don't know how much you know about my family, Mr. Banner, but apart from Maddy, I won't have a warm reception."

Alec watched him a moment, and then a small smile curved his lips. "It's Alec, and I'll be honest with you, Asher, I kind of expected that. However, your family politics don't concern me at all, other than how they may affect getting Jack home."

"Are you always like this?"

"An asshole or honest?" Alec's smile grew, and it looked damn good on him.

Asher laughed—inappropriate, maybe, but irrepressible. Alec Banner ticked boxes Asher didn't even know he had. "I'm guessing both."

"Then, yes, I am. But I'm good at what I do, and so are the people I work with. I make no guarantees, but I'll do whatever I have to do to bring your nephew back."

"Is that a good enough guarantee for you, Asher, or should we waste more time making sure the ex-FBI agent is good enough for *you*?"

"Hi, Dad." Asher had been so distracted by Alec he hadn't even heard his father approach or felt the cold shiver up his spine the man usually gave him. Maybe he was being a little dramatic about the cold shiver but...

"How are you holding up?" Regardless of his feelings for the man, not even he would go after his father when his only grandchild had just been stolen.

"Now isn't the time for breaking down, Asher. As Mr. Banner said, it is the time for us to come together and plan." His father turned on his heel and walked back into the living room. It was—or had been the last time he was here—the nicest room in the entire mansion and also the only one Maddy had been allowed to decorate when his parents had convinced his brother that he and Maddy should move in so his parents could help out when Jack had come along. Of course his parents' answer to helping out had been to hire a plethora of staff to do everything short of breastfeeding the baby—something he was sure they would have done if they could have.

Asher followed behind his father, the cold chill he usually experienced around his parents overshadowed by the comforting warmth of Alec walking beside him. The sensational scent wafting all around Alec was making it damn hard for Asher to keep his mind off what he and Alec could do together.

"Asher!" Maddy called and ran to him, throwing herself into his arms. Her whole body trembled, and his heart broke for the pain she and his brother must be enduring.

He held her in his arms, rocking her gently as his gaze sought out his brother. Kane was super intelligent, but he'd never had much of a backbone. Asher knew he hated being a lawyer and hated living at their parents' home, but Kane had been unable to say no to either. Kane put on an excellent public show, but the truth was he was incapable of standing up to either of his parents.

Despite what he saw as his brother's weakness of character, he loved him fiercely and knew Madeline did as well. The evidence that his son's kidnapping was breaking his brother's already fragile spirit was clear in Kane's haggard appearance and haunted eyes. When this shit was over, he was going to fight like hell to get Kane out from under the Winsome thumb.

Asher put Maddy gently back on her feet and walked toward his brother. They'd never really been ones for affection, but he scooped him into his arms and held on tight. The shaking in Kane's body was so noticeable he thought he must be literally holding his brother together.

"Hey, Kane. I'm so sorry, man. What can I do?" His brother's breath hitched, and he heard the barest whimper in his ear as Kane fought to hold himself together. They may not be the best of friends, but it hurt like hell to see the man so broken.

"I don't know. I don't know what to do. We've got a man here. He…I think he's going to take care of it," Kane murmured.

"Yeah. I met him. He seems like a take-charge kind of guy. I'm sure he knows what he's doing, but what can I do?"

"Just being here helps," Kane whispered. They both knew their parents scorned any kind of affection or sentiment.

"I'm glad. I wouldn't be anywhere else." Asher slapped his brother's back in the manly, not-getting-too-close, kind of way and stepped back. "Mother," he simply stated as he looked over at his mom, who sat perched on the sofa like an ice queen on her throne. He knew a hug or kiss would be unwelcome, even at a time such as this.

"Asher. You're looking...tanned." Well, her greeting was better than last time when she'd said he looked like a pot-addled hobo. She must be putting on her gracious manners for the sake of their guest.

Speaking of...he looked around and spotted Alec leaning on the wall, arms folded and watching the Winsome family dynamics with unconcealed interest. Actually, Alec's gaze was fixed intently on him, and it did crazy things to his insides. *Damn it.* Talk about bad timing.

The room fell into silence, and Asher didn't know what to do. At the best of times being around his family was awkward, but he had no clue what to do or say now, nor it seemed, did anyone else in the room.

"Right. Let's get to business," Alec broke the silence and further stamped his authority on the situation.

Asher moved to sit beside his brother, Maddy perched on the arm of the sofa next to her husband, and his father and mother sat side by side. There was a younger woman curled up on an armchair, and he suspected she was the nanny. Asher was torn between being angry at her for letting them take his nephew and feeling miserable for the trauma she'd suffered—and the guilt she must be feeling.

Alec remained standing, making it suddenly seem as though they were about to be interrogated. Such was Alec's presence, even his father was relatively subdued. Asher almost wanted to see Alec and his mother go toe-to-toe; he suspected it would be a confrontation worth witnessing.

"Okay. Jacey is working on the text message. Best outcome is she can trace the phone it came from or at least get a name. Realistic outcome is it will be a burner phone and give us nothing. I've also got Jacey organizing traces on all your phones, so when whoever has Jack calls, we may be able to pinpoint their location. It really all depends on how sophisticated these people are. This could be a professional operation or it may be someone with a grudge against your family." Alec's voice commanded the room, and Asher's body was definitely taking notice. He'd never been this instantly attracted to someone, and it both scared and thrilled him.

Asher glanced immediately at his father. If anyone was capable of achieving a grudge, it was his father. He was vicious in the courtroom, and his wins far outweighed his losses. There was bound to be hurt feelings out there but enough to do something like this to a child?

"Mr. Winsome, Kane, can either of you think of anybody from your professional world who may be looking for a bit of payback? Disgruntled ex-employees, clients, adversaries. Anyone along those lines."

Kane shook his head while his father answered, "No one specifically off the top of my head. I can think about it and let you know if anyone comes to mind, but I'm a defense attorney, so someone is always pissed off at me. I've had threats and some unfortunate conflicts in the past but nothing like this."

His father glanced over at Kane, who stood silently, his face pale, shoulders hunched. Asher understood what Alec had meant about him barely hanging in there. His brother's fragile demeanor was enough for him to worry about his brother too.

"Kane, is there anyone you can think of?" Maddy asked softly.

"No one specific but I'll think about it too."

"What about you, Mrs. Winsome? Is there anybody in your life who could be a concern?"

"I don't work, Mr. Banner." His mother's reply was clipped.

Asher had seen many people wilt under his mother's imperious manner before, but it seemed to bounce right off Alec Banner. "I'm aware, ma'am. Surely there are people in your life, though? I know you do charity work, organizing galas and the like—"

"Generally speaking, Mr. Banner, people who I work with organizing charity events tend not to be in the business of stealing young children from off the street."

"You know I've been doing this a long time, ma'am, and something I've learned is people will always shock the hell out of you. I don't rule anyone out no matter what they do, who they are, what color their skin is, or how much money is in their bank account. If I'm going to help get your grandson home, I need complete honesty from all of you. Now is the time to let me know if there are any angry lovers I should know about or any skeletons in your closets. I'm not here to judge, and I couldn't care less what you've all done in the past. The only one I care about is Jack and getting him home safely." Alec looked at each person in the room as he spoke.

Did everyone else feel as chastised as he did—and Asher didn't even think he'd done anything wrong. He spared a glance at his mother and was relieved to see from her downturned gaze, and the pallor of her skin tone, she had certainly felt censured by Alec's speech.

"Maddy, Kane, my best advice to you right now is to call the police. You need to get them involved immediately. While you're interviewing with them, I want you all to think if there is anyone in your lives who you might have even the slightest suspicion about. Don't dismiss gut feelings. We've got Jacey looking into the people around you for any secrets they may have kept from you, but if we can narrow down the list, it would be a big help."

Maddy was on her feet, pulling Kane with her before Alec had even finished speaking. She had Kane's phone out of his pocket and in her hand in seconds, turning her back on them while she made the call. His parents were quiet but didn't look terribly impressed.

"I'm going to step outside for a while. There are a couple of things I want to look into, and it'll give you all a chance to think." Alec walked out through the sliding glass doors at the back of the room, Asher's gaze following his perfect body as he went. As fabulous as the sight was, it wasn't doing much to alleviate the anger burning inside him.

"You didn't call the cops?" Asher accused as soon as Alec left the room.

"Maddy received a text message telling us not to."

"Jesus, Dad. You always call the cops. The bastards have got what...? A twelve-hour head start now." Asher tried to keep his voice low so he didn't disturb Maddy as she made her call.

"We did what we thought best, Asher."

Asher was thoroughly disgusted with his parents. He suspected the reason they hadn't called the cops was more about stopping any scandal than the kidnappers' threat. Mr. and Mrs. Winsome, doyens of San Diego high society, had hoped they'd be able to pay off the kidnappers and keep the whole saga quiet.

He was furious and needed to cool off—literally. He stood and threw a glare his parents' way before storming out after Alec.

Alec was nowhere to be seen as he approached the pool, and though he was disappointed, he needed the cool water more. He slipped his shirt over his head and slid his shorts down his legs, tossing his shoes off as he went. He walked to the edge of the pool in his boxers and dove in.

The water immediately cooled his heated skin but did little to ease his anger. He'd known what his parents were like for years, but this really went too far. He never thought they'd put their image above their grandson. He had to get his brother away from them.

Asher ducked and splashed in the water. He liked swimming laps but his soul needed levity right now, and playing in the pool was much better for that.

"You really love the water, huh?"

Alec's voice came out of the shadows, and Asher turned to find him sitting in one of the patio chairs with his elbows on his knees and his chin resting on his hands. He was staring intently at him, making a little thrill start fluttering away in his stomach again.

"Always have," Asher replied.

"Is that why the marine photography?"

"You have done your research."

Alec smirked and sat taller in his seat. "I just read it. Jacey did all the work."

Asher swam to the edge and levered himself out of the water. He moved closer to where Alec sat. A satisfied grin spreading on his face when he caught the other man looking at his package as he approached. He was semihard from simply being in his presence so wasn't too worried about the cold water making him...less than impressive. He should have been a little embarrassed about his Batman boxers, but he'd long ago learned not to care about trivial stuff such as wearing nerdy underwear.

Asher knew the instant Alec noticed the scarring on his thigh. His eyes widened and he looked up at Asher with the same horror most people did.

"It was a great white. Didn't even see it coming; though they reckon from the bite and the tooth they found in my thigh, she must have been about a twelve-footer. How the hell I didn't see the beast I don't know. Didn't like the taste of me, thankfully, because she took a nibble and then spat me out." Asher rubbed at his wasted thigh. He was lucky he still had his leg.

"You got bit by a shark and you're still a marine photographer?"

"Actually, I specialize in shark photography." Asher winked. He couldn't help himself; Alec made him all flirty.

"Jesus. That's…"

"Crazy? Stupid?" Asher suggested.

"Actually I was going to say amazing, courageous."

Asher preened pathetically under Alec's praise, his spine straightening and his chest puffing up, but like every reaction he had around the man, his body didn't care if his brain thought he was being foolish.

"I don't know about that, but people have car accidents and get back in cars all the time. Sharks aren't evil. She didn't want to hurt me; she was only looking for her dinner."

"You still love the sharks?"

"Of course. They're magnificent animals. Maybe I'll show you one day." Asher was surprised by his boldness, but he couldn't turn his back on someone like Alec Banner.

"Me? In the ocean with *Jaws*? I'm not sure I'm brave enough."

"Don't get Asher started on *Jaws*, Alec. You'll be hours listening to how that movie single-handedly demonized sharks for generations." Kane sounded better than he had since he arrived. Asher was glad to hear a bit of strength returning to his brother's voice. "Police are here," Kane finished and turned to go back inside.

"Shall we?" Asher asked.

"Lets. I'm sorry if I was harsh on your family before, Asher."

"Don't be. I'm with you all the way. The only thing that matters is getting Jack home."

Their eyes met, and Asher watched as Alec searched his. He didn't know what he found, but a faint smile touched his lips. "Glad you're on board. We'll get it done, Asher."

Alec slapped his shoulder as he passed. Asher relished the buzz on his skin from the brief touch.

"I hope so," Asher whispered, his heart aching for little Jack.

Chapter Three

ALEC

By the time he'd left the Winsomes to their grief last night, Alec had been more than happy to get the hell out of there.

The cops who'd turned up had been great. They'd been thorough in their questioning, leaving Alec with the impression they were the proactive type who wouldn't sit back and hope clues would easily fall into their laps. And they didn't seem to mind he had been called in by the family; in fact, they seemed quite open to working with him. Turf wars between people supposedly working for the same goal never sat well with him—and he'd seen it a lot. To him, that behavior was nothing but useless posturing and a waste of precious time.

The officers also got bonus points for giving the elder Winsomes hell about not calling them in sooner.

Despite not getting back to his hotel until a little after two this morning, Alec hadn't been able to sleep in. Years in the military and long hours at the FBI had taken care of any possibility of sleeping much past dawn. Though it was still early, he pulled on some boxers and his running shorts and slid his feet into his shoes—the temperature already hot enough not to bother with a shirt. He took a quick look at Google Maps and then set out for his run.

Running was not only his bliss but his thinking space. The fresh air, open space, and the pounding of his feet grounded him and cut through the bullshit in his mind. He'd solved plenty of cases in the middle of a five-mile run.

As he jogged along the empty footpath, he thought about the Winsome family. They were evidence the saying about money not buying happiness was true. Alec could read people well enough to know that even without the kidnapping nightmare those people were a miserable bunch.

The exception was Asher. As soon as he let himself think about the handsome youngest son, the man's face popped into his head and wouldn't fucking leave. Those silver-gray eyes and glorious hair...perfection. His wet body as he'd dragged himself out of the pool, the streaks of water trailing over the hard planes of his toned abs—and those fucking Batman boxers. *Jesus.* Not to mention the thing with the shark. He'd skimmed over the attack in the file, but to be confronted by the evidence of what the shark had done to him had been shocking. Give him bullets to dodge over a set of fucking teeth coming for him any day of the week. Asher must have nerves of steel to get back in the water after his attack.

Alec tried to push thoughts of Asher from his mind. He concentrated on savoring the burn of his muscles as he pushed himself to quicken his speed and did his best to focus on the case. The problem was he didn't have much of anything to go on. Something felt off about it all, leaving Alec to suspect this wasn't an average kidnapping—if there was such a thing. He'd bet his left kidney this was a personal grudge, some kind of payback. Revenge as a motive could either be bad or real good news.

On one hand, it may be whoever took Jack wanted one particular member of the Winsome family to suffer for a little while before they returned the boy unharmed. Or, on the other hand, they could want the Winsomes to suffer for, well, the rest of their lives, if they killed Jack. Either way, Alec didn't think a ransom was the motivator here. Greedy people would have called for their money by now.

Over the thump of music coming through his earbuds, the message tone from his cell sounded. He glanced at his watch and saw it was from Jacey. He'd left instructions for him to be called immediately if a ransom demand came through, but a quick scroll through the message told him she was letting him know she'd arrived in San Diego.

He turned and headed back toward his hotel. He'd be spending the day with Jacey, going through whatever dirt she had found on anyone connected to the Winsomes and then choosing likely suspects to focus on. Unless, of course, the kidnappers made contact, and then everything would change.

By the time he made it back to his room and showered, Jacey still hadn't arrived at the hotel. Given the drive time from the airport, he expected she'd probably be another fifteen minutes or more. He walked through his room with one towel wrapped around his hips and another in his hand while he rubbed his hair dry.

When the room phone rang, Alec leaned over the bed to pick it up. "Hello."

"Mr. Banner, this is reception. We have Mr. Asher Winsome here. May we send him up?"

Asher was here. Interesting. "Sure. Send him up."

Alec didn't exactly rush to dress, but even he balked at answering the door to a client in nothing but a towel. He slipped his jeans on but only had time to get a shirt in his hands before the knock on the door.

Asher's face, when Alec opened the door wearing nothing but his jeans, was priceless. Alec couldn't help the self-satisfied grin at the lust he caught behind Asher's glazed-over eyes.

"Come on in, Asher. I'm almost done."

"Oh, take your time," Asher answered, and Alec loved the hint of flirt in his tone.

Asher looked understandably tired this morning. His hair was tied in one of those man buns Alec hadn't quite made up his mind about but found deliciously sexy on Asher. His stubble was thicker, and Alec was fairly certain he had on the same clothes as last night. He probably hadn't slept much at all.

"So," Alec continued as he slid his T-shirt over his head. "What can I do for you?"

"I couldn't sleep and I had to get out of the frozen palace. So I thought I'd come see if you had anything for me to do to help."

"The frozen palace?" Alec raised an eyebrow at the term.

"I'm pretty sure you've noticed my folks are cold people. Kane and I called our house the frozen palace when we were growing up. The title stuck...for me, anyway."

Alec had wondered about the brothers' relationship—not everything could be garnered from Jacey's research, even as thorough as she was.

"Coffee?" he offered.

"Please. Black, one sugar."

"So you and Kane...do you get along okay?" Alec asked as he went to the tiny kitchenette and flicked the kettle on.

"Tricky question. Yes and no. Kane and I butt heads over Mom and Dad. I want him to get out from under their iron grip, but he's... Kane's not too capable when it comes to standing up for himself. He's a good man, but it was hard for him growing up."

"Harder than it was for you?"

"I learned early on not to give a crap what anyone, especially my folks, thought. I tried to go along with them for a while but...well, I don't waste time anymore trying to please people who will never be pleased, no matter what I do. Kane never learned that lesson. Mom broke him before he had the chance."

Alec stirred the sugar into the coffee and glanced at Asher. He seemed open to talking about the family, so Alec went for it. "Your parents were abusive?"

"I'd say emotionally, yeah. Never physically. I think they thought beating us was beneath them, and we always had everything we needed materially. Mom and Dad were so busy trying to create the perfect family with two perfect sons they didn't even notice they were breaking one of them. You get told often enough you're not good enough and you start believing it."

"How did *you* escape?"

"A great white shark set me free." Asher laughed, probably at the look of shock Alec knew was on his face. He marveled again how Asher could be so nonchalant about what had happened to him.

"I was nineteen when a shark had me in her jaws, and I thought that was it. I thought I was gone. Game over. I spent weeks in the hospital after the attack: blood transfusions, several surgeries, four hundred and thirty-seven stitches, the works. I had a lot of time to think. I realized if she'd have eaten me that day I would have died with so many regrets. Not least of which was I'd been living my parents' life and not mine."

Alec handed over the coffee, completely engrossed in Asher's tale. "A near-death experience, huh? They sure can change things."

Asher took a sip of his coffee and watched Alec for a moment. "You've had one?" he asked.

"Nothing like yours, but yeah, there were a few times while I was in the army when I thought my time might be up."

"Did it change you?"

"I don't think you can avoid being changed by something like almost dying. It kind of mellowed me out."

Asher spluttered his coffee. "You're mellower now?"

"Oh yeah. You should have known me before. I was a regular stick-up-my-ass kind of guy."

Asher smiled and watched him again before turning serious. "You'll get him back, won't you? I mean, we're all putting on our best stoic faces but inside—inside, Alec, I'm a fucking mess. I'm so out of my mind terrified I don't know where to put myself."

Alec really studied Asher then. Terror burned like fire beneath the surface of his amazing gray eyes. He wanted to take the fear away so badly he ached with it.

"Asher, I..."

"I know you shouldn't promise anything, but could you do it anyway, even if it turns out to be a lie?"

Asher's eyes were pleading with him, and he sounded so desperate that Alec had an overwhelming urge to pull him into his arms. Fortunately, he was saved from any potentially embarrassing gestures by a knock on the door.

"That'll be Jacey, our tech expert," he informed Asher before walking to the door and opening it to a smiling Jacey.

Jacey Locklear was everything he was not. Barely into her twenties, she exuded grace and confidence far beyond her years. Her hair was bright purple—this week—and she favored clothes that matched the birthstone color of whatever month it was. Alec had come across her a few years ago during one of his cases and had damn near arrested her ass. He'd chosen instead to put her to work for him, using her talent for good. She'd been lost at the time, and though not immediately grateful for the reprieve he'd given her, she was now. She was almost like the daughter he'd never have.

She was also a massive hugger, requiring they hug whenever they saw each other whether he wanted to or not. He'd never tell her, but he'd come to love those hugs—they were the only affection he had in his life.

He swooped her up and twirled her just as she liked it, her tinkle of laughter music to his ears. Alec liked men and women, but there'd never be anything between him and Jacey. They were father and daughter or brother and sister. Whichever—theirs was and always would be a strictly platonic relationship.

"Hey, you big ginger asshole. Tell me why I've had to leave the comfort of my living room and come all the way to Del Mar to see your ugly face again?" Her voice was lyrical, but there was nothing sweet about Jacey. She was tough as nails, but if you managed to get through her defenses, she loved fiercely.

"Good to see you, too, Lollipop."

She scowled and swatted at his arm. "Hey. I'm not a fucking lollipop. Oops, sorry, I didn't know you had company." Jacey halted when she noticed Asher leaning casually against the wall, coffee in hand and gaze fixed on them.

"Hey, you're Asher. I'm so sorry about your nephew, but Alec here is the best, and if anyone can find Jack, it's him. Hey, cool about your leg. I mean not cool as in a good thing, but it's kind of epic a shark tried to eat you. It mustn't like the taste of hot man, though, because here you are still alive and well." She flung her hand out and gestured up and down at Asher who seemed to be fighting off a grin.

"Jesus, Jace, we need to work on your small talk," Alec exclaimed.

"There's a reason I usually hide behind monitors, big guy." She turned back to Asher. "Sorry. I turn into a blabbermouth when I'm let loose into the world."

Alec rolled his eyes at the truth of her statement. "Asher, this is Jacey, and, Jacey, of course, this is Asher," he introduced unnecessarily.

"Good to meet you. No need to apologize. You're right that big old fish clearly had no taste. I mean all this"—he gestured down his body—"and she spat me out." Asher shook his head as though disgusted the fucking shark hadn't actually finished him off.

"Oh, Christ." Alec groaned. "Jacey, set up, and I'll get you a coffee," Alec said, trying to bring things back on track. Jacey winked at him and immediately began unpacking all her shit. She needed surprisingly little to work her magic.

"Asher, if you'd like to stay, Jacey and I will be going through the files she's put together about people in your family's lives. Maybe you could help sort through it and see if anything jumps out at you."

Asher nodded and wandered over in Jacey's direction. He quickly turned back to Alec and smiled.

Jesus, his fucking smiles...

"Thank you. This'll keep me from losing my mind."

Alec acknowledged the truth of his statement with a nod and a small smile of his own.

Several hours and a couple of blurry eyes later, they had three definite possibilities and a few others Jacey was going to look into further. Alec had contacted Maddy and discovered absolutely nothing had changed at the mansion. He didn't need to see Jack's mother to know she'd had a miserable night and no sleep—it was all in her voice.

Alec had also contacted Detectives Palmer and Leyland. All the news they had for him was their crime scene techs were at the park looking for anything: footprints, cigarette stubs, tire prints. They were desperate for any clue to kick off a trail for them to follow. They were also taking Emily back to the park so she could retrace her movements for them.

He promised to email them everything they found on potential suspects. They'd need to be careful, though; the cops had rules to play by and much of Jacey's information hadn't exactly been acquired legally.

Asher had been a trooper. The man must have been dead on his feet, but he plowed through as much of the research as he could. The Winsomes would have to think about calling in doctors soon. He'd seen before what happened when the family of the missing person couldn't shut their eyes for any length of time, and he didn't want that for Maddy or Asher or any of them, really.

"Hey," Asher's husky voice interrupted his thoughts. "How about a break? I could use something to eat, and no offense, but your coffee is crap."

"He's right, Alec. You suck at the coffee," Jacey added.

"Hey, it's hotel coffee; it's not my fault."

"Sure." Asher patted his shoulder and stood, stretching his arms high above his head. Alec didn't miss the patch of toned, tanned abs peeking from under his T-shirt as it rode up his torso. "There's a coffee place on the corner. I'll run down and grab us some decent stuff and maybe sandwiches? I could do with a bit of fresh air."

Alec pulled out his wallet and offered a few notes, which Asher promptly shrugged off. He scribbled their orders and passed it to Asher. Their fingers met as he handed it over, and a fizz and crackle of desire ripped through his body at the touch.

Asher barely made it out the door before Alec realized he missed him. Thoroughly disgusted with himself, he pushed the thought aside and turned back to his tablet and the reams of shit he still had to read through. He caught Jacey staring at him with a fucking smug smirk. He flipped her off and got back to work. Fuck his life.

Chapter Four

ASHER

Asher was glad to get out of the hotel room for a few minutes. He was a live and let live kind of guy, so trawling through the minutiae of other people's lives definitely wasn't his thing. But he'd dance through hell to get Jack home safely, so he'd forced himself to read through the tawdry affairs and petty crimes of people he'd known all his life and the darker secrets of people his father had defended.

If he was honest, he also needed a break from Alec. The former FBI agent was twisting his mind in all kinds of ways, and as heartless as it may be, he was glad for it. At least thinking of Alec gave him a few moments reprieve from torturous thoughts of what might be happening to his nephew.

He pulled his phone out as soon as he was in the lobby and called Kane.

"Hey, Asher. How's it going? Anything?" Kane's voice was flat and soft. His brother wasn't made for this kind of heartache.

"We've got a few people to look at but nothing concrete. Are you okay?"

Kane drew in a few shaky breaths before he answered. "I need him back, Ash. I can't do this, and I...I'm trying to be strong for Maddy, but I'm letting her down again. She's his mother and she's comforting me."

"You're his father, Kane. That's every bit as important, and you're stronger than you think. You can do this. You'll make it through. I'll help you. I'll be here." Asher was choking up, it hurt to hear the pain in Kane's voice, but damn, he didn't want to cry. His brother needed him, now more than ever. "I'll be a few more hours, and then I'll be home. You hang in there, okay, and you call if you need me."

"Okay," Kane whispered.

"Okay. Now take a deep breath and go and put a fist through a wall if you need to, but you're going to do this, Kane. I know you are."

"Thanks. I'm glad you're here. I've missed you."

Asher gulped and fought back the tears. "Missed you too. Now you go and hug your wife, and neither of you give up. Ever."

Asher nodded to himself as he hung up from Kane. He was going to take his own advice and not give up ever either.

Ordering their food and coffee took him less time than he'd counted on. Before he'd had much of a chance to relax he was making his way back to the hotel. He took a calming breath and knocked with his foot, his hands full of food and drinks. Alec opened the door, his lips breaking into a smile when their eyes met. Alec's damn cinnamon scent that drove him crazy, yet strangely also calmed him, greeted him. He held out the box of sandwiches for Alec to take and stepped over the threshold.

"Anything?" he asked, unrealistically hoping they may have found Jack in the fifteen minutes he'd been gone.

"Not yet," Alec murmured. Asher had no idea how Alec did this kind of work all the time. It'd break his heart, not to mention his spirit. It took a special kind of person to wade through this kind of shit.

He helped Alec organize the meal, and they all squeezed around the tiny table in the room. Alec pulled the table closer as he sat on the bed because there were only two chairs in the room. Jacey, rather unwillingly, left her computer on the floor where she'd been working and came to sit on the chair beside him. No one spoke as they ate.

A ping from Jacey's computer broke the silence, and she leaped from her chair. Asher watched her fingers fly over the keyboard as she worked on whatever had caused the ping. He hardly noticed her body flinch, but he definitely heard her sharp intake of breath.

"Alec, fuck." Was all she said, but Alec jumped from his spot on the bed to be almost instantly at her side. She stood with the laptop in hand and shoved it under Alec's nose.

It took a moment for Asher to stand to move closer, so he'd be able to see what she'd found, but his way was suddenly blocked by Alec.

"No." He hadn't heard Alec's voice quite so... commanding before, and that was saying something because Alec was definitely an authoritative kind of guy.

"What? What is it?" Asher's voice crackled with the panic insidiously working through his body. He was shaking in seconds, a cold sweat breaking out all over his body. What the hell had Jacey found?

"Asher, look at me," Alec ordered and he was unable to resist. Bad news was there in Alec's eyes as clear as day. "They've sent a link to Maddy. It's real-time footage of Jack—"

"Well, isn't that good? It means he's still alive...doesn't it?" Oh god, what was wrong? He had to be alive; he couldn't think of Jack any other way.

"He's alive, but it's an auction site, Asher."

Asher shook his head, trying to clear it and make sense of Alec's words. An auction site? What the hell was that? They were selling Jack? "What do you mean?" His voice was barely audible, but Alec must have heard him. His big hands came up and gripped onto Asher's arms, and for the first time, Alec's touch didn't shoot pleasure through him, only terror. Alec was holding him up because he knew whatever he was about to say next was bad.

"People auction kids online—usually to...pedophiles." Alec gripped him tighter and Asher was glad; otherwise he'd be on the floor.

"Oh, god, I'm gonna be sick," he managed to grit out seconds before Alec turned him and was pushing him into the bathroom. Asher barely made the bowl before the little bit of lunch he'd managed to finish came up. At some point, a wet cloth was held to his forehead and a large hand rubbed soothing circles into his back.

"We've got to get home. Maddy and Kane..."

"Don't know yet, Asher. Jacey set it up so any emails to your family went through her first on a delay. They won't get the email for another hour. We'll go there and tell them, but I need you to be okay first because they're going to need you."

Asher stood on wobbly legs and washed his face in the sink. He rinsed his mouth as best he could and looked himself over in the mirror. His appearance was awful. He was so pale, almost translucent, the shadows under his eyes almost ink black. He didn't look like himself at all, and he wondered if he ever would again.

"Asher?" Alec's voice was soft but steady. At least someone was holding it together.

He did his best to straighten up and turned to Alec. "Okay. I'm okay." Even as he said it, his bottom lip wobbled and tears threatened.

Alec grabbed his arms again and pulled him into his body, wrapping him tightly in his arms; he was warm and strong. The comfort and security of the hug was everything Asher needed right then.

Minutes passed as Alec held him; he had no idea how many, but every second helped soothe him, and he hoped some of Alec's strength was seeping into him because, god knows, he needed it.

Eventually Alec eased him away, looking intently into his eyes. "I know this is a terrible shock, but I'm not entirely sure it's what it seems, so this is going to sound trite, but try not to panic."

"What do you mean not what it seems?"

"If they were going to auction Jack, why would they send a link to his parents? That's unheard of. It's got to be someone trying to hurt or scare your family. I think they've only set up this auction to mentally torture at least one of you and maybe get some money while they're at it."

Asher rubbed his temples. He couldn't believe this was happening. Sure he'd heard whispers of things like this, but he had no idea. What kind of world were they living in? Would someone set this up just to get back at one of his family members? The notion seemed outrageous, but he held on to the hope it was the case because the thought of Jack being sold to a monster was intolerable.

"We should go. We can't let Maddy and Kane see this without any warning." Kane was hardly holding things together as it was. How was he going to react when he saw this?

"Good, yes we need to go. You're better?"

"As good as I can be, I guess." How good could a person possibly be under these circumstances?

"Okay. I'm leaving Jacey here. She's already started trying to trace the signal. She also called a colleague of mine and told him what's going on. He'll call in the FBI—I still have plenty of contacts there, and they need to be in on this in case it is legitimate."

With every word Alec spoke, Asher felt more and more as though he'd stepped through the rabbit hole. How could this be his life? And yet it wasn't only his. How many more people had gone through, and would go through, what his family was right now? Why wasn't more being done?

Asher's blood boiled with the anger growing inside him, flushing his cheeks and pushing aside the fear a little, and it felt good. He wanted to tear someone apart a piece at a time and make sure it hurt.

His anger must be written all over him because Alec nodded and said, "Hold on to your anger, Asher. It'll help you through this." Alec moved away from him, then. Asher immediately missed the closeness. Thank god, there were people like him in the world to fight back against the monsters—he only hoped there were enough.

Asher followed Alec out of the bathroom and offered a wan smile to Jacey as she looked up at him. "I'll get them, Asher. I'll find them. They can run, but they can't hide." There was a certain fierceness to Jacey he hadn't noticed earlier, and Asher was glad she was on his side.

"Thank you." He squeezed her shoulder as he passed by. He couldn't help a glance at her screen. In the top corner, was a minimized screen showing a low-lit room. In it, there was a ratty bed and nothing else. Curled up on his side was the tiny figure of his nephew.

"Can I see?" he murmured.

Jacey flicked a questioning glance to Alec, but Asher didn't see his response.

"Sure," she answered. Jacey moved the mouse and clicked to maximize the image.

It was definitely Jack lying there. Both of his little fists were curled under his pale cheek as he slept; his hair was messy, but he looked unharmed—other than the trauma of being snatched, of course. The bed he slept on was small, but he still looked tiny on it. Asher's heart ached at how fragile and vulnerable he looked. He'd give his life to be able to reach into the monitor and pull him out of there.

"Alec, Ben's going to call Harry and fill him in, and then he'll make his way down." Jacey was speaking, but he found it difficult to focus on anything aside from his sleeping nephew.

"Thanks, Jace. Call me when he gets here. I'll stay at the Winsomes. Harry and his team probably won't get in until late tonight, possibly even tomorrow morning, so send him everything you've got. I'll give Palmer and Leyland a call on my way to let them know."

He watched Alec grab his keys and moved toward him.

"Come on. We need to go." Alec spoke softly. Asher was never more grateful to have this man here helping them all through this. Asher tried to smile at him, but his lips pulled into more of a grimace.

"We'll take my car," Alec said. Asher didn't bother arguing. He was in no shape to get behind the wheel.

Asher tipped his head back and closed his eyes as Alec drove toward his parents' house. He did his best to listen to the tone of Alec's voice as he spoke to the police rather than the actual words he was saying. As much as he wanted to be there for Kane and Maddy, he was dreading what was coming so much that he was willing the drive to take as long as possible.

He'd lost his guts when he'd found out what was going on, so how could Jack's parents be expected to survive the news? With his help. He wasn't sure how, but he'd do everything he could to help them.

"We're about five minutes away," Alec told him, obviously finished with his call to the detectives.

"I don't know how to tell them."

"I'll tell them, Asher. You only need to be there for them."

"How do you do it? How do you tell people something like that?" Asher turned and looked at Alec's profile as he was driving. He looked as devastatingly handsome side-on as he did from the front.

"It's not something you get used to, but you do learn to manage it. You've got to do it quickly, not dance around. Stick to the facts, as simple and straightforward as possible."

Asher looked back out his window, the familiar neighborhood passing him by. He'd never been happy here, but after this was over, he didn't think he'd ever be able to come back. It would forever be a reminder of the most awful pain after this nightmare was over.

"Why do you do it?" He hadn't really meant to ask Alec the question, but it fell out of his mouth.

"Somebody has to and I can. I learned to compartmentalize in the army. I had to so I could survive; there's nothing pretty or exciting about war. I joined the FBI when I got out, and then an old army friend, Ben Cronin, asked me to join the company he's a joint partner in, specializing in missing kids. How could I say no to helping the most vulnerable of us?"

It was all so matter-of-fact and Asher could tell Alec didn't think of himself as any kind of hero, but his humility only made him more of one in Asher's eyes.

The mansion came into sight and Asher's stomach roiled, his body shaking with nerves. He had to do this, but frankly, right now he'd have preferred to be back in the jaws of his monster shark.

Alec came around to his side of the car as soon as they got out. His steady hands took Asher's shaky ones and squeezed. "You good?" Alec asked.

"No, but we need to do this, so I will be."

Asher turned to face the steps to the front door and forced his legs to move, one foot in front of the other, slowly, as though he were walking to his own execution. He would have preferred if he was. Alec stepped in behind him, and Asher almost sobbed when he felt his hand on the small of his back, urging him forward when he faltered. It was exactly what he needed to help him take those last few steps.

Chapter Five

ALEC

Fuck, he hated this part. Regardless of how tough he talked about compartmentalizing and being able to do this kind of shit, it was always so fucking hard having to break this kind of news to a family. He hoped to god he was right and it wasn't a real auction, but he wouldn't know for sure until the auction opened and bids started coming in. Bids they could verify.

The quickest and easiest way to do that was set up as a bidder himself to see if anyone outside the family could bid. He'd piggyback with the FBI if he could, but he wasn't afraid to go it alone if he had to. Ben and Ethan would have his back.

Asher was finally at the front door, but he made no move to enter. Alec rubbed his back a little and leaned closer. "You ready?"

"How is anybody ever ready for this?"

"You're right. Stupid question," Alec murmured, angry at himself for asking it.

Asher was trembling beneath his fingers, and he wished there was something more he could do for the younger man. He'd never hugged a client before, and although a few had hugged him, he'd always stood there like a wet blanket, barely able to return the embrace. But when Asher had lost it earlier, pulling him into his arms had seemed the most natural thing in the world to do. Everything he felt seemed magnified with Asher around.

Asher pushed the door open and Alec followed him in, staying close. The entire family was in the living room. Edmund had files spread around him; Phyllis had what looked like a martini in her hand while she stared blankly at the walls. Kane was sitting on the sofa, and Maddy was lying with her head in his lap while he aimlessly played with her hair.

"Mr. Banner," Edmund greeted him, but he gave no acknowledgement of his son. Christ, Alec wanted to put this guy on his ass.

"I have some news," he began and watched as Maddy practically leaped from the sofa. "Please stay sitting," he urged her.

"Oh…it's bad?" Maddy whispered and sat back beside her husband, grabbing his hand as soon as she could reach out.

"I make no apologies for the invasion of privacy, but I had my tech expert have any emails sent to your accounts rerouted to her first. Almost forty minutes ago an email was sent to your email address, Maddy. It was a link to a live feed of Jack." Alec heard the gasps but ignored them and carried on. "He's unharmed and we'll go to the link for you to see shortly, but I want to fully explain the situation."

Maddy shifted her glance between him and Asher, and the distress in her keen eyes told him she understood there was something terrible coming. She shifted closer to her husband and slipped her arm around him. He mirrored her movements, and they sat huddled together on the sofa waiting for the other shoe to drop.

Edmund and Phyllis didn't even move. Who would comfort them, because it certainly didn't seem like it would be each other.

"It's an auction site. Something like this is typically used to sell children. They may be sold to couples who want a child and see buying one as their only option, but they are also often used to sell children to pedophiles."

Maddy's tears were instant, and Asher moved to her other side to offer what comfort he could. Alec remained quiet, allowing them all a moment to parse what he'd told them. The elder Winsomes remained silent, though he finally noticed a tremble in Phyllis's hand as she gripped her glass.

"I can't…" Maddy's broken voice shattered the silence, and she stood, pushing away from both Kane and Asher. She made it two steps before her legs went from under her as she collapsed to the floor. Kane caught her a second before she hit. Both older Winsomes stood with their arms outstretched as though they'd catch her, too, which Alec had to admit surprised him. Asher helped his brother pick Maddy up and lay her gently on the couch. Asher raised her legs onto the armrest while Kane kneeled at her side, softly crooning to her.

Alec left the room in search of water and a wet cloth. He knew someone followed him out and wasn't at all surprised when he turned and came face-to-face with Edmund Winsome.

"What does this mean for my grandson, and what are *you* going to do about it?"

Alec eyed Edmund Winsome before answering. His face gave away nothing. Alec didn't like him at all. He was cold and austere, but even before he'd met him, Alec had had a real problem with defense attorneys. It burned like acid to see someone you'd hunted for months and knew to be guilty get off because of a ridiculous loophole their defense attorney exploited. It had happened to Alec, and probably everyone in law enforcement, and even years later, he was still pissed about it.

"*I'm* going to do whatever I have to do to get Jack home. What I need *you* to do is come up with someone who might want to get back at you. Someone who might want to hurt you like this."

"You still think this is personal?"

"I'd bet on it. Why else would they send the link to Maddy if not to cause you all pain?" Alec fished out a bottle of water as he spoke and then found a dish towel to wet. He gave another glance toward Edmund and then brushed past him on his way back into the living room.

Everyone was still hovering around Maddy's prone body. Her eyes were fluttering, so Alec knew she was coming around. He handed the water to Kane and then lay the damp cloth across her forehead.

He stood, placing his hands on his hips as he stared at Maddy while she fought her way back to consciousness. He kept watching her as he asked her father-in-law his next question. "What I need to know, Mr. Winsome, is how much you're willing to pay to get your grandson back."

Alec finally turned to face the older man and watched as he scowled and did his best to intimidate him with a glare. Alec was sure Edmund's threatening appearance worked on plenty of people, but it didn't bother him at all.

"I realize my wife and I must come across as uncaring, Mr. Banner, but I can assure you we will give everything we own to get Jack home."

"Glad to hear it because I'll need to know how much I have to bid with."

"We're bidding in the auction?" It was Asher who asked the question, and Alec heard the disbelief in his voice. When he turned toward him, he caught his startled expression masking, for just a moment, the horror and fear he'd worn since they'd met.

"Yes. Jacey, the FBI, and the police will all do what they can to track these people down, but we can't rely on that. As brilliant as Jacey is tracing people electronically, there are people every bit as clever at covering their tracks. We have to assume the people who have Jack have one of those IT people working for them. We need a backup. The simplest way I can see is to bid for Jack ourselves."

Alec looked around at five blank and shocked expressions. Once their brains caught up, they'd see the sense in what he was telling them, and it wouldn't be a hard sell getting them to agree. But he sure as hell understood their shock at what was going on here. It had taken him years to get used to the horrors of this world and these people had only been exposed to the real depravity of human nature for a little over a day.

Maddy recovered herself and moved to sit up aided by her fussing husband. She was pale and shaky, but her strength was returning. "What do we do now?" she asked through the tears still flowing over her smooth cheeks. Kane's eyes were dry, but while he'd been ghostly pale when they met, he now looked almost translucent. It was a miracle he hadn't gone down with his wife.

"We've already called in Special Agent Harry Doyle from the FBI. He's an old friend, and he and his team specialize in this kind of thing. Child exploitation is their sole focus in the bureau. I'll be liaising with him on how best to do this. Once we come up with a plan, I'll keep you informed. To be honest, I still think this is someone who wants *your* money, wants one or all of *you* to hurt. That's why they sent you the link."

"You think this is the ransom demand?" Kane asked.

"In a way, yes. They could have some legitimate bidders too. They might want to see who'll give them the biggest payday. Or it might be a private link, one only you can see. Jacey will be able to tell us more once she's investigated it thoroughly."

The doorbell chimed and Alec suspected Detectives Palmer and Leyland had arrived. It was far too soon for either Ben or Harry to have made it here. Asher moved to answer the door, and Alec's gaze followed his every move. His body tingled at the memory of holding Asher in his arms earlier.

Asher was followed back into the room by the two detectives plus another suited person he didn't recognize. Alec moved to intercept them before they reached the family. He shook hands with Palmer and Leyland, and Palmer introduced the mystery guest.

"Banner, this is Agent Darcy Cole. She's CBI."

"Agent Cole." Alec shook her hand.

"Mr. Banner, happy to meet you. I've heard good things. Harry called me and asked me to come and get a jump on things for him. I've worked with his team on local cases before. Leyland has filled me in, and Harry explained your presence here. He also said you have a ridiculously talented IT expert working with you, and my people should liaise with her?" Cole phrased it as a question, but it was really more of a statement. Harry Doyle was the best at what he did, and he didn't doubt Darcy Cole would follow his suggestions.

"Glad to have you here, Agent. Come and meet the family."

Within a few hours, Agent Cole had essentially set up a command post in the Winsome mansion. They'd had to call a doctor in for Maddy and Kane, both of whom had gotten progressively more hysterical as the meeting continued, especially when they'd been shown the live feed of Jack. They'd asked questions, ones they really didn't want the answers to, but at the same time had felt compelled to ask.

Doctor Morris was at their side now. He'd been doing his best to calm Maddy without having to resort to a sedative, but it was a losing battle, one Alec had witnessed many times.

Alec stood a little to the side watching, unsure of whether or not to intervene as the doctor began preparing the sedative, and Maddy became further distressed. They were in Edmund's study so as not to disturb the police and CBI agents who had multiplied over the last few hours.

"Alec..." Asher's tone was pleading, his face pale, his wide eyes showing how much he was struggling with the state of his sister-in-law. Maddy was a tough lady, but even the toughest people broke under the right circumstances, and a kidnapped child was the circumstance for Maddy, as it would be for most mothers.

Alec strode over to where Maddy was thrashing on the tiny sofa. He muscled both Kane and Asher out of his way as he sat beside her and grabbed her wrists. He tugged gently, turning her so she was facing him. "Maddy, look at me." His tone was necessarily commanding. "Jack needs you, Maddy. He needs you to be rested and on the ball. Dr. Morris is going to give you something to help you sleep so you can be what Jack needs."

She wriggled in his arms but not as forcefully as she had been. Kane rubbed her shoulders. "Please, Maddy. Just sleep for a moment. Being rested and strong is the best way to help Jack," Kane pleaded.

From the corner of his eye, Alec noticed Asher slip from the room. He couldn't see his face, but the hunch of his shoulders told Alec he was close to breaking.

Maddy quieted as the doctor gave her the shot, and Kane led her quietly from the room to go lay down.

"He'll need something soon, too, and he needs to drink. He looks dehydrated. She's at least been drinking, from what I can tell," the doctor addressed him and passed a bottle of pills over. "Give him a couple of those. I'll come back in the morning to check on them. She should sleep through, but the dose I gave her will allow you to wake her if needed."

"Thanks. I'll take the pills up to Kane shortly. I'll let him settle Maddy first. I'll make sure he drinks too."

"Good. The brother seems okay for now, but watch him. I'll go check on the parents. Make sure somebody calls me if I'm needed." The doctor grabbed his gear and left the study to attend to the older Winsomes.

Alec put the bottle of pills in his pocket and went in search of Asher. He found him in the pool—fully clothed and floating on his back, his eyes closed.

"Asher," he called and got no answer. "Asher." Still nothing. Alec put his phone and the pills on a small table, slipped his shoes off and walked to the pool stairs right into the water. Asher must have heard him or at least felt him displace the water, but he didn't move.

The water was only up to his waist when he reached Asher and he stood there looking at him. Fuck, he was beautiful, so fragile and yet tough. "Asher," he said softly, gently brushing hair away from Asher's forehead. Asher's eyes slowly opened and watched him with his piercing gaze.

"What are you doing here?"

Asher's eyes slid shut again. "The water's my favorite place to be."

"Even with the sharks?" Alec asked.

"Especially with the sharks."

Alec continued playing with the strands of Asher's hair that weren't submerged in the water. It didn't feel weird at all, even though it probably should. Asher kept floating, with his eyes closed, and Alec was content to simply be there with him.

"We're dealing with sharks now, aren't we? Human ones. Far more evil and dangerous."

"We are," Alec answered honestly.

"I don't know how to beat these ones, Alec."

"I do."

Asher opened his eyes and looked at him. He slipped a hand out of the water and grabbed one of Alec's, giving it a small squeeze before closing his eyes again.

They were still fully clothed in the pool, holding hands, when Ben walked out onto the patio a short time later.

Chapter Six

ASHER

"Your nephew is missing, and you're out there flirting with the help?" Edmund Winsome never yelled, but Asher almost wished he did. It would be preferable to the quiet condescension he employed instead.

"The help?" Asher huffed. "He's not the help, and we weren't flirting." Asher didn't bother trying to explain that what had happened in the pool was nothing but Alec trying to comfort him rather than some tawdry assignation. His father would think what he liked, as usual.

Through the window, he watched Alec still standing by the pool, with Ben Cronin, his work colleague. They were talking and gesticulating wildly, though it didn't seem to be in anger.

"You were both in the pool holding hands. What do you call that?" his father persisted.

"You should be grateful we had our clothes on, Father."

"Oh, for god's sake, Asher."

"What, Dad? What have I done so terribly wrong this time?" It wasn't the time for this, but his father knew how to push his buttons, and he was so emotionally raw anyway he couldn't stop himself. "I got here as fast as I could as soon as I was called. I'm doing my best to do whatever I can to help. So I needed a bit of comfort for a moment? It's not like I was out there sucking his dick—"

"Asher Winsome!" His mother's clipped and irritated voice came from the doorway. "Don't you dare speak like that in this house. I won't have crudeness." Her grandson was missing, close to thirty-six hours now, and yet his mother still looked immaculate as she walked toward him, her heels clicking on the tiled floor, makeup perfect, and not a hair out of place.

"I'm sorry," he conceded because he was. That had been unnecessary. "I shouldn't have said it, but, Dad, there is nothing going on—not that it's your business if there was. Alec was only comforting me. He's been strictly professional."

"Edmund," his mother said as she dropped her tiny hand on his father's forearm. "This is the time for us to come together. Let's not fight over the little things."

Asher was shocked when his father placed his hand over his mother's and dropped a kiss on her forehead. He'd never seen affection between his parents, but he was happy to see it now. They needed each other more than ever.

"I've just been to check on your brother. Maddy's sleeping quietly, and I think Kane will be out soon. I think the best thing for us to do is to try to get some sleep, as well. Agent Doyle will be here first thing in the morning. Doctor Morris left sleeping pills for all of us if we need them. Edmund?"

"No. I've got more files to go through. I'm trying to think who's doing this."

"Asher?"

Asher didn't want to fight with them, he really didn't, but the question burst out. "Why didn't you call the cops immediately? The truth..."

His parents glanced at each other, and it was his mother who answered. "Your father and I just wanted to pay the ransom and get Jack back. We thought if the police were called in they'd get in the way."

"Or people would find out, and we'd be dragged through the press?" Asher suggested.

"If I was so concerned about our image, I would hardly tell people what you do with your life now, would I, Asher?" His mother tried to deflect by attacking him, but he'd seen the truth in her eyes. They'd been too concerned with their image.

Her face paled as she stood watching him, proving his mother knew, as soon as the words were out of her mouth, that she'd fucked up, but Phyllis Winsome sometimes couldn't help herself. She'd always relished having a dig at him about being a disappointment; it was one of the reasons he stayed away. And, apparently, not even a family crisis could rein her in.

"Asher..."

"It's fine, Mother. We're all stressed and saying things we wouldn't otherwise. Go on up to bed. I'll head up later." He let the lie fall off his tongue—his mother had often said something related to her shame at his career, and it wasn't fine, but for now, he'd let it be. He turned and looked back out the window, not caring if his parents went up to bed or not.

Alec and Ben were now sitting on the outdoor lounger, their heads angled together as they spoke with each other. He wasn't even sure they were still talking about his nephew, but he did know he wanted to be out there with them. He wanted Alec's cinnamon scent and the warmth of his presence to shroud him with comfort.

He walked through the open French doors and headed for the two men still with their heads bowed and talking quietly.

"Hey, Asher. How're you feeling?" Alec asked as he approached.

"Better, thanks. Um…everybody's gone up to bed. And I was wondering if you were heading back to your hotel soon?"

Alec stood abruptly, almost knocking Ben from his seat. "Yes, sure. Sorry, Asher, we'll get out of your hair."

"No. No, oh shit. I didn't mean it like that. I was actually wondering if I could go with you. I mean my car is back at your hotel, and I could do with getting out of here for a while."

He flicked a glance at Ben, who was sitting, watching the exchange with a smirk and wide eyes. He was a good-looking man, a few inches shorter than his own height, but he looked like he could take care of himself. All he knew about Ben was he worked with Alec, but they'd been friends in the army previously. However they knew each other, Ben seemed amused by Alec right now.

'Oh. Okay then. All right, let's go. I'll have a quick word with Agent Cole on our way out."

"I'll take care of it, Alec. You and Asher head on to the hotel. You need to get out of those wet clothes. Ryan booked me the room next to Jacey's, so I'll stop in there too and can check in with her. Then I'll come up to your room, and we can talk some more." Ben winked, and Asher got the impression he was missing something. Perhaps Ben had read more into what was going on in the pool, exactly like his father had.

"Cronin…"

"It's fine. I'm capable of matching wits with the big boys, Banner. You go on with Asher—who by the way—" He turned to look quickly at Asher. "—needs to show me the wicked shark scar I've heard all about."

"I'm not even sure you're capable of matching wits with a first grader, but okay."

"Asshole."

"Douchebag."

Asher smiled at their good-natured banter. It reminded him of how much he missed his crew. He worked with many people in his line of work, but he had a core crew who were a constant in his life, and he missed them now. A few of them had wanted to come back with him, but he'd asked them to finish their current job first. If this nightmare wasn't over within the week, they'd start arriving here by next Tuesday.

"Ready, Asher?"

He nodded and headed back inside. Ben spoke softly to Alec, but he couldn't quite catch the words.

"I'm sorry about Ben," Alec offered as he caught up to him. Asher wasn't quite sure what he was sorry for; Ben seemed great. Under better circumstances, he could imagine they'd become friends.

"Don't be sorry. I like him and, Alec—" He stopped and put his hand on Alec's chest. "—with what I know about you, what you're doing for my family, it's not likely I'd question your judgment."

They were silent the rest of the way to Alec's car and for much of the drive back to the hotel. It wasn't until they were in the elevator on the way up to Alec's room that Asher finally broke.

"My dad thought we were flirting in the pool," he said softly.

"So did Ben."

Asher lifted his gaze to Alec and was met by large hazel eyes watching him with their usual intensity. He thought he could make out flecks of the brightest green in them, but he still wasn't close enough to see the full spectrum.

"Were we?" he asked.

Alec reached out and trailed a solitary finger down Asher's cheek and across his lips. "I'm not sure," he whispered.

Alec was brutally honest, his usual manner, as Asher was discovering. Maybe they had been flirting. At the time, all Asher wanted was for the nightmare to stop. He'd gone into the water seeking the calm it always gave him, but it hadn't been enough—not until Alec was in there with him. And when he'd gripped Alec's hand, so strong and sure, it might have been the only thing keeping him afloat because he suspected if he'd let go he'd have sunk to the bottom of the pool, dragged under by the lead weight of his pain.

"I don't think we were flirting," he said, holding Alec's gaze. "I think it was more."

Alec didn't answer, but he didn't pull away either, at least, not until they reached their floor. Asher followed behind as Alec strode to his room. He felt the ghost of Alec's fingers where they'd touched his face, but he wanted the real thing back. He was surprised by the voracity of his feelings for Alec. Perhaps all of his emotions were heightened right now due to the intensity of the situation he was in. He wasn't sure, but he did know whatever he was feeling for Alec had a strong pull. Maybe it would fizzle out when the nightmare was over. Maybe he just desperately needed someone to be there for him right now and Alec was convenient. He was confused and frightened and intrigued and bewildered. He was a fucking mess.

"Asher? You all right?"

Asher snapped out of his thoughts and looked around. He hadn't even realized they'd reached the room, but there he was standing in the middle of it probably looking like an idiot. Alec was looking at him with more concern than he remembered seeing on his own mother's face when he'd woken up in the hospital years ago with a big chunk of his leg missing. In the pit of his stomach, all of his overwhelming emotions bubbled, working their way through him until everything came spewing out in a mess of words.

"My parents didn't call the cops because they didn't want anyone finding out what happened with Jack. They were so damn concerned about their precious reputation; so much so, they couldn't even do the right thing for their grandson. My brother can't or won't stand up to them, and you've seen him—I mean, my god, he'll be lucky to survive this, even if we get Jack back safely. There's nothing to him; he's a shell of the man he should be. Maddy's hanging by a thread, and she's the toughest person I've ever met. I mean, she stood up to my mother the very first time she met her. Do you know how many people stand up to Phyllis Winsome? None. Nobody does. And my father accused me of flirting with the help—that's you by the way—the help! My god, could those people have less of a clue?

"I can't spend another night in their house. I wanna be there for my brother but I just... And every time I look at you it takes my fucking breath away, and how sick is it that I'm even thinking about you and how fucking gorgeous you are, when my nephew is missing? Your friend Ben—I actually felt jealous when I saw you sitting so close to him. It seemed so intimate, and I was fucking jealous. Everything is so—I don't know...I feel like I'm in a tornado, and I can't make anything slow down. I can't get any control. I'm trying so hard to be brave, but I'm lost and I'm scared. I'm so fucking—"

Asher's words were cut off by the warm press of Alec's lips on his. For the tiniest second, he didn't react at all, but then he was kissing Alec back with the same fervor.

Alec's lips were perfect the way they slanted across his own, pushing and pulling none too gently. Asher loved kissing, and this was by far one of the best he'd had. Alec nipped at his bottom lip, and he opened his mouth, easing his tongue out to soothe the sting. Alec took full advantage, sucking gently on his tongue before sweeping his own into Asher's eager mouth.

He had no recollection of how, but at some point, Asher wrapped an arm around Alec, pulling him as tightly against himself as he could. His other hand snaked into the mess of Alec's hair, gripping on to prevent him being able to pull away. He didn't want Alec going anywhere.

Alec's strong hands on his ass were pulling his pelvis in tightly against his own. He tried not to think about the hard cock urgently pressing against his own, because if he did, he truly thought he may come in his shorts. Alec's other hand tangled in the loose strands of hair that had escaped his bun.

Alec was all over him—he was all Asher could feel and see and smell—and the sensations were so good.

Even if for only this moment in time, there was no room in his mind for anything other than Alec Banner and the way he was making him feel.

Asher pushed back and sought out Alec's eyes. The hazel was glazed with lust, his pupils blown. But there was also hesitation.

"Asher—"

"Please. I need...you. I need you. For just a little while," he pleaded.

Asher gripped the hem of his tee and pulled it over his head. When Alec's lusty gaze traveled all over his torso, Asher was emboldened to carry on. He slowly worked the button and zipper of his shorts before slipping them over his hips. He shook his legs until the shorts hit the floor, and then he stepped out of them. He was conscious of having his Superman boxers on today and briefly wondered if Alec would think him childish for his superhero underwear fetish. If the look in Alec's eyes was anything to go by, those thoughts were the furthest thing from his mind.

Alec hadn't moved to take any of his clothes off—actually he hadn't moved at all—and for a horrible second, he believed he'd misread the whole thing. Well, he might as well go all in. He reached for the band of his boxers and carefully pulled them over this throbbing erection. His cock bounced on his stomach when he freed it. Asher was rewarded with Alec's slight intake of breath and a peek of his tongue as he licked at his lips while he watched Asher shimmy his boxers down his legs and off his body.

"Jesus Christ. You're fucking gorgeous," Alec breathlessly assessed. Asher wanted to strut around like a bloody peacock under the praise. Instead, he gripped his cock and slowly stroked it, his gaze never leaving Alec.

"No," Alec said and gently batted his hand away. "That's mine."

Normally, Asher wasn't a big fan of the "you're mine" kind of talk, but Alec made it sound so fucking hot, so he moved his hand and kept it away. Alec slowly sunk to his knees and put both hands on Asher's hips, whether to hold him in place or encourage his movements Asher wasn't sure yet, but they felt damn good there. Asher gently rested his hands on Alec's head, twisting his fingers through his gorgeous ginger hair.

"Oh fuck," he sighed when Alec licked a trail from the base of his cock to the tip, his tongue swirling around the head, teasing and tormenting him. Alec kept on licking at him, and Asher's hips swirled uncontrollably, searching for more. Alec was going to kill him.

When Alec finally sucked him into the warmth of his mouth, for a mortifying second, Asher thought he was going to shoot straight down his throat. If all his emotions were amplified by the nightmare he was in, then so was the pleasure. Alec's mouth was hot and wet and Christ he sucked so hard, keeping his mouth snug around Asher's cock.

Alec nudged his hips forward with his hands, and Asher got the message loud and clear. He gripped Alec's hair tighter and began moving his hips, thrusting them gently at first and then, as the pleasure increased, harder until he was fucking Alec's mouth with abandon.

God, he wanted to come so badly, but he wanted Alec inside him more than he'd ever wanted anyone. Top, bottom, he didn't really care; he enjoyed it all, but he'd never wanted as desperately as he did right then for Alec to fuck him until he couldn't think anymore.

With supreme effort, Asher pushed away from the decadence of Alec's mouth and stared at him.

"What, baby?" Alec murmured.

"I need you," Asher replied simply, and then turned and lay on the bed. He spread his legs wantonly and crooked his finger at Alec, calling him over.

Alec stripped his clothes with slow, purposeful motions designed to tease. Asher raked his gaze over every inch of skin Alec revealed. The man was fucking glorious. His skin was pale and smooth, and he had a light smattering of freckles on his chest. A sexy happy trail ran down his taught abs to his fucking beautiful cock. He was thick and long and Asher couldn't resist gathering a drop of precome on his finger when Alec came closer, bringing it to his lips. He leisurely swiped at it with his tongue, reveling in both the taste of Alec and the hitch of breath the action drew from him.

Alec suddenly turned and walked to his bag, rummaging through the contents. He proudly held up the condoms and lube with a giant smile. Asher was leaning on his elbows, watching between his legs, as Alec crawled up the bed and over his body, dropping openmouthed kisses all over him as he went.

They kissed frantically this time, hands everywhere, searching and exploring. Asher tipped his head back, exposing his throat when Alec began kissing down his neck. His whole body heated like it was on fire, burning until Alec could give him the relief he sought.

Alec kept nuzzling at his throat, even as his hand moved down his body, his fingers trailing featherlight over his scars where part of his thigh was missing. Such a gentle touch to a spot where once such violence had occurred.

Finally, his hand moved to Asher's ass. He trailed his fingers over his hole, circling and teasing. Asher willed himself to relax, waiting for the first breach of Alec's finger. But instead, Alec's hand moved away, leaving him bereft. Alec kissed down his throat and over his chest, and Asher could feel his hand shuffling around beside him.

When lube-slicked fingers returned to his ass, he realized what Alec had been doing. Alec played with him a little more before finally slipping a finger inside. Asher gasped, with relief, more than anything. That soon changed to pleasure when Alec added a second finger and found his prostate. He squirmed and wriggled beneath Alec, desperate for more.

"Now, now," he pleaded; his body completely unable to wait any longer.

Alec pulled away from him, and Asher watched, fascinated, as he covered his cock and lubed himself and Asher's ass. He closed his eyes and sighed with contentment when Alec's body came back down over his. The blunt head of Alec's cock nudged at his entrance, and he bore down as Alec pushed in.

Alec didn't rush and the exquisite torture of the slow-burning anticipation was so good that, before Asher knew it, Alec's balls were resting against his ass and the pain was already morphing into the pleasure. Alec held himself still, his hazel eyes watching Asher, his body trembling with the effort of not moving.

"You okay?" Alec moaned.

"Perfect," Asher replied because right then he was, Alec was perfect—everything was perfect.

Alec favored him with a flirty smirk and pulled back. He moved tenderly at first, gently probing for the right rhythm.

"Harder," Asher encouraged giving Alec the permission he seemed to have been waiting for. He began to piston his hips, jolting Asher with each and every thrust. Asher wrapped his legs around Alec and held on. He wanted to stare into Alec's eyes as he moved inside him, but he found it hard to stop his lids from fluttering closed of their own volition. Every surge forward had Asher closing his eyes, trying desperately to parse the overriding pleasure driving control of his body away from him and handing it to Alec.

He held no delusions that Alec wasn't master of his body in this moment. Every bit of pleasure he was feeling was given to him by Alec's movements, the feel of his cock inside, the brush of it over his prostate. Even the sensation of Alec's body lying over his, their skin slapping and rubbing in places, was almost too much good to bear. Alec was an assault to his senses, and Asher was reveling in surrender.

"So fucking beautiful, Asher. Feel so good," Alec moaned and his words of praise added to the conflagration of pleasure roaring throughout Alec's body.

He desperately grabbed at his cock, and barely three strokes later, he came. His whole body trembled with his orgasm, the likes of which he'd never experienced. His vision exploded in stars, and his body thrashed with the sensations tearing through it. He was entirely overwhelmed with pleasure.

"It's okay. It's okay, baby," Alec was crooning as he came back to himself. Asher was mortified to realize he was crying, and Alec was still hovering above him looking at him sadly. Oh, god, what had he done?

"I'm sorry, Alec. I don't know why I'm crying. This was perfect. You were perfect. I wanted it—no I needed it. Please... I—"

"Shh. It's all right, Asher. I know. I know."

This was awful. Everything had been so perfect; he'd come harder than he ever had, and now he'd gone and ruined it. Alec probably felt like shit, and talk about killing the mood. He felt miserable.

"Hey. Asher, it's okay. I understand. Everything is overwhelming right now."

"But I'm fucking crying. And you didn't even get to...finish." Oh, god, he was so humiliated.

"Um, yeah I did, actually. I came when you did. You looked so fucking beautiful I couldn't hold back even if I wanted to. I guess you were a little too busy yourself to notice." Alec pressed his lips to his and then carefully pulled out of his body. Asher watched as he pulled off the condom and confirmed his words.

"I'm so sorry. I just lost it. It was so good, Alec, and then I don't know what happened. Next thing I knew, I'm fucking crying like a baby."

Alec walked into the bathroom and came back with a couple of wet face cloths. He cleaned them both, then tossed the cloths back into the bathroom. He gently rolled Asher and pulled the blankets out from underneath him. Asher remained plaint, allowing Alec to move him where he wanted until they were both lying under a sheet with Alec as the big spoon.

Asher sank into the comfort of Alec's strong body at his back and his steady arm draped around him. Alec kissed his temple and pulled him tighter.

"It's okay, Asher. It's okay," he quietly crooned. Asher's eyes drifted closed, and he heard Alec murmuring words of comfort as he finally drifted off.

Chapter Seven

ALEC

Alec wanted nothing more than to stay curled around Asher in bed, but he knew it wouldn't be long before Ben turned up at his door. He wasn't looking forward to the grief Ben was going to give him over Asher, but Alec wouldn't change a thing.

Was it the smartest move to bed a member of his client's family? Hell no, but Jesus, Asher had been so needy and so fucking sexy peeling his clothes off in front of him the way he had. He was certain he was nothing more than a distraction, but he didn't care at all: he'd been worse things to others.

Once he was sure Asher was sleeping, he slipped from between the sheets and had the quickest shower ever. He dressed, wrote a quick note for Asher in case he woke, and quietly left the room in search of Ben.

Ben should be back at Jacey's room by now, so Alec headed in that direction. He wasn't even as far as the elevator before he heard the ding of its arrival, and Ben was disgorged from the steel box.

His best friend looked up and caught sight of Alec heading toward him. Ben's intense gaze traveled the length of his body before he smirked and nodded his head back toward the elevator. "Bar?" he asked.

"Yeah, that'd be best."

Alec followed Ben into the elevator and braced for the questioning he was sure was coming. At least Ben waited until the doors closed.

"So, you did it then?"

"Did what?" Alec tried to sound as though he had no idea what Ben was talking about.

"Jesus, Banner, don't try to be coy with me. You slept with him. I can smell it."

"Bullshit you can. I showered."

"So you did sleep with him," Ben smugly replied.

Alec wanted to slap his own forehead. He'd walked straight into Ben's trap. "Yes, okay. I slept with him."

"And..." Ben encouraged as the door opened to the lobby.

Alec quietly followed as Ben headed toward the hotel bar. He didn't want to talk about this for everyone around to hear. Ben led them to an out of the way table near the back of the room. They both turned their chairs so they were sitting alongside one another with their backs to the wall—old habits really do die hard.

"Corona or the hard stuff?" Ben asked.

"I better stick to the Coronas. Not sure I can handle the hard shit tonight."

Ben gave his shoulder a little shove and then strode to the bar. Alec watched Ben as he flirted with the bartender who couldn't seem to take her eyes off him. He'd yet to see anyone rebuff Ben when he got his flirt on, though of course these days it was all harmless. Ben had eyes—and everything else—only for Ethan.

It suddenly occurred to Alec that Ben might discipline him for sleeping with Asher. Technically, Ben was his boss, and his behavior with Asher wasn't the most professional thing he'd ever done, but not even the threat of disciplinary action could dampen the thrill. He'd loved every second of being with Asher. Even now, his cock stirred from the memory.

"So...tell me," Ben demanded as he returned with their drinks.

"Um...he was losing it and...all I could think of was to kiss him, and then we were touching and getting naked. He wanted me so bad, Ben." Ben watched him with an unreadable expression, and not for the first time, Alec began to doubt his actions.

"Oh god, I took advantage, didn't I? He's traumatized, and he needed comfort, and I went too far. Jesus, what kind of bastard am I?"

Ben huffed and cocked his head. "Ah, a confused one right about now, I'd say. Look, Alec, he's what, thirty-two, three? He knows what he's doing. So he needed something to take his mind off shit... We've both seen it before—we've both done it before. How many people did you fuck when everything was going to shit back in the day? Do you feel like they took advantage of you?"

While he'd been in the military, Alec had fucked just about any willing person who moved, especially when he was overstressed and the pressure was high, and no, he didn't feel taken advantage of. Those people had been there for him, offering him a moment's respite from the madness—and he'd likely done the same for them. It had never been Ben, though. In fact, it had never crossed his mind to chase Ben, which was odd because he was fucking hot. But they'd always been brothers, by choice if not by blood.

"He cried," Alec whispered.

"Jesus, what did you do?"

"No, after. He had this orgasm like I've never seen, and then, all of a sudden, he was crying. I don't know if it was regret or what. He says it wasn't. He said everything was piling on top of him. But what if…"

Ben sat back in his chair and watched him closely. He watched for so long Alec started to feel uncomfortable.

"You're different with him," Ben finally said.

"What?"

"I know he's going through a lot, so you're treading carefully, but I've seen you postfuck many times, Banner, and you're different with him. I can't pinpoint what it is, or what it means, but it's there."

"You're imagining things. I'm just feeling…" Alec wasn't sure how to explain what he was feeling.

"You got out of Cameron's pretty quickly the other day, and we could all see something was up. Are you ready to spill?"

He loved Ben, but Jesus, sometimes he went right in for the kill. "I'm out of sorts, Ben. I'm almost forty and completely alone. Don't get me wrong. I've loved the fuck-and-run years up till now. But I look at you and Ethan, Ryan and Lucas, and now Cameron and Zach…and I need more. I want someone for me."

"They're out there, man; your special someone is out there. And you'll find them. You're a catch, Banner; even with the red shit you've got growing there." Ben flicked his eyes up to Alec's hair and then tapped the neck of his Corona against Alec's. They both took a drink. He hoped to god Ben was right, because some days, lately, it felt like he'd missed the boat.

"Did you just compliment me, Cronin?" He smirked, enjoying the banter with his friend.

"These are crazy times we're living in, my friend."

Alec huffed in agreement and took a sip of his drink. "How'd it go with Jacey?" Alec asked, eager now to get the spotlight off him. He steadfastly kept his mind from wandering to Asher upstairs, naked in his bed, because if he started thinking about him, he'd ditch his best friend and run back for more of Asher's perfect fucking body.

"She's got a trace going on the IP address from the link. It's bounced her to Geneva. Doyle will no doubt call the locals over there, but we all know there'll be nothing to find. There's no way they're in Geneva. The Feds will have to subpoena the VPN Company to try to get any records or force them to track the owner. She's not sure if the auction is legit yet, because it hasn't opened up, but she did say others could definitely view Jack. Once an hour, the link opens and people can sign in and watch him for fifteen minutes. She's started tracking them, too, and she's sent details to Doyle's team. He's got a bunch of grunts doing nothing but monitoring the viewers. Nothing bad is going on—at least, while the cameras are on him. He sleeps mostly, so maybe he's been given something to keep him quiet. Might be for the best if he has."

"Why kids? I mean, we've seen it all, but I'll never get why adults drag kids into their shit show." Alec could never understand how anyone could look into those innocent little faces and hurt them.

Ben gazed into the distance. Was he thinking about the two little girls he and Ethan were raising—their daughters now for all intents and purposes? He'd never thought of Ben with kids, but he was an awesome father and loved those girls the same as if they'd been his own flesh and blood.

"Beats me. I look at Maya and Riley, and every time, I feel like I'm ready to throw myself on a grenade for them if I had to. There is literally nothing I wouldn't do to keep them safe. And they're so damn innocent, you know. Everyone is good in their eyes." Ben took another sip of his drink as Alec watched him. His friend had changed; he was a family man now, and he wore the title well.

"Are they still crushing on Zach?" Alec asked before taking a sip of his drink.

"Pfft, drives me fucking crazy. I know they love Ethan and me, but Jesus, Zach is fucking god in their eyes. I think they'd crawl over my cold dead body just to get to him."

"He's a sweet kid. You should be glad they're not idolizing someone like...well me." Alec smirked.

"That sweet kid is banging the hell out of my brother."

Alec laughed. Ben was an irreverent son of a bitch, and nothing was off limits. "Christ, Cronin, they're in love. Don't you have a romantic side? They're making love not banging."

"Don't you fucking start. Ethan almost had a coronary when I mentioned they were bumping uglies. You people need to learn to love me for my sweet, sweet self." Ben actually fluttered his eyelashes, and Alec couldn't help but laugh at the crazy fucker.

"We all love you plenty, asshole. Especially Ethan, though I'm still not convinced he knows exactly what he's gotten into with you—especially when all this hotness right here"—he gestured to himself—"would love to have a crack at him." Alec winked. Yeah he had a tiny crush on Ethan, and no, he'd never do anything about it, but it didn't mean he couldn't torment Ben a little.

"I think all that hotness has got a little shark bait of his own to deal with right now."

Ben's words took Alec right back to Asher. Asher who'd responded so beautifully to him, who'd been so giving and generous. Asher who'd made him feel more in the short time he'd known him than Alec had felt for as far back as he could remember.

"I just wish we'd met under different circumstances, you know."

"We've got a good chance of getting Jack home safely, Alec. Maybe then—"

"I can't even think about that right now. I was a distraction for Asher tonight, but I can't allow myself to be distracted by him. I've got to focus on Jack." Yes, he wanted someone of his own, but he knew meeting under these circumstances was a disaster waiting to blow up all the fuck over him.

Ben looked at him with disappointment in his eyes. "All right. So what's next?"

"We're gonna bid for Jack, and I'm thinking we'll have the family do it openly, but we'll get Jacey to create a fake bidder too."

"Good. Gives us more chances and better control over the situation. You gonna get grandpa for the family bidder?" Ben asked.

"I'm not sure. Part of me says yeah because he's the most likely one they want to hurt, but another part of me says they'll toy with him and sell the kid out from under him, really dig in the knife."

"Can't ask Jack's parents to do it," Ben mused and Alec knew where his thoughts were headed because his were already there. "You're thinking Asher?"

"Logical choice. He's immediate family but not the parents."

"It's a big ask, Alec. No one should have to step into this kind of swamp."

"No, they shouldn't, but someone has to, and I think Asher can do it." Asher was strong, and he loved his nephew. His love would give him the courage to keep going when things would otherwise seem too much.

"Have you asked him?"

"Not yet. I didn't get much of a chance—and no, Ben, let's not have any of your usual jokes and high school carry-on about my sex life." Alec smiled to show Ben he wasn't upset even though he was serious about no jokes regarding him and Asher.

"Still the same old 'sucking all the fun out of life' wet rag aren't you, Banner?" Ben stated in mock disgust. "Have it your way. I'll be the model of good breeding—for now." He winked. Ben didn't have it in him to be serious for long so Alec would have to enjoy it while it lasted.

"I'm gonna head back up and get some sleep—and yes I mean sleep, Cronin. Harry will be here early, and I'm guessing the auction will start tomorrow, so we need to get everything set up. We good?"

"We're always good, Alec. Meet you in Jacey's room at six?" Ben asked.

"She okay with that?" Jacey worked like a dog, but she was not a morning person. If Alec had to bet on it, he'd wager she'd be up all night tonight trying her best to track these fuckers down.

"She suggested five, but I told her no one wants to see your ugly mug so early in the morning."

"Humph. Love you, too, Cronin. See you at six."

Alec left Ben sitting at the table finishing off the last of his beer. He itched to get back up to Asher, and it wasn't so they could go for round two. He hated the thought of Asher waking up alone. He wanted to be there for him.

Asher was still curled on his side sleeping peacefully when Alec crept back into the room. He shucked his clothes before sliding in behind him. He wrapped his arms around Asher and tugged him gently backward. Asher wriggled and settled against him, wrapping his own arms around Alec's, holding him tightly.

"Where'd you go?" Asher whispered.

"Went to see Ben."

"Any news?"

"Nothing tonight. We can talk in the morning. Sleep now."

"He didn't even have his teddy bear or something to hold onto for comfort," Asher mumbled.

Alec squeezed him a little tighter. "We're going to get him back." Alec pressed a kiss into the back of Asher's hair. He smelled of chlorine and sex.

"We will—you will. I know it."

Alec was pretty sure Asher was asleep again as soon as he'd spoken the words. He had such faith in him, and Alec was determined not to disappoint him.

Chapter Eight

ASHER

For a split second, when he first woke up, Asher felt happy. He was wrapped up tight in the arms of a gorgeous, wonderful man, and his body still felt good from last night. But then he remembered what was really happening. And the memory chased him into reality and out of Alec's arms.

He slid from under the covers and sat on the edge of the bed. Last night with Alec filled his thoughts. Being with Alec had been better than perfect—until he'd cried. But Alec had even managed to make him feel okay about his tears.

All his emotions were so raw, on a razor's edge. He'd never felt so—well, so much of everything, and he knew it wasn't sustainable. Something would give. He had no idea how people coped with their loved ones remaining missing for years. Surely the unknown fate of people you cared for was the cruelest torment to endure.

His pile of clothes lay where he dropped them after stripping them off last night. He scooped them up and tiptoed to the bathroom. Alec had gotten in late, so Asher wanted to let him sleep a little longer. He set the pile on the basin and then turned on the shower.

The hot spray felt sensational on his aching body when he stepped in. He didn't want to be rid of the ache because it was of the best kind. The twinges were a reminder he'd been well fucked only hours ago. He wet the cloth, soaping it until nice and sudsy, and then began cleaning his body. He hoped the next time he showered they'd have Jack safely home. And that led to other thoughts: is this how he'd live if they didn't get him back? Constantly wondering where Jack was, what was happening to him? Was he crying for his parents? Did he think they'd all abandoned him? Always thinking maybe the next time he ate dinner or swam in the ocean or cooked a meal or watched a movie would be the last time before Jack came home.

How the hell were Maddy and Kane coping?

"Mind if I join you?"

Asher jumped at the sound of Alec's voice but recovered in time to turn with what he hoped was a calm look. "Course not. Come on in," he invited.

Alec stepped inside the shower. A tight squeeze, but Asher didn't mind the closeness at all. Alec pushed up behind him, and Asher relished in the feel of the firm body pressed against the length of his own, Alec's hard cock nudging between his cheeks.

Alec took the soapy cloth from his hand and washed every inch of his body—every nook and cranny. When Asher tried to turn and return the favor, Alec held him still.

"No. This is for you," he whispered, his words tickling Asher's ear.

Alec's arm reached around his body, and one of his hands wrapped around his aching cock. Asher's hips rolled and thrust as he sought release. Alec's other hand snaked around and toyed with his nipples before moving down to cup his balls. This man could play his body like a maestro. Asher moaned and grunted with each stroke and gentle roll of his balls.

It took only minutes under Alec's expert ministrations before thick streams of come were pumping from his dick, splashing the tiles and trickling down the drain. Asher groaned long and low as the pleasure swamped him.

Asher leaned back, trusting Alec to take his weight, and let his head rest on Alec's shoulder. This was the second epic orgasm this guy had given him, and Asher wasn't entirely sure he'd survive more.

He reached behind and wrapped his arm around Alec's ass, pulling him in tighter. He wanted to get on his knees for Alec right then and there and was half turned to do exactly that when a phone rang.

Alec quickly pressed a kiss to his hair and left the shower. "Finish your shower and get dressed. That'll be Ben making sure we're up. We're meeting him in Jacey's room. What can I order you for breakfast?"

Alec was already toweling off, and Asher didn't take his eyes off his body as his muscles bunched and strained under his actions. "Um...anything? I'm not really hungry."

"You need to eat, Ash. I'll order the works, and you can pick whatever you want." And with those words, Alec was out the door, apparently completely unfazed he hadn't come this time. Asher couldn't recall ever being with someone so entirely unselfish.

He wondered if Alec even realized he'd made his knees buckle twice in the space of a few minutes. First with the orgasm and then again when he'd shortened his name to Ash.

After taking a few moments to calm himself, Asher finished in the shower and dressed. He'd need to return to his parent's home soon for a set of fresh clothes and to check on his family, but first he wanted to check in with Alec and his team. He knew nothing major had changed because he trusted that Alec would have told him immediately.

Alec was waiting by the door when he stepped out of the bathroom. "Ready?"

He really wasn't ready to face yet another day of his nephew being missing, but what choice did he have? He'd heard many times how the lord didn't give people anything they couldn't handle, and he'd always thought the sentiment to be utter crap. Jack's kidnapping confirmed it for him because he knew he couldn't handle much more of Jack's disappearance.

"Yeah, let's go."

They walked silently to the elevator. The silence continued as they got in and traveled two floors down. He remained quiet as Alec knocked on a door and waited for it to be opened. He had no idea what to say to Alec. "Thanks for the orgasm; sorry we were interrupted before I could return the favor" seemed inappropriate.

"Come in," Ben said as he opened the door to them. "Breakfast is here."

Asher walked into the room and did his best to smile at both Ben and Jacey. Ben sat back at the small table and continued tucking into the huge serving of bacon and eggs he'd already started. Jacey was lying on her stomach on the bed. She was furiously tapping at her keyboard, barely looking up at them when they entered.

"Mm...sit down, Asher. Eat." Ben motioned to the chair opposite him with his fork. He really wasn't hungry, but Alec was right, he did need to eat.

The food smelled as it always did, but rather than the aroma of bacon making him salivate as usual, his stomach churned. He sat and pulled one of the plates closer. He picked at the food with his fork before finally taking a mouthful. He chewed and swallowed and then scooped up another forkful. The food was utterly tasteless to him, but he forced it down anyway.

"Anything new?" Alec asked, and Asher flicked his gaze to Jacey.

"Can't trace them past Geneva. The VPN company had some hardcore security, which I will crack, but a subpoena from the FBI will probably be quicker—either way it'll be a few days at least before they can help us. I'm writing a virus that I'm hoping to piggyback onto our bidding to allow me to bypass the VPN and get their real location. Auction's going to open at ten. I've set up a profile for a fake bidder, and I've included a seedy Internet history in case they check." Jacey didn't even look up from her work as she spoke.

"Jesus," Alec breathed. "Have you slept?"

"Got a few hours, but I'm psyched, Alec. I wanna get these fuckers. Just keep me stocked with Gatorade, and I'll be fine."

"How do we go about bidding?" Asher asked, willing and wanting to do anything he could to help. He didn't miss the glance passing between Alec and Ben.

"Actually, Ben and I spoke about this last night. We think you're the best person from the family to front the bid. We can't ask Maddy and Kane—it's too rough. We'll basically be setting up a profile for you, and we can do most of the work, but often toward the business end of the auction, they require you to Skype your bids. It's a precaution for them to confirm their bidders' identity. It's a risk for the bidders who're essentially showing their face while committing a heinous crime, but it usually proves their legitimacy."

"I'll do it. I'll be fine. Whatever it takes."

"Great. We'll get started on your profile, and then we'll head over to the local police station. Harry Doyle will be here by now, and some of his techs can help," Ben said around a mouthful of bacon.

"His profile is pretty much done, so when you guys are finished feeding your faces, I'm good to go." Jacey looked up briefly with a smile and a wink and then hunched back over her keyboard.

Ben stood and stretched. "All right. I'm going to head on over to the Winsomes. I'll update them all over there and stay with them until you guys arrive."

"Thanks, Ben," Alec said. Ben's response was a fist bump as he left the room.

Asher put down his fork and wiped his mouth on the napkin, but one glance at Alec told him he hadn't eaten enough, as far as he was concerned. Alec only raised an eyebrow, though, and then made a sandwich from the leftover toast and eggs on the plates.

"Let's go," Alec said and then shoved the sandwich in his mouth. Jacey was packed up and ready to go by the time Asher managed to wolf down a mouthful of coffee. He dropped the mug back on the table and followed Alec out the door.

The three trudged down to Alec's car and were quiet for much of the fifteen-minute drive to the local police station. The CBI and FBI were working out of there, so they could be close to the action and coordinate with the local police involved in the case.

Asher had seen plenty of movies and TV shows where there were jurisdiction disputes and the like, but thankfully, the only thing the people helping to find Jack seemed to be concerned about was actually finding Jack.

They were escorted through the station and into a large room toward the back of the building. The room was the fabled hive of activity. People were staffing workstations of all kinds, some with their noses buried in monitors and keyboards, others had earphones and their eyes closed listening to whatever was coming through. A couple more were hovering around a board with photos, maps, and what looked like a mind map.

In the center of the room talking to Detectives Palmer and Leyland was an extraordinarily thin man. He was average height but had to be well below average weight, so much so, that Asher wondered if he were sick. He was almost completely bald but wasn't doing it gracefully as he had a rather unfortunate comb-over going on. When he turned to look at Asher and the others as they entered the room, Asher also noticed the man had, without exception, the stoniest face he'd ever seen. He was handsome, but he looked thoroughly unmoved by the situation he was in. From the suit and his general bearing, he suspected the man was Special Agent Harry Doyle. Asher suspected that for Doyle to get as far as he had in the FBI, he had to be a ruthless hunter of human monsters and had learned to wear a stony impersonal mask.

"Banner, come on through. We're just finishing setting up." The hint of an inflection in his accent screamed New York though Asher wasn't good enough to pinpoint which borough.

He followed Alec as he approached the man with his hand outstretched. "Doyle, thanks for coming," Alec said as they shook hands.

"Thank you for calling it in. With luck, this'll be a personal thing, as you suspect, but we need to make sure it's not a new player coming in."

"Harry, this is Jacey—my IT wiz you're so jealous of." Jacey shook the agent's hand, and Asher didn't miss the once-over they gave each other. Jacey was a pretty young woman who clearly walked her own path, whereas Harry was the stereotypical, straight-laced federal agent. And there had to be at least a thirty-year age gap, but Asher was sure he hadn't imagined the flair of interest. "And this is Asher Winsome."

"Mr. Winsome, so sorry about your situation—" Harry Doyle shook his hand with surprising strength. "You've called in one of the best here, and in addition, the full weight of the FBI is working on this now."

"We appreciate anything you can do."

"Right. Let's get into it then. Mr. Winsome, may I call you Asher?" Doyle waited for him to nod before proceeding. "Asher, I know Alec would have kept you informed about these kinds of auctions and what to expect..." He flicked a glance at Alec as though to confirm what he was saying.

Alec nodded but added, "He knows, though I'm not even sure what to expect from this one. It's different. I'd bet everything this is not a legitimate auction."

"I tend to agree," Agent Doyle said. "We haven't picked up much interest. It's as though they don't have any contacts, possibly they don't know how or want to get into the usual traffic for this kind of thing. From what we can pick up, there's only been a few hundred sign-in attempts each time the viewing window opens."

"A few hundred," Asher gasped. "That many?" His head swam with the knowledge several hundred people were watching his four-year-old nephew with a view to buying him to do god knows what.

"Asher," Alec said quietly, "it's a really small number. Often, the number is in the thousands, tens of thousands, even."

"To buy a child? How the fuck are you letting this happen! What the hell are you people doing?" He turned his glare to Agent Doyle. "How could this be allowed to happen?"

"We do everything we can to stop it." Agent Doyle spoke plainly, no hint of anger at Asher's outburst in his tone; he'd probably heard it a million times before. "We're a handful trying to stop a horde. Human trafficking is a global plague, and I agree, we're not doing enough to stop it, but it's not from a lack of trying. I promise you that every man and woman on my team eat and sleep this shit day in and day out."

"I'm sorry," Asher said, suitably chastised. "I didn't mean how it sounded. I just... Why aren't there more agents or whatever you need?"

"That's a question above my pay grade, I'm afraid. Look, we're only a small group, but we do have wins so let's concentrate on winning this one."

"Okay." Asher nodded. Alec was standing close to his side, so close their shoulders were brushing, and the brief, light touch made him feel better. Jacey had wandered off to set up her computer at a large conference table, where several other people were already working away on computers of their own.

"Jacey's got our accounts set up and ready to bid. Asher's going to bid for the family, and we'll do counterbidding in case they don't want the family to buy," Alec explained.

"Good. We've got a couple of agents who already have an online profile in the community. They haven't heard a whisper of the auction, but they've been logging on to keep an eye on things. We can have a couple of them bid too. If money is their endgame, we need to push the price up quickly so they're satisfied; otherwise they may go to ground and resurface where we can't see. It's a miracle they sent the link."

"That's what makes me think it's personal rather than a legitimate auction." Asher had heard Alec say this several times, but he still couldn't wrap his head around the notion someone hated his family so much they'd choose this most vile of ways to hurt them.

"I tend to agree. Agent Cole is still at the house with the family. There's been no other contact—though I suspect you know already," Doyle said, nodding his head in Jacey's direction.

"Yeah, she's got everything covered—phones, emails, Facebook accounts, twitter. The works. Any way the family can be contacted electronically, she's already got staked out," Alec said, his voice full of pride. One day he'd have to ask the full story of how Jacey and Alec came to be.

"I hope you're paying her well, Banner, because I'm going to make her one hell of an offer." Agent Doyle kept his eyes on Jacey as he spoke.

"You can try, buddy."

Harry Doyle laughed, the sound so unexpected from the stone-faced agent that Asher actually jumped.

"All right. We've got a few hours till the auction opens. Come on into the interview room, and we can work through things in detail." Agent Doyle ushered them toward a small room that held a table, a couple of chairs, and two sofas, both looking comfortable enough to sleep on. Clearly this is the room where they interviewed the victims rather than the suspects.

Asher took a seat in the corner of one of the sofas. He sat rigidly, unable to relax at all. Alec sat beside him, almost as stiff as he was.

"Let me get some coffee in here. I suspect it's going to be a long day," Agent Doyle said and then left the room after taking their orders.

"Is that why you do what you do? You and Ben and the rest? Because there are so few of you trying to stop it." Asher asked as soon as they were alone.

"Mostly. It's a bit more personal for Ben. His partner, Ethan's, two nieces were kidnapped a little over a year ago. Ben and Ethan went in and got them. They're raising them now after their mother passed away. Anyway, at the time they were working for a security firm...they were bodyguards, and one of the men Ethan was protecting was affected by what happened with the little girls. He decided to open his own agency specializing in missing kids. He asked Ben and Ethan to go into it with him. Ben asked me to join and voila..."

"It's a wonderful thing you're all doing. I had no idea child abduction was so...prevalent." How many families went through what his was right now? How many little children suffered so horribly?

"This work is not something everyone can do. You see and hear some pretty brutal things. I *can* do it, so I *should* do it," Alec said matter-of-factly.

The door creaked open, and Harry came back in. He held three coffee mugs and had a couple of packets of cookies tucked under his chin. He passed off the coffees and then caught the cookies with his free hand, offering them to Asher and Alec. They both declined, which seemed to please Agent Doyle.

"So, Winsome Senior still hasn't come through with a solid suspect. He's handed a few names to Cole, but he seems pretty wishy-washy about them. What about you, Asher? Can you tell us anyone who might be involved?" Doyle sat after asking his question, his gaze fixed on him while he bit into a cookie.

"No. I don't have much to do with my family. I haven't seen my parents for well over a year. My brother I see every few months, but I see Maddy more frequently since Jack came along. She wants him to know his family," Asher answered, and despite the casualness of the meeting, he got the distinct impression he was being subtly grilled by the agent.

"Falling out with your parents?" A few crumbs fell from his mouth as the agent spoke.

"Of sorts. They don't agree with my career choices, so I find it best to stay away."

"And with your brother?"

"Not a falling out, no. Kane wants to please our folks, no matter what, and I've disagreed with him about it."

"And how are you doing for money? Marine photography pays well?" Doyle sipped his coffee, his eyes hawklike over the rim of his cup. Asher suddenly realized he was being interrogated.

"Harry—"

"You know I have to ask, Banner. Do you think Cole hasn't already done the same with the others?"

"They've been asked these questions—by me, the cops, and now you. The family is clean." Alec was tense beside him, and it occurred to Asher, for the first time, that perhaps Alec would be in trouble for sleeping with his client—or suspect, apparently.

"Look, Asher. I know it sucks, but we must look at you and your family through a lens of suspicion. It's the way it is."

"I understand, but I can promise you, Agent Doyle, I'd rather cut my own heart out than hurt that little boy. I've got a considerable trust fund from my grandparents, so I don't need money. And I can also assure you I'm not angry enough at my parents anymore to want to put them through this hell, and I was never angry with my brother. I'm not your guy."

Agent Doyle watched him for a good long while, his eyes searching. Asher endured it as best he could. "Good. Let's concentrate on the real perpetrators then."

Asher did his best to relax—an impossible task after practically being accused of Jack's kidnapping. He understood it, but it still grated. Doyle sat back a little, his gaze flicking between him and Alec.

"Okay, so the police got nothing from the abduction site. Too much time had passed and the area was too heavily trafficked. Footprints could be anyone's by the time they got there. They've been working with the nanny—Emily—but she didn't get a good look at their faces, not enough for the artist to work with, anyway. She can describe their bodies fairly well but no real features. Her bank accounts are clean, so it's not looking likely she's involved. The only way we're going to catch these guys and make it stick is get them red-handed."

"What've you got in mind?" Alec asked.

"Well, this is where Asher or one of our agents comes in. We've got to ensure we win the auction and then be there at the exchange."

"They'll have to be expecting us," Alec stated, and it was the first time Asher really thought about what happens after the auction. Surely the bastards who had Jack would have to know if the family won the auction the chances of the cops being at the exchange would be high, because of course they would. So why alert the family at all?

Alec had to be right, and this was all about causing pain to the family—as much as possible. And if that was the case, how the hell would they get Jack back?

The door suddenly pushed open, and Jacey poked her head into the room. "Alec, you guys better come see this."

They all followed Jacey to where she'd set herself up. A few other people stood nearby and several more busily worked away alongside her.

"What's going on, Jace?" Alec asked.

Alec flicked a quick look at him, and Asher got the distinct impression he was considering tugging Asher out of the room so he couldn't see or hear whatever the hell was going on.

"Okay," Jacey began, her finger pointing to something on the screen. "So the auction site isn't due to open for another hour, right?"

"Sure," Agent Doyle answered.

"Well the account I set up for Asher is still closed, but all others are opened. The bidding has started."

"What?" Asher tried not to scream, but the single word came out louder and more panicked than he would have liked. Alec's hand circled his upper arm and squeezed a little. Asher clung to the comfort it provided.

"The timer's still going under Asher's account, but everyone else is bidding."

"What about my guys?" Doyle asked.

"They're bidding." Jacey didn't even glance away from her monitor as she spoke. Her screen was split into a few workspaces, and her fingers were flying over the keys.

"How long does the bidding last?" Asher asked. He felt the pressure as Alec squeezed his arm again and braced himself for whatever was coming.

"Depends," Doyle said. "Sometimes they go until the bidding stops which can take a few minutes up to a few hours. If they don't reach the amount they're after, sometimes they bring the product out and—"

"Harry!" Alec's voice snapped like a whip, and his hold on Asher's arm tightened.

"Product?" Asher asked feeling sick to his stomach.

"I'm sorry, Asher, sometimes we have to distance ourselves, and we..."

"I get it. Excuse me," he cut Harry off and fled the room. He needed air. He needed for this to be over.

He ran through the police station, searching for an exit, ignoring a few offers of help. Heavy footsteps behind him told him he was being followed.

The sun was bright and the day warming up when he stepped outside. There was a large tree in the vacant lot next door, and Asher made a beeline for it. He sat with his back against it and closed his eyes. He took a few deep breaths, trying to calm down.

"Asher?"

"I'm okay," he whispered as Alec knelt beside him.

"I'm sorry about that. Sometimes we can be a bit tactless."

"I'm not angry, Alec, but I had no idea any of this went on. I mean, I knew, but I didn't...if that makes sense?"

"Perfect."

Asher opened his lids and looked at Alec; his hazel eyes squinted back at him, the gold in them highlighted by the sunshine. Asher bet he could find a hundred different colors in those eyes.

"I'm not helping much," Asher murmured. He felt thoroughly useless. Even when he'd been in the shark's mouth, he'd been able to fight back, but now he just felt helpless.

"You're here, which means Jack's parents don't have to be. Do you know how confronting it is for the parent to be in that room with the FBI, hearing real time what's going on?

I've seen them crack from it. You're sparing Kane and Maddy at least a little horror."

"Do you have family, Alec? Kids? Or nieces and nephews?"

"No kids, no. I'm an only child. My folks are still alive, though."

"Do you see them much?" Asher asked.

"I try to," Alec answered and swiveled his body around to sit beside Asher with his back against the massive tree. "They live up in Washington State, not far from the border. Mom was diagnosed with early onset dementia almost four years ago, so Dad quit work to take care of her."

"I'm so sorry. That must be hard."

Alec was quiet for a moment before he answered. "I cried the first time she didn't know who I was. It's harder for Dad, obviously. He never knows if he's going to wake up beside his wife or a woman who doesn't recognize him."

"He must love her very much." Asher's father would probably chuck his mom in a home if they were in a similar situation.

"Yeah, he does. He brushes her hair every day, and he learned to help with her makeup because she always liked looking her best. She never left the house without her hair done and her makeup immaculately applied. She couldn't give a shit now most days, but he does it for her anyway."

"They sound like the luckiest people in the world. I mean not the dementia, of course, but to have a love like that..."

"Dad tells me every time I see them not to be sad for them because they've been so lucky to have found each other and the years they had before."

"You never married or found someone to love, settle down with?" Asher asked, unsure if he wanted to hear the answer. He knew there'd be no one in Alec's life now because he might not know Alec well, but he knew he wouldn't be a cheater.

"No. Well, I actually wanted to marry someone once when I was too young. Thankfully she was mature enough to turn me down. Then the army happened and the FBI, and I guess I stopped looking." Alec nudged his shoulder with his own. "What about you?"

"I've had a few relationships, but none of them were with the one. I used to blame my parents for stunting my emotional growth, but now I think maybe I haven't met the right person yet."

"Still hopeful then?"

"Yeah. I want the works. Maybe even kids, but when I look at what Maddy and Kane are going through now, I'm not so sure." Asher wondered what Alec thought about having kids. He'd seen a hell of a lot more than what Asher was witnessing now. Would he want kids one day? Would he think having children was worth the risk?

Alec watched him silently until he eventually stood and held out his hand. "You okay to go back in?"

Asher put his hand in Alec's and allowed him to help him up. "Yeah. I want this finished."

Chapter Nine

ALEC

Alec kept one eye on Asher and the other on Jacey's screen. Asher was hanging in there, but Alec knew he was struggling. Who the fuck wouldn't be? The bidding had been underway for a little over an hour now, and Asher's account had finally opened. The first bid they'd made from Asher's account topped all other bids by twenty thousand dollars. They weren't messing around. They wanted to make it clear the Winsome family would outbid every other bid, that the Winsome family would be their biggest payday.

The plan was to drive off legitimate bidders, leaving only Asher and the agents bidding under their fake profiles. That way, they'd have as much control as possible over the situation. Alec wanted to get his hands on these monsters, but the top priority had to be getting Jack back.

"How much have we got to play with here?" Someone called out across the room.

Asher answered before anyone else had the chance. "As much as we need. My parents have a fortune in the bank, and if we need to sell everything we've got..."

"It won't come to that, Asher," Alec assured quietly. This would go higher than a typical auction because Alec believed this *was* actually a ransom payment, but he'd seen the Winsomes' accounts—they'd be able to afford it.

One by one, other bidders dropped out. There were only six left, one of them was Asher, four were agents, and one was an unknown bidder. The FBI was doing everything they could to track down the remaining legitimate bidder. People who bid for kids on the Internet, though, tended to know how to cover their tracks.

"Let's try to wrap this up. Put in a bid for Asher upping the last figure by another twenty thousand. And Jenny up your bid by ten after that. Hopefully, a thirty thousand dollar jump will knock the last bidder out." Harry's voice boomed through the room but showed no noticeable tension even though Alec knew they were all on edge. "Jacey, still nothing with the virus you got in there?"

"They're definitely local. It's going through a cell, though, so I can't get an exact address. All I've got is a signal pinging off a cell tower in Clairemont."

"Okay, good. It's something. I'll get some of the local PD in the area; make sure they keep a lookout. Let's make these bids then."

Alec watched as Asher made the bid. He'd insisted on doing it himself and he'd been allowed. Everyone understood the need to do something in this sort of situation, and this was all Asher could do, so they weren't going to stop him. He saw the dollar figure on the screen and hoped it'd be enough to satisfy these pricks. It was a far larger amount than anything he'd heard of previously.

"You all right?" He leaned over and squeezed Asher's knee.

"Yeah." Asher's voice was soft and cracked a little. He sounded as though he was hanging by a thread.

"I'm gonna give Ben a call. Update him and see how your family's doing. Why don't you give Kane a call? Check in with him."

"Okay." They both stood and walked toward the back of the room. Doyle would call them when another bid was needed.

Alec ushered Asher into the interview room they'd been in earlier and closed the door behind them. "You sure you're all right?"

Asher stepped up close to him and put his arms around Alec's waist, pressing his face into Alec's neck. Asher nodded as though he was okay even though he plainly wasn't. Alec wrapped his arms around Asher's back and pulled him closer. He pressed a kiss to the top of Asher's head. "It's almost done. Almost over."

"Is it?" Asher murmured into his throat, his lips tickling the sensitive skin there.

"Give Kane a call," he said, not wanting to lie to Asher but also not wanting to strip his hope any further. "Then let's go finish this."

Alec pulled away and pressed a kiss to Asher's lips before leaving him to his call. He stepped out of the room and found a quiet corner where he could make his own call. Ben answered on the third ring.

"Hey, Banner. What's the news?"

"We've got it down to one legit bidder now, and we've upped the bidding, hoping to knock them out. With luck, this part will be done in about ten minutes or so. How's things over there?"

"They're hanging in. The older Winsomes haven't moved from their seats. They're like fucking statues. Kane and Maddy are pacing like caged animals, but they're good. She's one tough lady." Alec knew Ben admired people who held it together under the worst of circumstances, so Maddy Winsome had probably earned herself a fan.

"Good. Asher's calling Kane now to check in. I'll call back when it's done and we've got the details for the exchange."

"This still feel hinky to you, Banner?"

Ben had always been good at reading people, and Alec had long ago given up trying to hide shit from him. "Yeah. I just don't see what they're thinking. How are they gonna make the exchange? They shouldn't have alerted the family, and by extension, us, to the auction. It feels wrong."

"I agree. It's completely illogical. We'll have to stay sharp because I can see this going sideways."

Jesus, he hoped Ben was wrong, but it didn't feel like it. "We can't let that happen, Ben."

"We won't, buddy."

Alec nodded even though Ben couldn't see him. He ended the call and made his way back to Asher.

Asher was on the sofa with his head bowed, talking softly, when he walked back into the interview room. Alec couldn't quite make out what he was saying, but he caught a few placating snippets. They were of a similar size, but Asher looked so small and fragile as he sat there trying to help his brother through a nightmare. Alec wanted to pull him into his arms and fight off the whole fucking world for him if he had to. He wanted Asher's pain to end.

He stood quietly, watching him while Asher finished his call. He thought about what Ben had said last night—that he was different with Asher. Was he? He was nothing if not a realist, and he knew Asher's heightened emotions had led to last night. He also knew anything starting under these conditions usually burned out pretty damn quickly. In the light of Jack's rescue, Asher would see things for what they were. He'd probably wonder what the hell he'd been thinking to get anywhere near Alec, and then the disparity between them would become real fucking clear.

Asher was tough, but it took a special type to get involved with someone who did the kind of work he did—and a hell of a lot of effort for the relationship to last. But he was getting way ahead of himself. Asher needed someone—anyone—last night. Alec was smart enough to know he'd been the convenient choice. And that's all there was to it.

"Alec?"

"Yeah." He jumped a little at having been caught with his mind wandering.

"Are you okay?" Asher was watching him with those gorgeous silver-gray eyes.

"Sure. Just thinking..."

"About?"

Well he couldn't blurt out all the shit in his head—even though, oddly, he wanted to. "What comes next." He hated his answer, but he had no other to give. His words were vague enough that Asher would think he was referring to Jack, so he hadn't needed to lie.

"Kane and Maddy seemed to be hanging in there. Kane said Ben and Agent Cole have been great. They sounded exhausted and scared."

"That's natural, Asher. Hopefully, this is the home stretch."

Asher closed his eyes as Alec had seen him do many times. Alec thought he used those moments to pull himself together before coming out to face the harshness of the world again.

"Let's go," he said when he opened his eyes. Alec followed him, a little bit more captivated by this man who had done nothing *but* impress him from the start.

Harry was bent over a screen when they walked back into the madness of this investigation. There was a flurry of activity going on, giving Alec the tingle people who were in his line of work often got when things were coming to a head.

"Banner, Asher, come on. The legit bidder is out and we've pulled two of ours out already and are just about to yank the third. That'll leave you and one of ours. We'll get you top bid and then halt the bidding. It'll be their call whether to take your top bid or our agent's bid as second highest. Nearly done," Harry finished, his keen eyes on Asher.

"Harry, this is it," one of the agents called.

"Okay. Final bid, Asher. Let's bump it ten grand."

Asher placed the bid, and everyone sat back and waited. And waited.

Alec was starting to panic; maybe they'd misread the situation, or somehow fucked up and lost their chance, when the acceptance with further instructions came through. Asher had won the bidding, and he had two hours to transfer half the money.

Everything had been tense until now, but Alec knew this was when the real pressure was on. From this point on, things would snowball and they could go terribly wrong. Winning the auction had given them as much control over this situation as possible—which still wasn't a lot—but everything was now in the hands of monsters.

Asher and Harry were immediately on a call to Edmund Winsome to arrange the transfer, and Alec took the opportunity to read through the instructions they'd been sent. Once half the money hit their account, they'd have Jack at the exchange location within the hour. The location would be revealed only when they got the money. Asher was to take his phone so he could transfer the other half of the money before the exchange.

"Dad's transferring the money now. Harry's got the bank tracing it, making sure it hits the account as soon as possible. We might have Jack back tonight." Asher spoke so fast all his words ran together as one long scramble of vowels and consonants, so Alec had to concentrate to understand him.

"We could, yeah, but, Asher, even with the bank onboard sometimes it can take a while for the transfer. My guess is they're gonna want somewhere populated for the transfer so there is a chance they could hold off until tomorrow. I know it's real easy to get excited now, but try to take things as they come." He hated saying those words, hated wiping the start of the smile off Asher's face, but he'd hate it even more if he had to watch Asher fall from too great a high.

They kept waiting because there was nothing else for them to do. Finally, close to an hour later, a call came in reporting the money had gone through. All they had to wait for now was the location for the exchange. If the kidnappers kept their word, they'd get it within the hour.

Asher was pacing, and as much as Alec wanted to get him out of there for a while, he knew he had no chance. As far as Asher was concerned, this nightmare was almost over. Alec hoped he was right.

"Okay, here we go," Jacey called out, and both he and Asher raced to her screen.

A message came through on Asher's email account. Alec skimmed through the words.

Harry groaned behind him. "The fucking zoo. Of course. Okay, so I'm guessing we're almost two hours from closing time, and they want to meet at the entrance—or at this time of day, the exit. It's going to be hard covering the entire area." Harry was merely thinking out loud at this stage. Alec knew from experience he'd start dishing out orders any minute.

"I'm going to call Kane," Asher enthused beside him. "Or should we wait? They'll probably want to come, and I don't know… Is that a good idea?"

"Call them, Asher. They need to know but discourage them from coming. If you can't talk them out of it, Ben will."

Just as Asher reached for his phone Alec's rang. The caller was Ben.

"Hey, Cronin, the exch—"

"Alec something's wrong, very wrong," Ben interrupted.

"What happened?" Alec asked, his heart thumping madly and his pulse quickening. The familiarity of his body's response to potential trouble was comforting.

"Edmund Winsome got a call from the kidnappers a few minutes ago. They want him to pay a million bucks within two hours, and they'll return Jack."

"We just paid them two million and another two coming when we exchange in under an hour. What the fuck? Could it be a hoax? Has it hit the media yet?"

Asher was watching him. From the look on his face, he'd been able to tell something was wrong. Jack's kidnapping hadn't felt right to Alec from the beginning, but what the fuck was going on? If the call to Edmund was legitimate, it didn't make sense. They'd given him two hours to transfer a million dollars, but potentially they could have Jack home safe within an hour—and why risk a two million dollar payday for half that amount?

"Doyle," Alec called, pulling the phone away from his ear. "We've got a snag."

Chapter Ten

ASHER

Asher felt as though everybody was looking at him. Granted, there were at least fifteen assorted law enforcement officers distributed throughout the crowd with their eyes on him, and who knew how many more spread through the parking lot and other areas in and around the zoo. But he felt like the entire crowd was watching him as he stood there holding himself together as best he could.

He knew Alec was somewhere nearby, but wherever he was, he was well hidden. He wished he could catch a glimpse of him—just a quick peek to help settle his nerves.

In his earpiece, there was minimal chatter. Mostly the voices were officers occasionally checking in or clearing anything and anyone who had raised any concern.

Asher was amazed at how quickly this had all been put together, especially with the added hitch of the mystery call to his father. No one could figure out what was going on, but Alec and Harry had been worried. They'd both tried to disguise it from him, but he'd seen straight through them.

There'd been hesitation in their eyes when they'd been discussing their options. Asher had seen it plainly. The call to his father had thrown them, and they'd been unable to account for it. It didn't make any sense, not that kidnapping a child or any of this made sense to Asher.

In the end, the decision was made to send a team to the mansion. Agent Cole would coordinate from there any exchange instructions which might come through, as though she was leading an entirely different operation from what they were doing here.

Harry had been pissed when they'd been unable to verify the authenticity of the caller. Jacey had all of their phones covered, and she was working on pinpointing the location of the caller or anything else she could find out. But Harry had been furious that his father hadn't let anyone know about the call until after the fact, and he hadn't asked the caller for proof of life. Asher had swayed a little when he'd heard those words—proof of life.

Even now, the idea of a grandfather thinking to ask strangers for proof his four-year-old grandson was still alive stunned him. How was any of this real?

Alec had spoken at length to Ben about what was going on. The decision was made for Ben to stay at the mansion to work with Cole and her team.

The time was approaching 4:30 p.m. and the park would be closing in half an hour. Streams of people were making their way to the exit. Happy families, mostly, and Asher wondered if the kidnappers were twisting the knife in a little more, as though they hadn't already done irreparable damage. Showing him what a happy family looked like when his own was on the midst of such bitter misery. Of course, Alec had explained the crowds, especially ones with plenty of children, would provide camouflage for the kidnappers, not to mention a certain amount of security. The FBI wasn't going to go in guns blazing in a crowd filled with families.

He hadn't seen Jack in close to four months—other than the terrible image of him on Jacey's computer—but Asher was confident he'd recognize him. He watched as many faces in the crowd as possible, searching, desperately hoping to see the sweet little one he loved so well. Jack favored his mother in looks, though he definitely had his father's dark gray eyes.

As far as Asher knew, Jack was a completely normal four-year-old, though his experience with children was limited. The last time Asher had seen him, Jack had been full of boundless energy and curiosity. Most words out of his mouth were questions. It terrified Asher a little because sometimes he didn't know the answers, so what the hell did he do then? Asher had made friends with Google that visit.

"Excuse me." Asher hadn't seen the man approach, but he felt him as he clipped his side in passing. He turned but only caught a glimpse of the back of the man's head. The large area was crowded so the shoulder bump wasn't really concerning, but the fact he seemed to be alone in a sea of families raised the hair on his arms a little.

"Asher, everything okay?" Alec's voice was in his ear, clear and strong and so comforting. Asher nodded. He'd been told to talk only if essential. His shaggy hair hid the earpiece so they were hoping the kidnappers wouldn't notice it. They'd sure notice if he stood there talking to himself though. "Okay. You're doing great," Alec added. Asher sighed, relieved because Alec must be able to see him.

As five more minutes passed, Asher was starting to panic. They'd been here for close to twenty minutes now, and they hadn't seen or heard anything. A phone rang, sounding close. It rang and rang, while Asher looked around for it. He wished someone would answer because the ringing was distracting him.

It stopped ringing but then immediately started again. Asher tapped his pockets. It wasn't his ringtone but maybe... He found the small unknown cell in his shorts pocket, and his mind immediately went to the guy who'd bumped into him a few moments ago. He pulled the phone from his pocket, bringing it to his ear while hoping the people watching would put it together and go after the guy who'd bumped him, because he couldn't waste time explaining it to them.

"Hello?" he answered, looking around, foolishly hoping he'd see someone else on their phone who might be the kidnapper. But what the fuck did a kidnapper look like?

"Look to your left, casually, so as not to alert all the eyes on you. Don't say a word for the ears listening in either. At the restrooms, you'll see what you're looking for. He's alone, but he won't move because he knows we're close by, so don't think of getting to him yet. Take out your phone and transfer the other half of the money. I'll wait."

Asher's legs shook so badly he didn't know how they were holding him up. Alec was in his earpiece pleading with him to tell him what was going on, but he ignored him. He shook his head no when he heard someone else suggest they go in and see what was going on.

A tiny figure was standing against the wall of the restrooms. He was too far away to know for sure if it was Jack, especially with the cap pulled down on his head, but he was about the right size. Besides, what choice did he have but to believe the child was Jack?

He reached for his own phone and opened up the tab to transfer the remainder of the money. He kept his gaze on Jack. He was so close. So fucking close. He couldn't mess this up.

"Asher. Asher, listen to me. Is it them on the phone?" Alec was asking in his ear, but he wouldn't risk answering. "Nod if it is."

He nodded, just once, as furtively as he could manage.

"Don't transfer the money till you're sure Jack's here," Alec continued.

Asher continued on, desperately wanting to alert Alec to what was happening. If he could get him to understand that Jack was right there, maybe Alec could get to him. But he couldn't risk it. The guy on the phone said they were watching. He said there was someone close to Jack. He had no idea how far these people would go so he couldn't do anything to risk pissing them off.

"Asher, have you already spotted Jack?" Alec's voice was low and soothing—so very calm it helped ease his own spiraling nerves. He so desperately wanted to answer, he wanted to scream at Alec to run and grab the little boy. Instead he only gave the barest of nods. "Okay. I know they'll be watching so if there's any way you can give us the tiniest hint...I'm watching you, Ash. I'll see it. I promise."

Asher continued logging in to the banking details his father had provided. When this was over, he'd have to give his parents points for not bitching about the two...maybe four million dollars they were willingly handing over. For most people, it'd be a no-brainer, but his parents weren't most people, and money and prestige had always been everything to them.

"Steady, Asher." The kidnapper's voice came through the phone he still held close to his ear. He was juggling to transfer the money and hold onto the kidnapper's phone and listen to both Alec and the kidnappers. His pulse was racing, the sweat dripping down his back in sheets, his hands shaking hard enough it was a miracle he hadn't dropped the phones. He was fucking terrified. The weight of his responsibility in saving his nephew was pressing him into the ground.

"It's transferred," he said as soon as his finger hit the button. He waited for more instructions, but nothing came through the second phone. He waited and waited—for something, but there was only deafening silence. Without thinking, he flicked a glance toward Jack. The little boy was still there, exactly where he'd been left. Why weren't the kidnappers saying anything?

"I've got him, Ash." Alec's voice came in clearly. "I can see him."

Asher was half relieved and half terrified. How could he tell Alec that Jack was being watched? Or would he already know? If he tried to warn Alec, the kidnappers would know. What would happen then? Or possibly nothing would happen. He'd transferred the money, so maybe they'd simply walk away.

There was still no word coming through the kidnapper's phone, but the line was still open. He pocketed his own cell and turned toward Jack. There were still so many people milling about, especially near the restrooms as parents took their kids for one last toilet stop before the long trip home.

Asher took a step, hoping that if he was doing the wrong thing the kidnapper would stop him before he got too far. Nothing...no voice came through the phone. He kept walking, taking slow, tentative steps.

From the side of the building, a man emerged—alone. Did he look suspicious? Was he looking at Jack? Heading for him? Was it even Jack? He still couldn't be sure. He moved quicker now. Each step a lead fucking weight as he waited for something to go wrong.

Every person around Jack looked wrong to him now. How many were there? He couldn't see Alec, but he had to be close. Jack. Jack. The little boy filled his vision, nothing else mattered. He was standing there like a fucking statute— or a four-year-old too damn terrified to even twitch. His next steps were close to a run. The voices were silent in his ear and on the phone. He had to get there. Had to save Jack.

The bang from his right snatched his breath and shattered his heart. He was no expert, but he recognized a gunshot when he heard it. His gaze instinctively darted toward the sound. He caught flashes of people running, others throwing themselves to the ground or over their children, their mouths moving in screams, but the sound of the screams was muted—far away.

A face. A face in the crowd. One he knew. He knew that man. A blue ball cap and a gray T-shirt. Ordinary clothes meant to disguise, but Asher knew him.

In the split second, he'd looked toward where the gunshot had come from, turned back to check on Jack, and then turned again when it registered that he recognized somebody, the man was gone. Didn't matter. Jack was right there; his little legs straining with the effort of not moving despite his brain probably screaming at him to run from the obvious danger.

"Jack," he called, unsure if it would scare the boy more. It had been months since they'd seen each other, and that was a lifetime for a four-year-old. "Jack, it's Uncle Asher. I'm coming. Stay there."

He was almost there, just a few more steps. It was only now he registered the constant noise in his ear. Officers were squawking, shouting through the earpieces. Harry was throwing out instructions—fast and succinct. He had no idea what they were doing, but he trusted they were doing everything they needed to, everything they could.

It had only been seconds since the gunshot, and so far there hadn't been another one. He was right there—six feet, four, two, and then he had Jack in his arms, scooping him up, pulling him close, and running for the protection of the toilet block. The tiny body in his arms shook violently. Two enormous gray eyes flooded with tears looked up at him as he peered down.

"It's all right, Jack. It's me. Uncle Asher. You remember me?" he asked as calmly as he could through his panic. The little face nodded and then buried into his chest. Asher wrapped his hand around the tiny skull, crooning softly to the terrified child. "It's okay. It's okay. I'm going to take you home to Mommy and Daddy. It's all right now."

"Asher," Alec yelled, but his voice wasn't in his earpiece this time. He turned toward the sound. Alec was running full tilt toward him.

"Alec, he's there. Blue cap, gray T-shirt. I know him," Asher screamed back and pointed in the general direction he'd last seen the man.

Alec's gaze flicked over him and Jack, his indecision plain in his cool hazel eyes. He understood, because he wanted Alec right there beside them, preferably with his strong arms holding them both close, but he wanted that son of a bitch more. It had to be him. It couldn't be a coincidence.

"We're okay. I promise. Go get him, Alec."

Alec nodded and ran. Asher missed him immediately, only recognizing the safety he'd felt with Alec's presence when it was gone again. He walked farther into the restroom block.

Jack cried quietly in his arms, and Asher pushed his lips gently into the little boy's hair. He cradled him close, one arm wrapped around his waist, the other still cupped around the back of his head.

Asher moved a little closer to the door so he could see what was happening. Outside, the initial shock was over, and with the absence of more gunshots, people were starting to move, running toward the exit. Asher could hear agents now calmly ordering people to move this way or that. He poked his head farther out of the restrooms and almost sagged in relief when he found himself face-to-face with Harry Doyle.

"Asher, you got him?"

"Yeah. It's him. It's Jack. He seems okay."

"Are you?" Harry asked.

Asher finally noticed it wasn't only little Jack shaking like a fucking leaf. His entire body was shaking so hard it actually hurt. He couldn't stop the sob that burst from him— a mixture of fear, relief, anxiety, and joy.

"Come on. Let's get you both checked out," Harry said softly.

Asher started to follow the agent when he finally came to his senses. "Alec. Shit, Alec's gone after the guy. I think it's the guy. He was there...right there where the shot came from, and he was calm and alone, and I know him."

"Tell me," Harry demanded.

"It was Morgan Fincher, the grandson of one of the partners at Dad's firm—Piers Fincher. I've seen him at functions over the years. What are the chances it's a simple coincidence he's here?"

"Slim to none," Harry drawled. "Which direction?"

Asher pointed to where he'd last seen Morgan and had sent Alec. Harry turned and followed the trajectory of his finger.

"Get to Agent Sparks at the exit there; she'll get you to the paramedics." Harry turned back to him and squeezed his upper arm before gently touching the top of Jack's head. "We'll get him." He smirked and then took off.

Asher ran toward safety with his precious bundle securely in his arms.

Chapter Eleven

ALEC

All hell had broken loose with the single gunshot. He suspected the shot was a blank. Something to scare the crowd and cause the chaos Alec was struggling to get through now. It had worked well. Parents were scooping their children into their arms and running, some were lying over them, shielding them with their bodies. Doyle's people were doing what they could to safely usher them away from the chaos.

After the initial screaming and shock had stopped, all energy seemed to be focused on getting to safety. Near the entrance to the toilet block, Asher crouched with Jack huddled in his arms. Everything in him was screaming to get to them as soon as he could.

"Asher," he shouted. Asher turned toward him, and even from this distance, Alec could see stark terror in those gorgeous gray eyes. Asher's face was pale, and he was trembling badly.

"Alec, he's there. Blue cap, gray T-shirt. I know him," Asher called to him, pointing somewhere over his right shoulder. Alec never took his eyes off Asher and the boy. He had to know they were okay before he did anything, even though his body burned to go after the asshole who'd done this. "We're okay, I promise. Get him, Alec."

Alec allowed himself one more gaze over Asher to make sure there wasn't a hole in him, and then he turned and ran.

When he'd heard the gunshot, at first he'd been so fucking terrified they'd shot Asher, but then he'd seen him moving toward Jack. Now he'd heard Asher's voice, he knew he was okay, so his thoughts turned to the monster who'd caused all this insanity.

Adrenaline pushed his legs to work harder, his senses heightening, and his body poised, prepared to fight.

He trusted Asher when he'd told him to go after this guy. Some guy Asher apparently knew. If the man turned out to be innocent...well, Alec didn't really give a fuck. Better to tackle an innocent guy to the ground than let an asshole who kidnaps and sells children go.

He headed toward the crowd running from the area Alec had pointed to. He was tall enough so he could see over most heads. At the front of the crowd, he thought he caught a glimpse of a blue cap, so he kept heading that way. He couldn't make out anything more—no gray T-shirt, no gun swinging idly in his hand, but Alec suspected there could be. The actions of the kidnappers so far were all over the place. Alec couldn't decide if they were professionals or not, but he wasn't taking any chances either way.

The guy he was chasing was buried in the crowd, which was concerning for Alec. Too many convenient hostages around, too many chances for collateral damage. Firing a gun to panic the crowd had provided perfect cover.

"Banner," Harry spoke in his ear.

"Blue cap, gray tee. Heading toward the farthest left exit gate." He didn't waste breath saying more; Harry would know.

The crowd was starting to press closer as they approached the gates and were being funneled into the tight space. Alec pushed through the horde of people, ignoring the protests and shouted curses. Ball Cap was almost out of the gate.

Alec moved out of the stream heading toward the exit, took several full strides to his left, and vaulted over a turnstile. In doing so, he avoided the pileup at the opened gate. He landed cleanly and pumped his legs to regain ground. He was only a few feet away from Ball Cap, who'd reduced his pace to a calmer fast walk rather than the running pace he'd been doing earlier. Ball Cap must think he'd gotten away cleanly.

Alec used his momentum to tackle the man center mass, both of them crashing to the ground in a tangle. They rolled as Ball Cap tried to struggle away from him, but Alec was strong, and he was fucking motivated to get this guy.

Ball Cap tried to punch up from beneath Alec, when Alec had him on his back, but only managed a glancing blow to his shoulder. Alec grappled Ball Cap's lower body with his legs, his thighs squeezing the man's legs tightly so he couldn't move. The butt of a gun peeked from Ball Cap's waistband. He grabbed it with his left hand while his right arm cocked back to deliver a punch of his own. His fist caught Ball Cap on the chin, whipping his head back and to the side. Alec tightened his legs even more, holding him securely, knowing from experience that right now was when the man would choose to either fight harder or give up.

Unfocused brown eyes looked up at him when Ball Cap's head rolled back from Alec's blow. The body beneath him loosened, showing Alec he'd landed his punch well. Ball Cap didn't have the wherewithal to fight back even if he wanted to.

Alec glanced around, searching for the backup he knew would be close. Two agents approached, weapons drawn, from his left, and on the right was Harry, a smug smirk pulling his lips, zip ties already in hand. The crowd still moved, but slower now, giving them a wide berth, their frightened gazes constantly flicking back toward him and Ball Cap, in case the bad guy got loose, and they all had to run screaming again.

As the two agents cautiously approached, Alec handed off the recovered weapon to one of them. Once his hands were free of the gun, Alec relaxed his legs and moved from where he was sitting astride the man, kneeling beside him instead. He flipped him onto his stomach and then held his hand up for the zip ties as Harry approached. He took great delight in tightening them.

Harry moved in to have the pleasure of reading the fucker his rights and hauling him to his feet. There was nothing gentle about the way either of them treated Ball Cap, and Alec couldn't have given a shit even if there were a dozen cell phones focused on him recording every move he made.

"You good, Banner?"

"Never better, Harry." He winked, as he drew in deep breaths. He wasn't getting any younger, even if he was in excellent shape, and the adrenaline rush was already starting to ease up.

"Asher and the boy should be with the paramedics by now," Harry said, giving Alec a knowing glance. Sometimes he fucking hated that he worked with people who were trained to read others. There was no hiding anything from them.

"Thanks. I'll go check on them." Alec barely glanced at Ball Cap as he walked away. The only thing he cared about this man was the fact they'd caught him.

There were dozens of emergency vehicles in the parking lot now. Police, fire, ambulance—they'd all shown up as they should. The second the shot went off someone would have called 911 to report a public shooting. They were so fucking common these days that every city, town, and fucking backwater village had procedures in place to respond. Harry and the locals would be hours sorting out the fucking mess. Thank fuck, he didn't have to deal with that shit on a daily basis anymore.

The public had been herded into an unoccupied section of the parking lot normally reserved for tour buses. They were surrounded by uniformed officers who'd likely be nervous after being called to a shooting. He could also see SWAT off to the side, their Colt M4 carbines held purposefully in their arms, their steely eyes raking the crowds.

The paramedics were milling through the mass of people, attending to anyone in need, but mostly they were offering a soothing touch to the shocked multitudes. Alec made a beeline for the ambulances parked in a cluster. Asher and Jack would have been taken there.

Suddenly, he felt his phone buzzing in his pocket, the sound still off. He pulled out his cell and caught Ben's name on the screen before bringing it to his ear.

"Yeah," he answered.

"Jesus, Banner, what the fuck is going on? I'm at the fucking mansion literally holding back this entire fucking family because they've seen on the news about shit going down at the zoo. Tell me some good news 'cause I don't want to have to get violent with the fucking victims, man, and it's gonna come to that in a second—I can see it in Maddy's eyes."

"Well, if you'd shut up and let me speak," Alec answered. "We've got him. Jack's safe—unhurt as far as I know. So is Asher. I'm on my way to the bus now to check on them."

"He's safe. They're both safe, so you can all calm down now while I try to find out what's going on," Ben called out, trying to appease the family, only to be bombarded with a barrage of questions. "Fuck, Banner, give me something more to tell them."

"I'll call when I know what hospital we're going to. And tell them we've got him...well, we think we've got one of the bastards who did it. Asher says he knows him, but I don't know anything more yet."

"All right, I'll calm these guys. Let me know ASAP where you'll be, or I swear I'll let Maddy loose on your ass. And man, she is one fierce lady I wouldn't want on *my* fucking ass."

Alec allowed himself a chuckle and then hung up. His entire body was itching to see Asher again. Make sure 100 percent he was safe and unhurt.

The backs of the ambulances were all open. A few people were sitting in them, probably with grazes from the panicked stampede and a couple more being stretchered in. Panic attacks most likely or maybe even heart attacks. He followed law enforcement—they'd be milling around wherever Asher and Jack were, for sure.

The biggest crowd was packed around the third ambulance from the front, and Alec made a beeline for it.

Helicopters buzzed overhead, and media vans were already setting up in the distance. The vultures had arrived to pick over the carcass of the latest hot news item; the gleeful reporters would be doing their best to transmit shock and horror at the scene, all while imagining the accolades they might receive for best coverage of yet another human tragedy.

As he approached the ambulance, he saw Asher sitting up in the back, Jack in his lap, and a too-young-looking paramedic talking calmly as she carefully eased a thermometer into Jack's ear, removing it seconds later. Asher's eyes were fixed on Jack, occasionally flicking up to the paramedic as she spoke.

Some of Doyle's team was standing around the vehicle, nodding at Alec as he approached. He pushed through them, managing to walk right up to the back of the ambulance before Asher even noticed him.

"Alec," Asher whispered, sounding thoroughly relieved when he finally noticed Alec's approach.

"Hey. How're you both doing?" Alec asked quietly, doing his best not to startle the little boy in Asher's lap.

"We're fine. Both of us." Asher beamed. "Did you...?"

"Yeah, I got him."

Asher's eyes closed briefly, and he blew out a sigh. Alec watched his body relax as some of the tension drained away.

"Sir," the young paramedic said, "we're getting ready to take them to Scripps Mercy."

"Okay, thanks." Alec turned his attention back to Asher. "I'll follow you there. I'll be right behind you," he added when a hint of panic crept into Asher's eyes.

Asher nodded. "All right, I'll tell them to let you through," he murmured, never once easing up on the grip he had on Jack.

"Your family knows. I'll let them know where to meet us. You lie there, relax, and hold on to that little one," he said, nodding at Jack.

Asher sighed. "I'm not sure I'll ever be able to let him go." He kissed into the hair on top of Jack's head. "I was just about to call Maddy and Kane now. I bet they want to speak to Jack. Thank you, Alec. Thank you."

Alec nodded, suddenly overwhelmed by the image before him. Christ, he was getting fucking soft. He reached out and squeezed Asher's arm. "I'll see you soon."

He sent a quick text to Ben, letting him know which hospital to take the family to and went in search of Harry.

The agent wasn't hard to find once he'd turned away from Asher and Jack—and what a fucking struggle leaving them had been. Usually, once a case like this was finished, Alec had no problem walking away from the people involved, regardless of how much he'd come to care about them. Asher was a whole new ball game, but Alec was sure he might have been the only one playing in this game.

Harry was holding court with—well it looked like every law enforcement and news agency present was huddled around Special Agent in Charge Harry Doyle. There was no way Alec was going to fight through the crowd only to have the questions start as to who he was and what the hell he was doing in the middle of this mess. Alec was a low profile kind of guy.

"Hey, Sparks," he called quietly to the agent he recognized leaning against one of the SWAT vans.

"Banner, you good?"

"Yeah. Listen, tell Doyle I'm going over to Scripps Mercy with Asher and the kid. I'll be there when he's ready to grill me." He was tired and sore and the last thing he wanted to do was sit through an interview with Harry so he could get his story, but he also knew his statement was essential for the case against dirtbag Ball Cap, so he'd suck it up—after he got his fill of ensuring Asher was absolutely safe.

"No problem, Banner. You might wanna get them to check you out. I can see the bruises coming up already." She smiled and turned back to her boss.

Ball Cap hadn't landed any significant blows, so he must have roughed himself up tackling the bastard and rolling around on the hard asphalt with him. He sure felt like it. As the adrenaline kept easing, the pain started seeping in. The ache was nothing unbearable—not at all—but he'd feel it tomorrow. Then again, so would Ball Cap, and that put a fucking smile on his face.

All he had for ID to get past the uniforms guarding the perimeter was a fucking visitor pass Harry had given him, but thankfully, a few of the locals from the station were there and waved him through. He did his best to keep his head down as he drove past the media camp.

It took him less than fifteen minutes to get to the hospital. He found a lot, huffing at the excessive fee he'd have to pay for the privilege to park so close to the hospital, and headed for the entry.

An elderly man staffed the information desk, and he smiled warmly as Alec approached. "Help you, sir?"

"Yes. I'm looking for the ER."

The man smiled consolingly at Alec. "If you take the elevator on your right there to the basement, head left as you get out and follow the signs."

"Thank you."

"Pleasure, sir."

Alec headed toward the elevators, lengthening his stride to shave seconds off the time before he saw Asher again. Jesus, as much as his logical brain tried to talk him out of this Asher thing, his fucking lizard brain kept cooing to him, "Asher. It's Asher you want" over and fucking over. Looked as though it was going to be a battle to the death to see which brain won. What Alec had to remember, though, was he'd been a distraction for Asher and likely nothing more.

He found a nurse as soon as he walked into emergency. He explained who he was, but she seemed to already know.

"Mr. Winsome instructed us to let you through." She smiled. "Follow me."

Asher was lying on a bed; the head elevated high so he was practically sitting. His eyes were closed, but his arms were wrapped tightly around Jack, who was still lying in his lap, his little body relaxed against his uncle. Alec was dying to know if anyone had tried to separate them and what had happened to them.

"Ash," he whispered as he approached. Asher's eyes flew open, and he pulled Jack even tighter against him. "It's just me. It's Alec."

Asher's body sagged as he understood there was no immediate danger. Jack's large gray eyes were fixed on him, untrusting and never looking away. Alec wondered if the little boy would ever trust again.

"Hey. You must be Jack. I've heard a lot about you," Alec tried and cringed as the little boy flinched.

"It's okay, Jack. This is Alec and he's a friend of mine, and your mommy and daddy. He helped us today, helped save you." Asher rubbed Jack's little arm as he spoke.

Jack looked at him before turning slightly and curling farther into his uncle's body. Alec couldn't blame the kid at all.

"Your family's on their way," he said to Asher.

"Good. I wanted to call them, but I didn't want to leave Jack."

Alec nodded. "No, of course, I understand." Suddenly he felt so awkward with Asher, but he had no fucking clue why. "How are you? Are you all right? Really?"

"I will be. But Jesus, Alec, I—"

"Jack? Oh Jack, Jack." Maddy's voice cried out behind him. Ben must have broken the fucking land-speed record to get them here so soon.

Jack immediately sat up at his mother's voice, and he instantly burst into tears. By the time she reached him, he was wailing, "Mommy."

Asher handed Jack off to Maddy, and the little boy was lost to sight as mother and father wrapped him up between them. Edmund and Phyllis stood back a little, but they both wore smiles.

Ben was standing even farther back with Agent Cole. Alec went to join them. They silently watched the happy family reunion, and if there was a little tear in Alec's eyes at the sight, well, though unusual, Alec decided the sentiment was okay.

Chapter Twelve

ASHER

Asher was dead on his feet. Everyone had urged him to go home hours ago, but he'd refused. He'd been determined he wasn't stepping out of the hospital until his nephew did.

Now, finally, at five in the morning, Jack was cleared for release. Physically, the little boy was fine, but Asher didn't need someone with initials after their name to tell him Jack was suffering mentally—emotionally. Jack had been timid, clingy, and jumpy ever since Asher scooped him into his arms at the zoo.

Mercifully, Jack was sound asleep now on Kane's lap while the doctor signed the papers to allow him to leave.

"Are you sure we can't offer you a bed, Mr. and Mrs. Winsome?" the doctor asked, not even raising his gaze from the notes he was making.

"No. Thank you. We just want to get him home," Maddy replied.

"Of course. I understand. Try to get him plenty of rest. If he has nightmares, which are likely, make an appointment with one of the psychologists I've recommended to you. They're all exceptional, and honestly, I'd make the appointment as soon as possible anyway. Children are resilient, but he's been through a lot."

"We will. Thank you," Kane said softly so as not to wake the sleeping child in his arms.

"Okay. Well, that's it for me. Good luck and don't hesitate to call or come back if you've got any concerns." The doctor shook each of their hands. Asher couldn't even recall the poor man's name. He was so damn tired.

As soon as the doctor left, Kane was on his feet, his son cradled gently in his arms. Jack wasn't a baby anymore, but Asher suspected Kane wouldn't even register his weight; he'd find it even harder than Asher had to let Jack out of his arms.

"All right. Let's get home," his father said, the first words he'd uttered in hours. Edmund Winsome looked shell-shocked. He'd been told who'd been arrested over this, and he seemed to have grayed overnight because of it. "Well, I guess your services are not required any longer, Mr. Banner."

Asher cast his glance over to Alec, who was still leaning against the wall on the far side of the room. He'd been there for hours, silently standing watch over the Winsome family, and his father had repaid him with cold indifference bordering on rudeness. His father's disrespect was all there in the disdainful tone. Asher was never more ashamed of his father than in that moment.

"Actually my 'services' will end when the little boy is safely back in his own home and not a second earlier," Alec drawled, never shifting his gaze from the older man's eyes.

"I think we can manage to get him safely—"

"Edmund," Maddy snapped, "this man was involved in rescuing my son and keeping my brother safe. As far as I'm concerned, he can have the world if he wants it. Mr. Banner, please...we'll do whatever you think is best."

God, Asher wanted to cheer Maddy. He loved his sister-in-law, but she was extra awesome whenever she took down one of his parents. He also loved how he was never an in-law to her—always a brother.

"I don't expect any more trouble, but I will escort you home. Let's not forget—" Asher watched as Alec turned the full force of a raging glare on his father. "—you paid a million dollars to a second caller who hasn't been located, and we have no idea how they fit into any of this."

Asher had forgotten all about the other call in the mayhem, and he could tell from their faces the rest of his family had too. This must be over, though. They'd gotten their million bucks; surely they'd be happy.

"Right. Well now that's settled I suggest we get Jack home. I suspect we could all do with some sleep ourselves," Asher's mother said. She was always the one to wrap things up—make the final decision and act on it. Happily, this time she was spot-on. "Asher, I trust you'll get a lift with Mr. Banner?"

"I'll be happy to bring him home," Alec answered before he had a chance, and Asher was unreasonably delighted he'd sounded so eager to give him a ride, to be alone with him.

It struck him, suddenly, that Alec would be leaving now. If not today, then certainly tomorrow, this man would be out of his life as though he'd never been. Was he ready for him to go? To say goodbye. He absolutely felt a strong pull toward Alec, but was it nothing more than circumstances magnifying everything he felt? Or was the potential for more there? Would Alec even be interested in more? And how would it work anyway? Asher didn't even know where Alec's home base was. Obviously he traveled for his job but where did he call home? Where did he hang his hat?

Asher had his own place at Coronado Cays so he could keep his beloved boat close. He'd spent a lot of the money from his grandparents well, but he was hardly ever there. He traveled the world photographing sharks, mostly to Guadalupe Island, which wasn't too far from home, but still, he was rarely there. His lifestyle was one of the reasons none of his relationships lasted very long.

"Good. Then we'll see you at home, Asher." His mother kissed his cheek as she passed. His father didn't acknowledge him at all.

Maddy threw herself into his arms. She was still trembling. Would she ever stop? Would she ever let Jack out of her sight again? How could she, after this fucking nightmare? She'd never been one of those helicopter parents, hovering over their child, Bubble Wrap in hand. She was always loving and attentive but was willing to allow Jack to explore his world, within reason. How would she be now? Would Jack ever manage to wander out of sight of either of his parents?

"Thank you. So much, Asher," Maddy murmured into his ear. He'd lost count of the number of times she'd thanked him since she'd arrived at the hospital, but every one of them had been unnecessary. He'd have fought the hounds of hell for Jack with no thanks necessary.

"I'll see you soon," he whispered back.

Asher quickly pecked a kiss to Jack's head as Kane passed by with him still asleep in his arms. Asher had always thought maybe one day he'd have kids of his own, but after this, he didn't know if he was strong enough. If he lost them…? He didn't know if he was brave enough to risk such a tragedy.

"Come on. Let's get out of here," Alec said from behind, close enough for his breath to tickle his ear.

Asher walked quietly beside Alec as they made their way to Alec's car. The urge to hold Alec's hand itched beneath his skin, but he wasn't at all confident the gesture would be well received. He tried to sort through the thoughts swirling around in his head. It would be best if he and Alec could talk now while there was no chance of his family walking in on them. But what did he say? What did he want?

"What're you thinking so hard on over there, Asher?" Alec asked, and apparently Ash was gone and they were back to Asher.

"You," he replied honestly. It might be his imagination, but he was pretty sure Alec paled, just a little.

"Anything I can help you with?" Definitely apprehension in his tone.

Alec beeped the key fob in his hand, and Asher made a beeline for the passenger seat. He knew they needed to have this conversation and yet a little delay surely couldn't hurt.

Asher settled in and pulled on his seat belt while Alec did the same. The car purred to life when Alec turned the key. Asher braced himself to open up. They had maybe a half hour trip, but it would be a really, really long ride if this went to shit.

"So, um...what I was thinking about was us," he began as Alec pulled the car away from the curb.

"Us?"

"Yes." This conversation was more painful than a root canal—or so he'd heard.

"Okay."

Jesus. Alec was giving him nothing so all he could do was jump right in. Asher was plenty of things, but coward wasn't one of them. "I was thinking about what was going to happen now. Between us, I mean." Could he sound any more pathetic? He was coming across needy and whiney when all he'd really wanted was to clarify things and see where Alec's head was at—if he wanted more.

"Nothing has to happen, Asher. I understand what went on between us. I'm not expecting anything more," Alec replied, his gaze never leaving the blacktop in front of him.

"You understand what happened between us?" Asher didn't understand this conversation, let alone what had occurred between them.

"Sure. It's fairly common, something of a phenomenon really. People find themselves in high pressure, extremely stressful situations; everything is heightened and they need a distraction—some relief. I get it."

Asher was speechless. He'd expected a polite letdown or maybe even a tentative acknowledgement of something more—something special between them. What he got was Alec telling him he understood Asher had been using him as a distraction.

"Oh." He was unable to think of a single thing more to say in response—suitable or otherwise—so he remained silent, looking out his window at the early morning light bringing the city slowly to life.

"You okay, Asher?" Alec asked after maybe ten minutes of uncomfortable silence.

"Yes. It's just that I thought maybe... I wasn't using you, Alec."

"It's not a problem. If anything, I should be apologizing to you. I shouldn't have taken advantage of you. My behavior wasn't very professional."

"Then why did you?" Asher snapped. This was becoming the worst talk in the long history of bad conversations.

Alec quickly flashed him a look before turning back to the road. "Lapse in judgment, I guess."

Asher was furious. Lapse in fucking judgment? As though what they'd done—as though *he*—was a fucking mistake. Jesus Christ, he actually considered leaping out of the moving car he was so angry at the man beside him.

He remained stonily silent. He'd always been told if you can't say something nice, don't say anything at all, and right now there was nothing *nice* he could say to Alec fucking Banner.

He didn't even wait for the car to come to a complete stop in his parents' driveway before he was out the door, slamming it as hard as he could manage. He wished he was a little stronger so the window would shatter from the violence, but all that happened was the car shook and the bang shattered only the silence.

"Asher?" Alec called. Asher turned to see him standing outside the car, looking at him with utter confusion.

"Goodbye, Alec. Thank you for what you did. You have my apologies for *using* you the way I did." Asher turned his back and stomped inside, leaving Alec where he stood, and if Alec was shocked and confused, Asher didn't even give a tiny rat's ass.

Asher stormed through the house and straight out to the pool. He managed to yank his shirt and shoes off this time before striding down the steps and into the cool, soothing water. He needed the ocean. The pool water was good, but it was the ocean that calmed him—the salty smell, gentle lapping waves, its vastness. To find comfort in the ocean waters was amazing considering the violence he'd endured in it.

"Asher? Everything all right?" Kane's voice was soft as he approached the pool. His brother looked worn out, battered, and Asher suddenly realized he had no right to be bitching about his life after what they'd all been through.

"Yeah. Sorry, Kane. I'm just..."

Kane kept walking right down into the water, fully clothed as Alec had done—was it only two nights ago? It felt like a lifetime.

"I saw you with Alec out front. It looked...um...tense."

"You don't need to hear it right now, Kane."

"Asher, you and Alec...you got my son back. I'll never, *never* be able to repay you for what you did. If you need to talk about something, you can bet your ass I'm going to listen."

They floated around each other. They hadn't been close as brothers in too long, but Asher wanted to change their relationship. Kane was a good guy; he needed to grow some balls and get out from under their parents, but he was decent. Maybe this whole thing would help him escape.

"We um...we fucked," he quietly confessed.

"You and Alec?"

"Yeah."

"Wow. Okay. And now...?"

"And now I tried to talk to him about it. See if maybe he wanted to start something with me." Asher swallowed, the memory of the awful conversation horrifying him all over again.

"And...it didn't go well?"

"He apologized for taking advantage of me, accused me of using him as a distraction and said it was a mistake that shouldn't have happened."

"Ouch."

"Yeah," Asher murmured.

"He's a fool," Kane said. Asher looked at his brother. His tone had been vehement—as though he would go after him if Alec were standing there right now. "I can't hate him because of what he did for Jack, but I can think he's a fucking idiot to let you slip through his fingers. You're a catch, Asher, and he should be trying to hold onto you with every one of those big brawny muscles of his."

Asher laughed, really laughed for the first time in days. Kane might be weak, when it came to their parents, but he had Asher's back—always had. Asher had never been afraid to come out to Kane. He'd always known Kane would support him no matter what.

Affection of any kind was rare in his family, and Asher felt a little choked up at his brother's display. Perhaps Jack's kidnapping, and the nearly worse tragedy of being sold to strangers, would be a turning point for his entire family.

"Thanks, Kane. I shouldn't be dumping this on you right now."

"I'll be honest, Ash, what happened with Jack is going to mess with me—with all of us—for a long, long time, but we've got him back. He's safe and a big, big part of that is thanks to you. And I'm not going to stop living; I'm not going to ignore my brother when I can tell he's hurting."

Asher splashed his way through the water and pulled his brother into a hug. He held on tightly because he needed it; he hadn't realized how much he needed it, and if he wished he held Alec in his arms, well, that's just how he felt.

"Promise me you'll get out, Kane. Live *your* life. Not theirs," he whispered in Kane's ear.

Kane nodded and agreed, "I promise. No more, Ash. My family comes first now—Maddy, Jack, and you. If Mom and Dad want to be a part of our lives, they'll have to accept me on my terms."

They held on to each other for a little longer, and as soon as they pulled back from each other, Kane splashed him. For a split second, Asher was too shocked to retaliate, but it didn't last. He pulled back his arm, scooped it through the water, and splashed it all over his brother. Kane's countermove was immediate, and it didn't take long for it to degenerate into a full-blown splash fight.

They were both laughing and doing their best to dunk each other when their mother called, her voice breaking up their fun. He stood, shook his head a little, and wiped the water from his eyes.

His mom was standing at the sliding door. Alec stood inside, a little behind her.

"Boys, Mr. Banner needs to leave. He needs to be deposed about the events of yesterday."

Kane made to move out of the pool and flicked a quick glance to Asher. He smiled and shook his head the tiniest bit. He'd said his goodbye to Alec Banner, and as far as he could tell, there was nothing more to say.

"We've said everything we need to say to each other, Mother," Asher called. He didn't miss the flinch in Alec's body. He turned and dove under the water, splashing away from a man, who, for a brief moment, Asher thought might become important to him—may have been the one.

Chapter Thirteen

ALEC

Four Months Later...

Alec groaned when the trill of his ringtone yanked him from sleep. He didn't get nearly enough shuteye these days, so he coveted whatever he could get. He pushed at the heavy arm draped over his waist and cursed. *Shit.* He must have been fucking exhausted to allow last night's random fuck to stay the night.

The hairy arm made a grab at him, its owner obviously misreading Alec's intention in the haze of slumber. Alec clutched at it and threw it away from his body then lunged for the still ringing phone.

"Yeah," he grunted, not even looking to see who was calling. He fucking hoped the caller wasn't Ryan or Ben with another case. He'd been working nonstop for months, and he needed a break.

"Alec? Alec Banner?"

"Yeah. Who's this?" he asked, not recognizing the soft female voice.

"Alec, thank god. It's Maddy. Maddy Winsome."

Alec sat bolt upright at the mention of the name. He was wide awake now. He hadn't heard from the Winsomes in months, though he knew the trial was coming up and he'd see them then—all of them. His thoughts flashed to Asher, but he pushed them away. He was still working hard to forget the youngest Winsome brother. He'd fucked his way through scores of partners trying to forget him, but he hadn't been able to stop comparing every single encounter to that one night with Asher.

"Maddy. Is everything okay?"

"No. No, it's not at all. Did you hear about Morgan Fincher?"

Morgan Fincher? The man who'd kidnapped her son and tried to auction him online? The last he knew he was safely locked up and awaiting the upcoming trial. "No, I haven't. What happened?"

"Four days ago, he was beaten. In prison. They tortured him and left him for dead. Doctors aren't sure he's going to make it."

This wasn't really surprising news. Morgan Fincher had hurt a child, threatened to auction one to pedophiles. Criminals had their own justice for people like Morgan. Alec was only surprised it hadn't happened sooner. The question was why Maddy Winsome, his victim's mother, was apparently upset about it?

"No. I hadn't heard. I'm not surprised at all, though. Um...and I'm not sure why you're calling me..."

"It's Asher," she said and, with those words, Alec was on his feet, pacing the room. His bedmate was watching him with bleary eyes, now sparking to lust as he ogled Alec's naked body.

"What's Asher got to do with it?" For a split second, he wondered if Asher had been responsible for the beating. He couldn't have physically done it himself, but it was way easier than people might think to pay someone to beat or even kill a person in prison.

"Look, Alec, I know this is asking a lot, but could you come out here? It's complicated, and I—Asher—needs your help."

"I'll call you when I arrive. Are you at the mansion?" Alec didn't even hesitate, and he had the feeling Maddy knew how he'd react.

"No. We moved out. I'll text you the address. Thank you, Alec."

"Is he all right?" Alec whispered, terrified of the answer.

"He thinks he is, but no he's not. And, Alec...he's in danger too."

Tricky girl. So, Asher wasn't just in actual danger, he also wasn't doing so well after the kidnapping four months ago. Not for the first time, he wished he could have been there for him, but he hadn't wanted Asher to feel obligated to allow him to hang around, and he was convinced that's all it would have been.

"Danger?" he asked.

"Someone's already tried to kill him once, but he refuses to believe it. We need your help, Alec."

Someone had tried to kill Asher? A blaze of white-hot fury surged through his body, and he wanted to rip someone limb from limb. And what the fuck did it have to do with Morgan Fincher being bashed in prison?

"I'm on my way," he answered. He didn't even wait for Maddy's reply before hanging up and tossing the cell on the bed.

"Hey, everything okay?" Bill or Will or fucking Ezekiel asked. He felt bad. Alec always tried to make his partners feel special, even if for only one night. He usually always remembered their name, but he never let them stay.

"No, actually. I have to go. It's an emergency." He turned and started shoving his meager belongings in his bag. He'd been heading home today anyway, so most things were already packed.

"Okay, sure. Um…maybe I can get your number?" Dean—fucking Dean—hesitantly asked.

"Look, Dean. Last night was great; you were great, but I'm not interested in more—with anyone." *Liar*, his brain hissed at him.

"Oh. Okay, sure." Dean sighed and Alec was tempted to explain to him the bullet he'd dodged. Alec was no catch for anybody. But he had somewhere he needed to be, and from the sounds of it, he had someone he needed to talk some sense into.

MADDY AND KANE Winsome's new home wasn't too far from the mansion, but the fact they'd moved out at all was a start. Cases like the Winsomes, where they'd almost lost a child, could make or break a couple, and happily, it seemed to be working out okay for them. Their home was large and modern. The house was nowhere near the ostentatiousness of the senior Winsomes, but there was no doubting there was plenty of wealth here.

Alec sat in his rental across the road and watched the house for a while. He'd been pep talking himself ever since Maddy's call, steeling for a face-to-face with Asher again.

Asher's expression the last time Alec had seen him haunted his dreams. He'd been so angry and so hurt, all Alec's fault. Hurting Asher was the very last thing Alec wanted to do. He was so sure he was only a distraction for Asher; it never occurred to him that maybe there was more—at least not until he'd dissected their last conversation, and by then it was too late. He'd already blown it.

Ben was furious with him when he'd told him what he'd said to Asher. He'd expected teasing for fucking up so badly, but his friend was angry. And then sad. He asked Alec if he truly knew what he wanted because it seemed to Ben he'd thrown the very thing he claimed he wanted away with both hands. Alec was too much of a fucking coward to admit Ben was right—too much of a coward to go back and try to make things right with Asher.

As he sat across from Maddy and Kane's home now, he was terrified. Frightened Asher may be in real trouble and equally scared Asher would tell him to fuck right off. He couldn't imagine knowing Asher was in danger and not being allowed to help.

Alec was scared most days of his life: of getting shot or blown up, or letting someone down, or letting a killer get away, or losing a child. There was so much in his life to be afraid of, but like every other day, he pushed the fear down and stepped out of the car. He sucked in a breath and crossed the road.

A short driveway led up to bright-white front doors. Without even seeing inside, Alec sensed this was a happy house. He picked up the door knocker and let it rap a few times on the solid timber. The echo of the bangs reverberated inside the large house. Within seconds, he heard the *click-clack* of heels on hardwood flooring, and then Maddy stood at the open door, a small smile on her pretty face.

"Alec," she said, before throwing her arms around his shoulders. "Thank god. Come in, please."

Alec followed her through the door and to the right. He walked into a large living area, which was clearly the home of a happy four-year-old boy. Toys of all sorts were strewn throughout the room. There were cars, Legos, dolls, and what looked like a mini-wooden storefront complete with cash register, wooden cereal boxes, fruits, and vegetables.

"Please, have a seat." Maddy gestured to a comfortable beige armchair. "Can I get you a drink? Kane will be here in a moment. He and Jack are just getting out of the pool."

"A cold water would be great; thanks, Maddy."

Maddy patted his shoulder and walked out of the room. Squealing and laughter echoed through the house, getting closer. It stopped when Jack and Kane entered the room.

Jack's smile fell immediately when he noticed Alec, and the little boy clung to his father's leg, hiding his face.

"Jack, look at Daddy," Kane urged softly. "This is Alec. He's the man Mommy and I spoke to you about. He's a friend of ours and yours. He helped Uncle Asher get you back from the bad people. Remember?"

Alec watched as a little face peered out at him, big eyes squinting, before turning up to look at his father and giving the tiniest nod. From the brief glimpse he'd had so far, Alec thought Jack looked well. He'd lost the haunted, terrified look, though he'd seen it there hovering at the edge when Jack had walked in the room and found a stranger in his home.

"Come say hello, and then you can go play with Maxy, if you like." Jack nodded and Kane walked him closer. "Jack, this is our friend Alec."

"Hi, Jack. It's good to see you again." Alec held out his hand.

"Hello," the little boy said and shyly slipped his fingers into Alec's open palm and shook. He glanced up at his father, who smiled down and scuffed his hair.

"Good job, Jack. Go find Maxy, okay?"

Jack beamed a smile and ran from the room.

"Maxy?" Alec asked.

"German Shepherd. Psychologist suggested a pet might be good for him, and Maddy and I instantly thought guard dog." Kane laughed and stuck out his hand. "Good to see you, Alec."

Alec stood to shake the proffered hand and then resumed his seat. Kane sat opposite him, his expression turning serious. There'd also been a huge change in Kane. He looked stronger and happier, no longer ready to break in an instant.

"What's going on, Kane?" Alec had made some calls on his way here regarding Morgan Fincher, and what he'd been told wasn't pretty. The man was lynched in the prison bathroom. His body was a mass of wounds when was found: burns, cuts, bruises, broken bones, and there'd been evidence he'd been violated. That he was still alive was something of a miracle. What Alec still couldn't figure out was what it had to do with Asher.

Maddy came back in the room carrying a tray with a jug of lemon water and a few glasses. She placed it on the coffee table and poured three glasses, handing one to Alec, one to her husband, and taking one for herself.

"Maddy told you about Fincher?"

"Yeah. I read the details...ugly," Alec answered.

"Well, a day after Fincher was almost killed in prison," Kane began, "Asher got a call. The caller was hysterical, screaming abuse at him. He told Asher what had happened to Fincher was all his fault, and he was going to pay for it."

"Asher happened to be here when he got the call," Maddy continued. "Otherwise I don't think we'd ever have known about it. He wanted to ignore it. We thought maybe it was someone close to that monster. Someone who was obviously upset because of what had happened to him." Maddy huffed and rolled her eyes. "Don't get me wrong,

Alec. I'm usually an incredibly loving woman, but if they'd have cut that man's heart out and fed it to him, I wouldn't have been at all sorry about it. He stole my baby—tried to sell my baby to...well, I can't even think about it. But you get it, I'm sure."

Alec did get it. Forgiveness was great if you could do it, but he certainly understood not being able to find it in cases like this. "I get it, Maddy." He smiled a little to prove he really did. "So Asher got a threatening call, but they've escalated?"

"The very next day, Asher's house burned down. Oh, the investigators haven't confirmed it yet, but I know it's going to come back as arson. And here's why," Maddy said, leaning forward, as though she was about to share the biggest secret in the universe. "Asher had sprinklers in his house, but the water had been turned off, so had the main power—no smoke alarms." She sat back, and Alec could tell by her look she was thinking, "Well, how do you like them apples?" Alec didn't like them very much, at all.

"Was Asher home?" Alec asked, his heart in his fucking throat. Obviously he wasn't harmed because they'd be doing this in a hospital right now, but he was still almost breathless with fear because it had been so close.

"He was and he was damn lucky. Fire started at two in the morning. If he'd have been asleep—" Kane's voice choked off, and he looked at Alec. "He's had trouble sleeping since Jack—we all have, but it saved his life. He got out, but the house burned quickly—too quickly to be saved. He lost it all."

"And he doesn't think it's connected to the call?"

"No. I don't know if it's willing ignorance, or he really doesn't see it. I'm hoping when the report comes back as arson he'll take it seriously."

"I'm still not really sure why you've called me…"

Maddy and Kane shared a look like they were having one of those wordless conversations married people seemed to have all the time. "Asher won't listen to us. We've all tried, but he won't have a bar of it. You and him…you guys… um…you had a connection before, and we know Asher respected you and your opinions, so we thought maybe you'd have more luck making him understand," Maddy finished hopefully.

For an unkind moment, Alec wondered if they'd called him to try to set him and Asher up, but they weren't the scheming, frivolous sort of people. The Winsomes had been touched by crime, and they knew something like this was no trivial matter to be used in a game of matchmaking.

"Where is he now?" Alec asked. His eyes quickly dashed around as if Asher might jump out of hiding any second.

"He's gone to Guadalupe Island. He's filming down there for a Discovery Channel Shark Week show."

"And you think he'll be in danger down there?" Alec didn't know too much about Guadalupe Island, though, with Asher there, he suspected the water around it was teeming with sharks. Asher's bravery at getting back in the water with those giant fucking killing machines never ceased to impress him, and his defense of sharks was remarkable. Alec was pretty sure he'd want every man and his dog out with harpoons if one of those beasts had tried to eat him.

"We don't know, but we're worried enough to call you and pay for you to go down there." Kane looked upset, and so did Maddy, and their concern was enough for Alec. An arson report in his hand would be great, but he'd go without it because he couldn't fucking stand the thought of Asher in danger.

"Okay, I'll go, but I need you guys to take this to the police. Get the fire report when it comes in and shove it under every cop's nose until someone takes this seriously. I'll do what I can with Asher." Alec stood, more than ready to get to Asher to see for himself he was safe. "How the hell do I get to Guadalupe Island?"

Maddy laughed and stood with him. "Come on, I'll show you. And, Alec, I'm not really sure what went wrong with you guys... Well, Kane told me some of it, but it doesn't make sense to me for anyone to let Asher Winsome slip through their fingers. What I'm trying to say is don't hurt him again."

Fuck. She'd said it politely, even pleasantly, but Maddy's words were like a gut punch. He felt ashamed and angry at himself and plain fucking sad because he'd made such a mess of something that could have been so good.

THE HOUR-AND-a-half bus trip from San Diego to Ensenada was nothing, but the fucking eighteen-hour boat trip out to Guadalupe Island was wearing thin real quick. Alec had never spent a huge amount of time on the water. He didn't mind it—loved swimming and the surf, actually— but being cooped up on a 112-foot boat filled with great white shark enthusiasts was a little beyond the limit of his patience.

Despite the warm, sunny day, there were low-lying clouds around the island, giving it a menacing, ominous feel as they approached. Given what Alec knew was under the surface of the crisp blue water, he believed the feeling of menace was incredibly appropriate. The island seemed spooky, like it was home to King Kong, sending a shiver up his spine. He stood portside on the boat, and even though he was keeping his eyes open for the cruiser he knew Asher was on, his gaze constantly darted to the water, sure any moment he'd spot a dorsal fin breaking the surface and the infamous *da-dum* tune would sound in his head.

Every other passenger, aside from crew, was lined along the railing, desperately hoping to be the first to spot one of the large predators. Alec had no idea so many people were into sharks. He didn't see the fascination himself; they were huge, and they could eat you. End of story, and that was all he needed to know.

"Mr. Banner?"

"Yes." He turned sharply at the sound of the voice. One of the crew—deckhands, Christ, he didn't know the nautical terms—stood before him.

"We've spotted the *August Moon*. She's anchored half a mile away on our starboard side. If you'll come with me, we'll get you in the launch and take you across to her."

"Did you radio them?" Alec had asked for them not to give any details, only to tell the crew of the *August Moon* someone with urgent news for Asher was on their way and would be boarding soon.

"Yes, they know you're coming. Asher Winsome is in the water, so he hasn't been informed yet."

"Good. Thank you. I'll grab my gear and meet you at the launch."

It took him only minutes to get his bag. He was already packed and ready. When he got to the back of the boat, his eyes boggled at the tiny little "launch" they expected him to get into in shark-infested waters. The boat was a fucking inflatable. His own teeth could probably rip a hole in it, let alone a row of shark's teeth.

"Is this safe?" He didn't care what he sounded like; he needed reassurance he wasn't about to be breakfast for some hungry fish.

"Perfectly." The crewman smirked, making Alec suspect he hadn't been the first to ask that question.

It took less than ten minutes to motor across to the smaller boat Asher was working from, and Alec's entire body was clenched tight the entire time. He wasn't even sure he breathed. Crew from the *August Moon* helped him aboard, and he quickly thanked his escort from the *Nautilus*.

"Mr. Banner. Welcome aboard. I'm Steve, the captain. I'm not sure what's going on, but you sure seem to be in a hurry to get to Asher, so I have to assume it's important." Captain Steve was anywhere between forty and sixty. His skin was sun-weathered, almost like leather, making it hard to guess at his age. His head was covered by a cap, but Alec could see silver wisps poking out from under the brim. He was shorter than Alec and stocky. The start of a beer belly pushed out his T-shirt. Alec didn't much care what he looked like, or if the captain was friendly, at this point. Given where he was, he was far more interested in the man's competence at keeping this boat afloat.

"It's very important; otherwise, I can assure you I wouldn't be out here."

"Not a shark lover then?"

"I love them just fine...so long as they're far, far from me."

The captain laughed and then turned away, gesturing for Alec to follow him. "Asher's still down, but he'll be coming up any minute. Drop your bag there; we'll get you settled later. Come watch."

He dumped his bag as told and followed Steve to the rear of the boat. There was a fair bit of commotion, a stream of bubbles popping on the surface. The top of the cage poked through the water and suddenly a gloved hand was pushing at the lid. A second hand passed a large camera looking device up as a hooded head popped up.

Alec watched as the diver pulled his goggles up, resting them on the top of his head and then took the regulator from between his lips. "Some big ones out today. Jasper got up real close, and we got some awesome footage. The big sixteen-foot girl from yesterday was back, as fucking nosy as ever. Kept poking the cage with her snout. Awesome," Asher babbled excitedly, Alec's chest bursting with a little simmer of happiness at the sound.

Asher's face was almost hidden by the black neoprene hood of his wetsuit, but his handsomeness was still visible. And then, suddenly, large, beautiful gray eyes locked on his, and Alec's heart stuttered at the connection he felt. He was in so much fucking trouble.

Chapter Fourteen

ASHER

Alec Banner was here on this boat. Alec fucking Banner, who Asher understood now had the power to break his fucking heart. He hadn't truly gotten over the events of four months ago. Not his nephew's kidnapping, not learning more about the depravity of mankind than he ever wanted to know, and certainly not over Alec fucking Banner.

Four months had passed, and yet he was still able to clearly conjure Alec's face and perfect fucking body in his mind's eye. He could still smell the delicious cinnamon fragrance wafting around him, still hear his deep voice telling him how beautiful he was. Fuck him for turning up here and pushing himself back into Asher's life.

Asher hadn't even asked what he was doing here before pushing past him and heading for the showers. His legs were wobbly both from hours in the water and the shock of finding Alec on board. He rested his forehead on the shower wall and let the water sluice over his body—hoping it might calm him.

Every nerve ending was tingling as though Alec's proximity fired them up. Damn it, he wouldn't have it—couldn't have this. He'd put himself out there for Alec once before, only to be spectacularly shot down. And Asher was the type to learn from his mistakes, so that sure as hell wouldn't be happening again.

Despite his bold thoughts, though, his body didn't really seem to give a shit, too busy being damn excited to see the man again. And Asher certainly didn't want to go back out there and face Alec with a raging hard-on, so he circled his hand around his cock and stroked. He used his thumb to caress the head every few strokes, and for once, allowed himself to imagine Alec while he played.

For the last few months, he'd tried to forget about the pleasure he'd found in Alec's arms, which he could manage when he was out of sight. But ignoring how Alec had made him feel was damn well impossible to do when he'd been face-to-face with the gorgeous man only moments ago. Memories of Alec flared to life behind his closed eyes, and Asher stroked himself harder. He remembered the feel of Alec's fingers on his bare skin, the cinnamon smell, and the perfect fullness when Alec's cock had been inside him.

He came with a muffled groan into his bicep, his seed painting the shower wall. The same deflated feeling he'd felt for months after getting himself off followed quickly on the heels of his release. It would never be as good, as satisfying when the actual man who brought him so much pleasure was missing.

Asher quickly rinsed off, toweled his body, and slipped on his shorts. He regularly wore nothing but a pair of cargos while he was on the boat, and he saw no reason to change now. He dumped his gear in his cabin and headed for the aft deck, where he heard muffled voices.

"Yeah, no, I wouldn't stand there, man, those big babies can breach right up onto this deck if the mood takes them. Seen it happen," Damon's voice boomed, tinged with humor. Asher knew he must be fucking with Alec, because everyone else onboard knew better, and they were used to Damon's fuckery.

"Breach? Like jump out of the water?" Alec sounded unsure, maybe even a little scared.

"Sure, man. Haven't you ever seen *Air Jaws*? You got any cuts on ya, 'cause they can smell blood from a quarter mile away, and don't get me started on how they can sense fear." Well, at least there was a tiny morsel of truth in this statement.

"I thought they didn't like humans for food? And doesn't the blood have to be in the water?"

"Nah, they'll smell it anywhere, and they'll eat anything," Damon continued.

"Don't scare the poor man, Damo. That's bullshit what he said about them sensing fear, mate. But they can smell blood in the water—and arousal. And the way you were looking at Ashy before when he dropped trou... Well, I don't know, I think there'll be some pretty riled-up white's beneath us." Kelly, his crazy Australian shark expert, had apparently decided to get in on the torture-the-new-guy act.

"Enough, Kels," Asher called out good-naturedly. He was kind of amused. He thought he might enjoy watching the two of them go at Alec like a couple of white's ripping apart the same carcass.

When he stepped out into the dusk light, Alec was standing in the very center of the deck. Damon and Kelly were leisurely reclining on the railing they'd warned Alec to stay away from, with smug grins on their faces, and Asher couldn't stop one of his own forming. Especially when Alec turned to him, eyes wide in either fear or shock, his face a delightful shade of puce.

"Here's our boy. We were just meeting your friend, Ashy," Kelly said. As an Australian, she felt not only a responsibility, but a cultural requirement, to shorten almost every word she could—and then stick an *O* or a *Y* or a *ZA* on the end of it. Hence, Damo, Ashy and Wazza for their poor deckhand Warren. Afternoon was arvo, a gas station was a servo, and a bottle-o was where you bought alcohol. Asher wasn't sure she was actually speaking English half the time. He was still trying to work out what she meant by it being her bizzo.

"Yeah. Guys, this is Alec Banner. He's the ex-FBI agent who helped us get Jack home safely. Alec, this is Damon and Kelly."

"I'm Kels," Kelly said, coming forward and offering her hand. As Alec took it, Asher was amused to see a slight hesitation. "This big bastard here you can call Damo. Alec was it? Nope." She shook her head. "You're gonna have to be Banno."

"She's Australian," Asher said by way of explanation. "Apparently they're the laziest people on earth because they have to shorten every word."

"Not every word, asshole. And it's a show of affection. If I shorten your name, it means you're in."

"Technically, Kels," Damon added. "You didn't shorten his name. Alec is only four letters and Banno is five unless we're dropping an N and then it's still four, which is the same as Alec." Damon looked suitably proud of himself.

"Fuck, Damo. You don't have to ruin everything with your big brain and your logic. I'm just taking the piss." Kelly playfully swatted at the big man, and they both wandered off, laughing among themselves. They were assholes, but they were his, and Asher loved them like family.

"They're um...unique," Alec said when they'd walked inside the cabin.

"What are you doing here, Alec?" Asher's humor had left with his friends. All that remained was shame at what had happened between them and a healthy dose of anger at this man who had burst back into his life.

"Maddy called."

"Jesus. Is this about the house fire? The threat?"

"She and Kane are worried about you, and I think they've got a reason to be, Asher."

"Why'd they send *you*?"

"I'm not real sure, to be honest. But I really think you need to take this threat seriously." Alec was still standing dead center of the deck, and Asher wondered how he was going to get him in the water. Because he was getting Alec Banner's ass in the water with the sharks.

If he had to put up with being in close proximity with him for the next four days, until they headed back to Ensenada, then Alec was going to come to meet his sharks.

"It was a house fire, Alec. An accident."

"Stop being so fucking stubborn, Ash."

"No. You don't get to call me Ash or even fucking Ashy. I'm Asher to you. Nothing but a client, someone you either pity fucked or allowed to *use* you as a distraction. Nothing more. I'm not Ash to you." Asher really hadn't had a handle on how angry he was at Alec, and his ire was probably undeserved. Asher could have fought harder to make Alec understand, but Alec's reaction when he'd approached him on the topic of "them" had shocked him—humiliated him.

"Jesus," Alec whispered. "I'm sorry, Asher. I didn't mean to hurt you."

"Yeah. Well, you didn't," he lied. "Guess you better come and meet the crew since you'll be here awhile. Dinner will be soon. If you don't get in before Damon, there's not a lot left."

Asher turned to head back into the cabin. He was on cleanup tonight, like most nights, because his cooking fucking sucked. It wasn't until he was in the cabin that he realized Alec wasn't following him. He huffed and walked back onto the deck.

"Alec?"

"Going to be *here* a while? I kinda thought we'd head back in." Alec looked decidedly pale.

"Why would we do that? Even if I did believe someone was after me, I couldn't be anywhere safer. I've known everyone on this boat for years. And besides, you're here now."

Alec took a deep breath as Asher watched him literally fighting his fear. His fists clenched, and he straightened his spine. "I just didn't give it much thought, and now I'm...well...I'm stuck in the middle of the ocean with man-eaters right below my feet." Alec's body shuddered, and for a moment, Asher felt a little sorry for him.

"Why *did* you come racing out here?" Asher murmured as he stepped closer to Alec, both afraid of, and ridiculously curious about his answer.

"Because it was you," Alec whispered back, "and I can't let anything happen to you."

They watched each other for a moment. Asher had been scrutinized by predators before, and that's how he felt under Alec's gaze now. It would be so easy...

"Dinner, and then we'll talk," Asher said, pulling back from Alec's orbit. Keeping his distance was going to be harder than he thought.

Asher led Alec down to the galley. There were no bells and whistles on this craft. Crew dished out their own food and then found a seat around the table. They could comfortably seat six, but there were already eight on board, and Alec made nine. From the delicious odor wafting through the cabin, he could tell Jasper had cooked tonight. He was by far the best cook of all the crew, and it seemed like tonight's fare of burritos would be no exception.

"Here." Asher handed Alec a plate. "Dig in," he advised and then turned to put together his burrito.

Asher waited until Alec finished and then led him to the table. It seemed word of Alec Banner's arrival had spread because, for a change, everybody was at the table and surprise, surprise, they all shut up and turned to stare when Asher and Alec walked into the room.

"Jesus." Asher rolled his eyes. "This is Alec Banner, and I'm sure Kels already told you all about him, and I'm just as sure you assholes listened when we spoke on deck, so if there's any questions or comments, let's get them out of the way now..." Seven arms shot up in the air, and Asher laughed. How his father ever expected him to work behind a desk when this was out here for him was beyond him. "Oh, fuck no. I've changed my mind. Eat your food and leave him alone."

Asher squeezed in beside Jasper. There'd be enough room for Alec if he didn't mind being sandwiched up against him.

"Here, Banno. There's room here." Damon patted the seat beside him. Alec was on the taller side, but Damon had him by at least four inches and almost double the width. Asher could see Alec's indecision, but fuck, if he was going to help him out.

"Come on, squish in," Kelly encouraged. "And I'll do the proper introductions." She glared at Asher while Alec did his best to share a bench with her and Damon. "That's our captain, Stevo. First mate, Mickey. Our jacks-of-all-trades and deckhands extraordinaire, Wazza and Connie. And the one beside Ashy is the one you've really got to look out for—he's Jasper."

They all shook hands with Alec, which made for an awkward experience, given how packed in they were, and then they settled into their meals.

"Why do I have to look out for Jasper?" Alec asked and Asher knew what he was thinking. Jasper was what Asher would describe as petite. He looked as though a strong breeze might blow him away. He was also timid and jumpy around people. Asher had known him for six years and still knew next to nothing about him. He strongly suspected someone had done a real number on him at some point in the young man's life, but he never said, and Asher never asked.

"'Cause he's the damn fool who swims outside the cage," Damon said fondly. Of everyone in the crew, Damon was the one who got along best with Jasper. He had a feeling Damon knew Jasper's story, and the big man often went out of his way to safeguard him, whether that meant literally chasing off someone giving him a hard time or subtly intervening when Jasper became flustered in a social setting.

"Outside the cage? Like where the sharks are?" Alec asked, his stunned gaze on the small man.

"Well, yes, that would be where the sharks are, Alec," Asher mocked. "He can't do it here though. Diving outside the cage at Guadalupe is illegal. But pretty much everywhere else we go he swims outside of the cages."

"But don't they...I mean...how do you not get eaten?"

Asher prepared to answer, knowing Jasper usually avoided conversation with strangers, so he was surprised when Jasper beat him to it.

"They don't like the taste of humans, so generally we don't get eaten by them. If they bite, it's because they're trying to figure out what we are. Besides, I'm not much of a meal for those guys, more like an appetizer," Jasper joked, and Asher caught the small nod and look of pride from Damon, followed by a fist bump between the two men.

"You'll see everything in action tomorrow," Asher added.

"What? Like from the boat?" Alec asked.

Asher laughed, couldn't help it. "Oh, hell no. You're coming down with us."

"No. No, that's really not necessary."

"Oh, but it is," Kelly joined in. "It's kind of like an initiation. You come onboard; you go in the ocean—one way or another." She laughed wickedly, and Asher watched the color drain from Alec's face.

"I just... I'm not sure... It's been a long—"

"Don't worry, Alec," Asher interrupted, thoroughly enjoying Alec's discomfort. "I'll be there if you need a hand to hold, and you sure won't be the first one to pee yourself when those big guys come in—hell, you're in the water anyway, so no one will know—and I'm pretty sure sharks aren't attracted to the smell."

Alec was quiet for most of the rest of their meal. A few of the others asked questions, which Alec answered good-naturedly, especially considering the grief they'd dished out to him. He even came and helped Asher with the cleanup, which was much more than Asher deserved after the way he'd been treating him since he got on board.

After dinner was free time. Mostly, they were all exhausted from their long days, but they often sat around talking or discussing plans for the next day. Tonight, though, it seemed as if everyone had cleared off to bed, leaving Asher completely alone with Alec on the flybridge.

The earlier cloud cover had lifted, and all Asher could see were stars, brighter and more numerous than they ever were in the city. The dark of the night sky melted into the black of the water, which was so calm tonight the surface was like glass. It produced a mesmerizing reflection so it looked as though they were floating in the sky, completely surrounded by stars. It was beautiful.

"Wow," Alec breathed.

"Yeah. It is wow."

"If it wasn't for what I knew was swimming around underneath us, I'd say it's perfect out here." Alec was looking out over the ocean and the light from the stars gave him an almost ethereal quality. As far as Asher was concerned, Alec was every bit as wow as the stars.

"They're not monsters, Alec. I've met a real monster, and he wasn't swimming around in the ocean."

"You really love them...this out here, don't you?" Alec turned and faced him.

"It's everything to me. I don't know what I'd do, otherwise," Asher admitted.

"How did the shark get you?" Alec asked.

Lots of people asked that question either when they saw his bite or heard about it. People were morbidly curious especially when it came to someone almost being eaten. Asher had a sterilized, condensed version he usually shared, but even before he started speaking, he knew it wouldn't be enough with Alec.

"I've always loved the ocean; swimming in it, surfing, paddle boarding, whatever. I had a group of friends from childhood who I went surfing with every weekend, same spot, same time of day. One day, we went out exactly like we'd done every other time. It was the most beautiful, crisp, clear day, and the waves had been a little slow, but we didn't care. We hung out on our boards, talking and mucking around." Asher let his mind wander back to that day, let the memories wash over him and sweep him back to what had been, until four months ago when his nephew had been kidnapped, the most terrifying moment of his life.

"I'd rolled off my board to cool myself off while I waited for a wave to take me in. I had my arms hanging over the board while I was talking to my friend when something hit me from below. I don't remember a sharp pain, only this incredible force more like a bus had hit me. My friends told me later the shark lifted me almost entirely out of the water.

"I remember looking down into this enormous face that had my leg in its mouth, and it almost looked like she was grinning at me. Her eye rolled like they do, and she started dragging me under. I tried punching her in the snout, and then I dug around for her eye and kept digging till she spat me out—but not all of me. She took a souvenir." Asher reflexively glanced at his ruined thigh.

"Next thing I knew, my friends were pulling me out of the water onto one of their boards and hauling ass for the shore. All I can remember of the trip in is I kept thinking I could see this big dark shadow trailing us, and I was waiting for her to come and finish me off. If she hadn't made off with half my thigh, I'm pretty sure I would have walked on the fucking water to get out of there. By the time we made land, I was almost unconscious from the blood loss. I don't remember much after that until I woke up in the hospital."

"Fuck..." Alec cursed.

"Yeah. But even though the shark took a piece of me, she gave me stuff too. Do you know what real courage is, Alec?" He waited until Alec shook his head before continuing. "It wasn't me being bitten. Courage was my friends staying in water full of my blood, knowing there was a shark in there with them, until they got me out and back to land. They could've taken off, left me, and no one would have blamed them. They're the brave ones. That shark showed me the best of humankind."

"You still see them?"

"Yeah, we get together at least once a year. Out of four of us, only two still go in the water, though."

They remained quiet for a while. Alec was probably trying to parse Asher's story; most people needed a moment to think it over. Asher took the opportunity to stare at Alec's profile. He was so gorgeous. So powerful physically, but there was also definite vulnerability in the mix, and for some reason, the combination flipped his switch.

"I'm sorry for what I did—last time, you know," Alec eventually said.

"I wanted something more with you," Asher softly admitted.

"I didn't realize it at the time. I should have listened to you, instead of jumping to the wrong conclusion," Alec spoke out over the ocean, not turning to look at him.

Asher reached over and gently curled his fingers around Alec's chin, pulling and forcing him to look at him. "Yeah, you should have. Everything could have been different."

Asher allowed a small flicker of hope to ignite inside him, but he wasn't going to make it easy for Alec, not at all. Alec's long fingers threaded through Asher's hair as they watched each other.

"You let your hair grow even longer," Alec murmured.

"Yeah."

"It looks fucking sexy."

Asher swallowed and fought the feelings coursing through him. The lust, the fucking desire—he'd never experienced them so potently, but it only led to trouble and heartache. So Asher did what he'd been doing for four months. He pushed everything he felt for Alec Banner down and kidded himself he wasn't interested—that he didn't care at all.

"So you really think I'm in danger?" he asked.

"I do...and, Asher, I'm not going to let anything happen to you," Alec vowed.

Asher nodded and smiled up at him. That would do—for now, Alec's promise was enough because if he stayed out here much longer, listening to Alec talk to him in his sexy voice, promising him safety and the possibility of more, he'd fall into bed with him again. And he wasn't going to risk heartache this time.

Chapter Fifteen

ALEC

"I'm not so sure about this," Alec said for the millionth time for everyone to hear, hoping somebody would finally come to his rescue. But apparently, judging by the utter lack of response, no one was listening to him.

His entire body ached from being cramped all night in the small bunk he'd been assigned in Asher's cabin. Asher had laughed his ass off at him when he'd tried to coil his body into some kind of comfortable position in the narrow berth. Asher, meanwhile, had eased into his like a pro and was asleep even as the last peals of his laughter were echoing through the small room. Ten years ago during his stint in the military, that bunk would have been a luxury. But Alec was softer now—too used to his extremely comfortable, and ridiculously expensive, king-sized bed. Even the moderate comfort of hotel beds he spent so much of his time in had softened him.

"I'm really just as happy to stay up here and watch," he tried again, even as he followed Jasper and Damon toward the cage.

Why he hadn't thought to lie and tell everyone he had no idea how to dive he couldn't explain. It would have been an acceptable out. But when Asher had asked, he'd foolishly bragged about the dive training he'd received in the army. So now he found himself being led toward a flimsy-looking cage like the proverbial fucking lamb. He fucking hoped there'd be no slaughter today.

"You'll be fine, Alec," Damon quietly reassured. "You'll be in the cage. They'll try to eat Jasper first, and if that happens—run, or swim fast." He laughed and Alec thought maybe everybody onboard this boat was a little crazy. *Ben would fucking love it here.*

Alec turned to look at the slender man preparing to get in the water. "So you'll really be out of the cage?" he asked.

"Sure."

"How long will we be down there?" Alec looked at the water surrounding him. It looked mirrorlike in the calm conditions, but what was happening underneath was what scared the crap out of him.

"Ashy likes to stay down until he's got the shots he needs—or until he's out of air."

"Uh-huh," Alec murmured distractedly. He'd spotted Asher off to the side, talking to Kelly. His wetsuit was half on and hanging around his trim waist, leaving his torso bare. Though a similar height to Alec, he was broader, and he was nicely toned in the "I don't go to the gym" kind of way. Asher's body came from hard work and an active lifestyle. His skin was perfectly smooth and darkened by the sun. The sight of it provoked the unreasonable urge for Alec to lick every inch, especially all the way down the plains of his back to the peek-a-boo hint of ass crack. Alec's mouth watered as he let his gaze wander lazily over Asher's perfect body.

When he finally made his way back up to Asher's face, he found amused gray eyes watching him. He flushed at being caught staring, but then allowed his tongue to peek out and lick slowly along his bottom lip. He smirked when those gray eyes widened, and a slight shiver rippled through Asher's body. If he was going to be forced into the water with those giant, scary-ass fish, then he was going to play with some prey of his own.

"You ready?" Asher called. Alec even admired the sound of his voice.

Alec walked closer and inhaled Asher's scent, all sunscreen and salt water with the underlying spice Alec had yet to identify. He'd heard somewhere once that attraction often starts with smell, and as Asher's scent permeated through him flaming his lust, Alec knew it to be true.

"Is this my punishment?" he asked, offering Asher a wink.

"Maybe...or maybe I know what an amazing experience it is and don't want you to miss out. Ten years down the road, I don't want you regretting you were too scared to do this." Asher gave him a wink of his own, and Alec's knees actually fucking trembled.

Was Asher talking only about the shark diving or was he hinting at something else—a much bigger regret? Had he been talking about them?

"All right. But if I get eaten, Ash, I'm gonna haunt you for the rest of your days."

Asher looked him up and down, slowly and purposefully. Alec wondered what he saw. "I think I can handle being haunted by you."

"Oh my god. Are you two gonna be like this for the next four days? 'Cause, I swear to Satan, I'm jumping overboard if you are," Damon boomed.

"Leave them alone, Dame. It's kind of oddly sweet," Jasper added.

"It's gonna make me chunder," Kelly called from someplace where Alec couldn't even see her.

"Chunder?" he whispered to Asher.

"Vomit."

Asher pulled up his wetsuit, dancing a little to get it on. He smiled broadly and, damn it, if Alec didn't wish that smile could always be there. Alec reluctantly turned away from him to check his equipment for the tenth time. He didn't want anything going wrong down there that would take his mind—or his eyes—off those sharks.

"Don't worry, Alec. I'll look after you." Asher's lips were right at his ear as he spoke, his breath tickling. A shiver danced up Alec's spine, and his fingers twitched with want. There was nothing he wanted more right now than to get his hands on Asher—except maybe the feel of dry land under his feet.

"Okay. I trust you." And his words were true. Alec didn't trust often or easily—he'd seen too much of this world—but it occurred to him that, for whatever reason, he trusted Asher.

Asher was watching him with an unreadable expression before curling his hand around the back of Alec's neck. Alec's skin tingled where Asher's fingers touched him. He looked into serious gray eyes. "I mean it, Alec. I'll look after you," Asher said. And for the second time, Alec wondered if he was referring to something more than diving with sharks.

The atmosphere was heavy with desire and something feeling suspiciously like promise. Alec wanted to lighten the moment a little. "One more thing...that gap in the cage—"

"Oh don't worry about it, Banno," Kelly interrupted. "Only babies can get through the tiny gap."

Alec kind of wanted to point out that even a baby great white was not something he wanted to get too close to.

"Okay," Asher began, "we're gonna start you off in the surface cage. It can get a bit rough in there with the swell so be aware of where you are; otherwise you'll be tossed into the cage bars."

"And you don't wanna start bleeding in there, man." Damon laughed.

Alec did his best to ignore the big man's attempts to unnerve him and concentrated on what Asher was telling him. "Jasper's going down in the deep cage with Kels. We'll just get whatever shots we can and, hopefully, give you a bit of a show."

Alec watched, his heart thumping madly, as Jasper and Kelly were lowered in their cage. Jasper reached over and fist-bumped Damon as his feet hit the water. Alec wasn't sure exactly what was between those two, but there was something, and he wondered how Damon could stand to watch Jasper do participate in such a dangerous activity every day.

"Kelly's doing her research while we're down there. We know next to nothing about how they breed, but these waters are a mating ground. We've had a few big females in the water for the last few days—and some aggressive males. Kelly's hoping to tag one of the females so she can track their path, maybe find their nursery." Asher's eyes were alive with excitement, making Alec realize he was one of those few truly lucky people who'd found their calling.

Despite one nearly ending his life, Asher now lived for the sharks. His devotion to them was as admirable as it was amazing. He pulled his gaze from the cage being lowered in the water and concentrated on Asher. As he fiddled with his camera, Alec's eyes were drawn to his fingers. Asher worked his camera lovingly, his long digits almost caressing it as he fiddled with different parts.

"If you do freak out or want to get out of the water, let me know by giving me a signal. I don't mind giving you a nudge to do this, but I don't want you to stay in there if you're terrified." Asher spoke almost absently as he kept tinkering with his camera.

"You'll know if I need to get out. Promise. I'm no hero, Ash," Alec said, casting another nervous glance at the water.

Asher handed his camera off to Damon and got the remainder of his gear on. Alec made his way to where Warren stood on the platform, waiting to help them. The water was crystal clear, so Alec could easily see past the bottom of the cage. When he didn't see any dark shadows, his pulse lowered a fraction.

Asher joined him, his excitement obvious on his handsome features. "Here we go," he said, wasting no time backing onto the bridge and stepping down into the water and the safety of the cage. Damon handed over his camera and then Asher was gone, submerged beneath the surface of the blue waters.

Alec took a giant calming breath, put his regulator on, and with a last, longing look at the safety of the big boat, backed onto the bridge, his gloved fingers gripping the rail so tightly he thought they might break.

Damon gave him a nod and a wink, and Warren wished him good luck as he dropped one foot into the water, closely followed by the second. He could already feel how the swell was banging the cage around as he lowered himself deeper and deeper into the ocean. His heart was thudding against his chest so hard he wondered if it might break through the bone, tissue, and skin and pop right out.

Once he was completely under, he turned, coming face-to-face with Asher. He gave him a tentative thumbs-up, which was enough for Asher, who responded in kind and moved to the edge of the cage farthest from the boat.

Alec took a deep breath and joined him. For a while they just hung there, bumping around in the cage like a bumper car. Alec struggled to keep from knocking into the bars with every rise and fall of the swell.

The visibility was amazing, so he understood why this was such a popular spot to observe sharks. Alec relaxed into the tranquil peace of the ocean as minutes passed by in relative calm. And then Asher's hand tapped his and pointed.

Alec followed the length of Asher's arm and peered down into the watery blue. His entire body tensed, and his heart thumped impossibly harder in his chest as he watched an enormous gray shape swim gracefully and surely toward them. The shark swam as though he knew he was king down here. Alec was awed and humbled by its size and graceful presence.

Asher moved his camera out through the bars, causing Alec to worry the shark might take his arms off, but Asher seemed completely at home and relaxed. Alec watched, mesmerized by the swish of its massive tail as the shark came closer and closer and then eventually skimmed past the bars of the cage. It had to have been at least twelve feet long, and though not especially big for the species, the shark was quite big enough for him.

When Asher tapped him again, he turned to see another shark, of similar size, approaching from the right. Several feet away, a giant fish head hit the water, hook and line still attached. The second shark headed straight for it. Alec was shocked when the fish head appeared to be dragged toward the cage and the people in it—including him.

Less than four feet from the cage, the shark caught up to the fish head. Its giant mouth opened, and its teeth descended as it lunged for its meal. Teeth and gullet filled his field of vision. And then it closed its jaw, latching onto the bait. It shook its massive head. Alec watched, unable to look away, as it moved past the cage still thrashing violently with its catch in its mouth.

Any fear Alec had been feeling disappeared in the face of the awe and respect he felt for this mighty animal. The shark was graceful in a way something of its monstrous size shouldn't be. He'd often heard of sharks having dead eyes, but Alec would have sworn he saw intelligence, or at least keen interest, as the first shark made another pass by the cage. Its pilot fish swam gamely along with it, and Alec was humbled by nature. That the sharks knew not to eat pilot fish because they ate their parasites only proved to Alec how well Mother-freaking-Nature knew what she was doing.

Alec was surprised to realize his hands were gripping the bars of the cage, but no longer in fear. He felt almost as though he wanted to pull the bars apart and join the giant fish on the other side. He was also surprised when he noticed several more sharks had joined them, gliding effortlessly through the water but never getting too close to each other.

Asher tapped him again and pointed to his left. Alec turned and saw a shark coming closer than any previous ones. Its nose nudged the cage and though Alec was sure it was a gentle touch, the cage swayed in the water, knocking Alec off balance—if one could be unbalanced in water. Without thought, Alec stuck his hand through the bars and skimmed his gloved fingertips along the shark's flank as it passed. He'd never experienced anything like it.

As suddenly as they came, the sharks seemed to disappear. Alec looked across at Asher, expecting him to be relaxed, but instead, he seemed to be on heightened alert. What the hell was going on? Asher's head was swiveling all around as though he knew there was something to see but had no idea where to look. Alec joined him but saw nothing.

Suddenly Asher grabbed his arm and tugged him back away from the bars and gestured right. Alec turned and immediately started to shake. Swimming parallel and at eye level to them was an absolute giant. She had to be close to twenty feet and totally dwarfed the sharks swimming around only moments ago. Alec tried not to think about the fact twelve-foot killing machines were so scared of this one that they fled the area.

His mind flicked to Jasper, and he thanked god the man was safe in his cage—or were the cages even safe with an animal of this size? Asher had edged closer to the bars and had poked his camera barely through as he recorded the monster-sized fish who had turned and was coming back for another look. Alec held his breath as it passed by and hoped it didn't share the same curiosity as a cat. It could swallow him whole, never mind take a little investigative nibble.

The big shark circled them for the longest ten minutes of his life. Alec was fascinated by the distinctive white belly and the massive dorsal fin—a symbol of so much fear. And then, as suddenly as she'd come, she disappeared.

Shortly after the big one left, the smaller ones returned, and then Asher gestured toward the surface. A part of Alec was itching to get out, but a bigger part wanted to stay. He had another four days, and he was dying to hear what Asher had to say about the twenty footer.

Alec managed to get himself onto the deck of the boat with relative ease, despite his shaking legs and the natural high he was on. And he was on a high. He shucked his equipment and pulled the top of his wetsuit down for better comfort. He could hear excited voices but wasn't really registering the actual words, until he heard Asher's voice.

"Did you see the size of that girl? Holy shit, she was easily twenty feet. She had some recent bites, too, so she may have been mating. God, she was so fucking beautiful!" Asher enthused, his voice high and loud with his excitement.

Alec turned, the excitement and the high he was on making him reckless. He took three paces back toward Asher and scooped him up around the waist, twirling him. "Woo-hoo, Ash. That was fucking awesome! I damn near shit myself when the big one came, but Jesus Christ, I see what you mean now. They were fucking amazing." He laughed as he kept spinning with Asher in his arms.

Thankfully, Asher was laughing, too, so he tried not to worry about making a colossal fool of himself. He planted Asher's feet back on the deck and, swept up in the moment, pressed his lips fiercely to Asher's. This kiss was quick and dirty and perfect. "Thank you," he said after the brief kiss. "Thank you for making me get in there. That was amazing. When can we get back in?"

Asher laughed again, before smiling fondly at him. "We can go back in this afternoon, once I've uploaded this footage. And Alec...maybe you should listen to me more often. Maybe I might know what could be good for you."

Alec thought that maybe Asher was absolutely right.

Chapter Sixteen

ASHER

Later that night Asher was once again alone on the flybridge with Alec. The sky was cloudier tonight, harder to see the stars. Dinner was a rambunctious affair as they all talked over the top of one another about the big girl who'd come to play with them today. She was the biggest fish any of them had ever seen, and they weren't able to rein in their excitement. Even Alec excitedly joined in the conversation, asking questions and making observations.

Alec had gone down in the cage twice more, without hesitation. Apparently, Asher had converted another doubter into a shark enthusiast.

"Here," Asher offered a beer to Alec as he reclined on the sun lounger.

Alec pushed himself up a little and reached for the bottle. "Thanks." He tapped the neck of his bottle against Asher's and took a sip.

Asher leaned back on the rail and admired the way Alec's throat worked as he swallowed his beer. Alec's eyes were closed and he looked so thoroughly content that Asher was expecting a purr from him any moment.

"So, do I see a change of career in your future?" he asked.

Alec opened his eyes and let his gaze travel all over Asher, so intensely Asher felt the weight of it raking over his skin. "Well, I definitely prefer the monsters you work with to the ones I do," Alec answered noncommittally.

"No contest," Asher agreed. Asher knew plenty of people would never understand why he chose to do what he did, especially after nearly being killed by a great white, but the work Alec did was way worse. He had no idea how someone could do that kind of work—how they could touch the vilest evil—and not go insane. "I've told you before I don't know how you do what you do."

"You did it."

"Once, and for my nephew. You can and do help complete strangers, you fight for them. That's bravery I'll never understand."

Alec was still watching him closely. Maybe he should feel uncomfortable under the scrutiny, but he didn't. "You were brave when it mattered, Ash."

"Tell me a little about your work," Asher murmured, seeking greater intimacy with this man who had intrigued him since the day they met.

Alec patted the sun lounger and widened his legs. Asher was like a moth to a flame and went easily. He was a fool if he thought he'd be able to stay away from this man. He sat between Alec's spread thighs, leaning his body back onto Alec's chest. He wasn't sure, but he thought he felt the light brush of Alec's lips in his hair.

"I'll tell you a little, but I'll give you the sanitized version. Deal?" Alec asked.

"Deal."

Alec wriggled a little and settled farther back on the chair, taking Asher with him. "Most of the cases we get turn out to be one parent taking their kid and running from the other parent after a separation. Sometimes it's because of abuse; other times it's nothing more than revenge. Those cases make us mad because we know the parents are not thinking of their child at all. All they wanna do is hurt their ex."

"You find them easy enough?"

"Mostly. There have been one or two who skipped the country. For those cases, we have to call in the authorities, because there are all kinds of legal shit to deal with, and if you don't do it right, it'll work against the parent trying to get their child home."

"Wow. It's hard to believe people would want to hurt someone they once loved so badly. How do things go so wrong?"

Alec shrugged behind him, his movement momentarily dislodging Alec from his chest.

"Last case I had was...rough. Twelve-year-old girl. Parents woke up one morning, and she wasn't in her bed. They called us in because they thought the police were too busy focusing on them as suspects and not doing enough to find her." Alec awkwardly took a sip of his beer and grunted when Asher wriggled a little.

"They always suspect the family first, don't they?" Asher asked. He'd watched crime shows—hell, his own family had been suspected when his nephew was kidnapped—he knew how it worked.

"Yeah, and if people knew the statistics, they'd understand why."

He felt Alec's nose moving through his hair and this time he couldn't mistake the kiss he pressed to his skull. A little shiver ripped up Asher's spine, but he counseled caution. It would be so easy to fall back into bed with Alec, but he'd been singed by the flame of desire before.

"Did you find her?" he asked.

Alec huffed. "Yeah, we found her. She'd run away because the Dad was coming into her room every night, and the Mom was too fucking weak to stop him. He just wanted his toy back."

"Jesus..." Asher gasped.

"She's safe now, but she'll wind up in the system, and that can go either way. Poor kid, she's got it all stacked against her, but she'll be okay."

"What makes you say that?" Asher asked.

"Because she had the balls to fight for herself when no one else did," Alec stated with admiration thick in his tone.

"How do you cope?"

Alec huffed a laugh. "I run and my boxing bag gets a good workout."

"I bet it does."

"It's tough sometimes not to take a swing at the perps. The Dad, smug bastard, was lucky I didn't put my fist through his teeth. Swore black and blue he never touched her. The kid's lucky...it was a good act, and some would have believed him. Some would have sent her right back into hell."

Asher relaxed again as silence fell between them. Being around Alec was so easy and comfortable. Why did Alec walk away from this—from him? Had it been a misunderstanding? Or did Alec not want him?

"Alec? Will you be honest with me?"

"You know I will," Alec murmured in his ear.

"Did you ever think about having more with me than just a quick fuck?"

"You were never just a quick fuck, Ash. The truth is I haven't been able to stop thinking about you for the last four months. But I know I fucked up."

Alec put his arm around Asher's waist and pulled him tighter against his chest. What Alec said tasted like truth to Asher. Was he ready to give him another chance though?

"What if I gave you another chance?"

Alec shifted behind him and was quiet long enough for Asher to wonder if he'd overreached.

"I can't make any promises, Ash. I haven't been serious about anyone for a long, long time. I want a relationship, a real one, but I'm not really sure I'm cut out for it. But if you wanted to try...I can promise you, I'd give it my all."

Asher nodded gently, still unwilling to drop his guard. "I'll keep that in mind." He closed his eyes and lay back, putting his head on Alec's shoulder. Asher wasn't much smaller than Alec, so he might be starting to get uncomfortable with Asher leaning on him, but he decided to stay for a few more minutes.

"Can you make *me* a promise?" Alec's voice was low and gravelly, sending a shiver up his spine. Asher probably would have promised him anything right then.

"I'll try," he answered honestly.

"Good enough. Promise me you'll take this threat seriously. Promise me you'll do whatever you have to do to stay safe."

How could he not promise when Alec's concern was so genuine? When his house burned down, he'd honestly thought it was a terrible accident. But if the water was off and the electricity out... He had to stop living in denial and concede the chances were high someone was after him.

"I will. I promise."

"Thank you," Alec whispered.

"What do you suggest?"

"Maddy and Kane are already taking their concerns to the cops. We need them to investigate to try and find out who's behind it. The timing makes it pretty likely it's something to do with Fincher. But who?"

"Dad told me his grandfather disowned him when he was arrested. Won't have anything to do with him and refuses to let the firm represent him." Asher wasn't sure how he felt about the man losing the support of his family. Obviously Morgan Fincher was a bad guy but to be disowned, to have his family turn their backs on him...

"Do we know anything else about him? His parents or other family?"

Asher thought about it. The times he'd met Morgan at his father's firm's social functions he'd been there alone, with only his grandparents. Asher had only had a few trivial conversations with him but nothing about his family. He had no idea who Morgan had around him or which of them might want revenge for what had happened to him in prison.

"I don't really know, to be honest. But it seems unfair to me. I mean, I get that I played a part in catching him, but it's his fault. He chose to do what he did." Truthfully, it made him angry someone was threatening *his* life because Fincher had chosen to commit a heinous crime.

"Nothing about crime is fair, Ash. Nothing. But we're not going to let them win. When we get back to Ensenada in a few days, I need you to come back to San Diego with me. I've got contacts and we can get you protection while the cops work this all out." There was a hint of pleading in Alec's tone, and Asher didn't want him to worry any more than he already was.

"I'll come back...but can't you be my protection?" Asher did not want to be surrounded by strangers watching his every move, and that's all he imagined when he thought of protection or bodyguards.

"I won't be going anywhere. Not until we catch this guy."

Asher leaned away from Alec before turning to look at him. He looked relaxed and, dare he say it, happy. Asher didn't want him to go anywhere—even after they caught the guy, but he wasn't ready to admit those feelings quite yet. He got up on his knees and straddled Alec where he lay on the lounger. He sat back, resting his ass on Alec's thick thighs. He watched Alec for a moment before he leaned forward and touched his nose to Alec's, gently rubbing them together. Alec's scent was so potent this close Asher's stomach flipped pleasantly.

"What happened here?" he asked as he gently touched Alec's scarred lip.

"I had a cleft lip when I was born. Not a bad one and the doctors did a good job fixing it," Alec answered.

"They did." He pressed his lips to Alec's and flicked his tongue along the seam. The kiss was perfect, Alec's soft lips working with his own to deepen the connection. He moved his body so he barely rolled against Alec's. Strong arms held him close as the kiss stole his breath. He reached up and twined his fingers through Alec's hair, holding him tightly so that—at least in this moment—there was no way he was getting away.

Asher's erection pressed against Alec's rigid length. The feel of their bodies rubbing together was delicious. It would be so easy to be with Alec again. But he reminded himself nothing truly worthwhile ever came easily.

He pulled away from the heat of Alec's body and the safety of his arms. He pressed one last quick kiss to his lips before he stood. He looked down at Alec, letting his eyes trail all over him. He leaned down and put his thumb to Alec's bottom lip, tracing where his own lips had just been.

"Night, Alec," he whispered and then turned to head down to his cabin. Asher couldn't help the small smile breaking over his face when Alec groaned in frustration behind him. He had no intention of tormenting him for too long, but he'd always heard it didn't hurt to keep them guessing.

Chapter Seventeen

ALEC

Being cooped up on the boat with Asher lasted for four of the best days of his life—and four days of torture. They'd been ridiculously affectionate with each other, constantly touching and kissing whenever they had the chance, like giddy teenagers. Alec's lips were actually tingling from the constant abuse, not that he was complaining at all. He could happily kiss Asher for hours—days—on end. But Asher had also kept him at arm's length, refusing to, as he put it, "go all the way" with him.

They'd spent their days in the water with Asher's beloved sharks and their nights talking and laughing. The rest of the crew had become experts in subtly excusing themselves, leaving Asher and Alec alone under the stars. It had been insanely romantic, without either of them ever really trying.

Now, thirty miles outside of San Diego, Alec knew he was going to miss those days terribly. He'd also miss being able to relax. The *August Moon* had been a safe space for Asher. The likelihood of an attempt on his life coming on the boat from anything other than what was in the water was remote at best. There was no way in such a remote location. But as soon as they'd docked in Ensenada, everything changed. And now Alec was looking for danger in every face in the crowd.

"I'm going to my boat, Alec," Asher said, again.

They'd had this same argument the entire time Asher had been driving them back to San Diego, and Asher was wearing him down. "You heard the arson report, Asher. We know the fire was deliberately set. We know it was an attempt on your life. Going somewhere they'll be waiting for you is plain foolish." Alec was proud of the serenity he'd managed to keep in his tone, especially given how much he felt like throttling the gorgeous, stubborn, frustrating man beside him.

"We're not gonna be there long. We'll get on the boat and head out to the ocean. You told me yourself how safe we were on the *August Moon*. It's the same thing," Asher argued.

"No, it really isn't. Look, Ash, there's a big difference between tracking someone down to Mexico with an eighteen-hour boat trip off the coast, to turning up to wait at a San Diego marina where your target's boat is known to be moored. It's not safe to go back there. We can hire a boat if it'd make you feel safe or we could take off somewhere until the cops have it sorted." Alec was starting to get a little desperate.

He didn't want Asher going back to his boat, but short of physically restraining him, there was no way to stop him. Maybe the time had come to get the family onboard. Perhaps Maddy or Kane would have better luck with the stubborn man.

"No. Please, Alec, the *Nautibuoy* is my home, more so than my house ever was. I want to get to her. I don't want her blown to hell too."

"The naughty boy?"

Asher huffed a laugh. "Yeah, but it's spelled n a u t i b u o y. You can blame that one on Kane, and an awful lot of tequila."

Alec laughed, suddenly imagining a happily drunk Asher thinking it was an awesome name for his boat. "What if we send someone else to pick her up?" Alec could be dogged, too, and he didn't like the idea of going to Asher's boat at all.

"Well, we're only about a half hour away, and I'm driving so I'm not quite sure how you're planning on stopping me." Asher turned and flashed a shit-eating grin at him. Alec was torn between laughter and strangling him.

"You know I could stop you if I wanted, right?" he grouched.

"Sure, big boy. Sure you could." Asher winked this time, and Alec felt like screaming—but, oddly, in the best kind of way.

Asher reminded him a lot of Ben, at least the Ben he'd first known before war and death had given him the hard edge always lurking right beneath his surface. "I could, you know," Alec said, cringing at his sulky tone.

Asher remained silent as he kept driving. What was he thinking about so hard? "What's on your mind, Ashy?"

"Oh no. Don't you dare start calling me that, or I'll start calling you Bluey."

Alec flinched at the hated name. According to Kelly, Australians called people with ginger hair and blue-hazel eyes Bluey. He had no idea why they did. Why these people couldn't simply use a person's—or object's—proper name was beyond him. He'd have to have a serious talk with Ryan about it one day. Banno he could have lived with, but Bluey? No, just no.

"So Ashy was the best she could do?"

"Well she likes to change her mind a lot. Mostly it's Ashy, but I've also been Ash-a and Ash-o and there was brief flirtation with Drongo."

"Drongo?"

"Yeah. Apparently a Drongo is like an idiot. So she called me one after an unfortunate incident with a set of barbeque tongs and a tiger shark." A flush crept up Asher's neck as he spoke, making Alec determined to get the story out of him one day.

"I'm gonna need to hear that story."

Asher flicked a glance to him again, and Alec got the distinct impression he was sizing him up for worthiness to hear the tale. He didn't think he'd ever wanted for anything more than to be found worthy by Asher Winsome.

"So Kane's meeting us at Old Town, right?" Asher asked, possibly hoping to distract Alec from the tiger shark story.

"Yeah, Café Coyote. It's a popular tourist spot, so there'll be lots of people around. Even if someone is following your brother to get to you, they won't try anything there. It'll be safe." At least he hoped it would be. He'd already lost the battle to keep Asher away from his family.

"I know I should stay away from them and disappear, but I need to say goodbye in case...well, in case I don't get another chance," Asher said, his normally strong voice faltering.

This was the first time Alec had heard a hint of fear in Asher because his life might actually be in danger. Hearing about the arson report had gone a long way in convincing him because he'd still been hanging on to his denial. At least until he heard the investigators had found evidence of gasoline all through the charred ruins of Asher's home.

"I understand. But, Asher, after this, there can be no contact."

"Yeah, I know," he whispered. "It's funny how I'm more upset at not being able to see Maddy and Jack than my parents. They've changed a little since Jack's kidnapping but, I don't know, they're still... I guess some people are wired to not be able to show they care."

"You know I wouldn't count on not seeing Maddy here. She said she'd stay away, but from what I know of your sister-in-law, I'm betting she'll be here with bells on to say goodbye."

Asher laughed and nodded his head. "You know her pretty well," he agreed.

Alec had no siblings so couldn't understand the bond between them, but he supported it. That relationship was the only reason he'd reluctantly agreed to this meeting.

CAFÉ COYOTE WAS overflowing with customers. The Mexican restaurant was the most crowded in the area, and Alec was grateful Kane had picked it for their meeting. The building was a massive space, and according to Kane's text, he was on the ground floor, just inside the door to the right.

Asher sidled his way through the crowd, Alec staying close on his heels, his eyes scanning for any danger. He wasn't at all surprised to see Maddy sitting beside her husband as they approached their table.

"Alec said you'd be here," Asher said as he greeted his family.

Maddy turned her smiling face toward him and stood up. "Is that FBI profiling you've done on me, Alec?"

Alec allowed the hug she gave him and smiled at her when she pulled away. "Doesn't take a profiler to work out some people, Maddy." He winked.

"Damn, and I always thought I was a little enigmatic."

"Not when it comes to your family." Alec looked around again and saw nothing to give him pause. He was as sure as he could be that Asher was safe here. "I'm gonna make a call. You guys see if you can talk Asher out of going to his boat," he said, bracing for the outcry. Kane and Maddy didn't disappoint.

"Asher, don't be so stupid," Kane began.

With a smirk and a wink at Asher, Alec walked away to make his phone call. He didn't go far, just enough so he wouldn't be overheard but could still keep an eye on Asher.

"Banner, what's up, man?" Ben answered on the third ring. In the background, he could hear squealing, and he wondered what Ben's twins were up to.

"I need advice about Asher."

"What about him? Any more news about the fire?"

Alec had called Ben on his way down to Ensenada to fill him in on the attack on Morgan Fincher and the resulting threat to Asher. Now arson had been officially confirmed, and since it appeared Asher would need protection, Alec was turning to his best friend for advice. Ben and his partner, Ethan, had both worked as bodyguards before leaving to form Chasing Hope, so he wanted to pick Ben's brain about how best to protect Asher.

"Definitely arson but we knew that. I've talked him into lying low, but I've never done this before...protecting someone. Usually I'd transfer them to the Marshals if they need protecting. What do I need to do?"

"Okay. Where are you taking him?"

Alec was kind of nervous about telling Ben about the boat. He knew he wouldn't approve, but unless he could change Asher's mind, there was nothing, short of kidnapping, he could do about it. "Ash wants to get his boat. He wants us to get in it and sail off—"

"Into the sunset?" Ben laughed. *Asshole.*

"Hilarious, Cronin. But I'm serious. I've tried to talk him out of it. I've suggested someone else go to pick it up. I've even told him whoever is after him is probably watching it. But he's a fucking mule."

"It's damn hard when two mules are butting heads, believe me I know. You do whatever you have to do, Banner, to talk him out of the boat. I'm gonna talk to the Krispin's Security people to see if we can get some bodyguards down there. If someone is after Asher, it's not a one-man job to protect him. You can't be awake and aware twenty-four seven." Ben spoke with all professional seriousness now.

"Thanks, Ben. I know Kane's willing to pay whatever to keep Asher safe. It's a matter of getting Asher to agree to it."

"The Krispins have plenty of safe houses dotted around, too; I'd try to get him to one of them. The boat would be isolated, sure, but as you'd know, it'd be easy enough to track, given its Asher's boat."

Maybe he could talk Asher into a safe house. He looked over at him and watched fondly as he laughed at whatever Maddy was saying, with her hands gesticulating wildly. The man stole his breath every time Alec caught him laughing with abandon. He loved how his head tipped back, his eyes crinkled at the edges, and his mouth spread wide with his laughter. He looked wild and free and beautiful.

"Okay. So send me a list of the safe houses, and I'll get him there one way or another," Alec finally said to Ben.

"You bet. Let me know where you're headed, and I'll get Krispin's Security staff there to meet you. And Alec...you take care, and I don't mean of just Asher."

"You know I will, Ben. Thanks. Talk soon," Alec finished. He ended his call and leaned on the wall for a moment, watching Asher.

Alec had been successful in all of his chosen careers: the military, the FBI, and now working at Chasing Hope. He'd had very few failures, so the thought of failing Asher now was too much for him to take. He couldn't allow it. If he had to go caveman and drag Asher to a safe house, he would. If Asher ended up hating him because of it, then Alec would have to live with that. Nothing—absolutely nothing—was more important than keeping Asher safe.

"Everything okay?" Maddy asked as he approached the table.

"Yeah. I was talking to Ben." He looked over at Asher, holding his gaze as he spoke. "He's sending me details about safe houses and arranging for bodyguards."

Kane attempted a small smile, relief written all over his face. "Perfect. And we've talked this numbnuts out of going to his boat."

"They blackmailed me," Asher groused. "They actually told me I wouldn't be allowed to see Jack until he was a grown-ass man if I was fool enough to go there."

Alec didn't care at all how it had been done, only that it had. "Perfect." He blew right past Asher's outraged "Hey." "I'm thinking we'll keep heading north tonight, find an out of the way hotel along the way. We need to put distance between Asher and San Diego."

"Well," Maddy said as she stood. "Both of you give me a hug before you go. And you promise me you'll keep each other safe."

Asher stood and hugged both his brother and sister-in-law. When it was Alec's turn, he shook Kane's hand and allowed Maddy to hug him again. He didn't know a lot of huggers, but Maddy was likely one of the best.

All four walked out of Café Coyote together. He and Asher turned right while Kane and Maddy went left. The crowds had died down somewhat, and there were only a handful of people walking the sidewalk now.

The first Alec knew of something terribly wrong was when the tiles on the wall exploded into shards right in front of him, pricking the tender skin on his cheeks.

Chapter Eighteen

ASHER

Alec's body hit him with a power he'd been totally unprepared for, slamming them both onto the concrete sidewalk. The contact would have been worse if Alec hadn't taken the brunt of the fall. Asher was quickly rolled under Alec's body as he listened in confusion to the *pop pop pop* shattering the normal noise of midafternoon in busy Old Town, San Diego.

His cheek burned as Alec's weight pressed him harder into the pathway. Where his body was not covered by Alec's, Asher could feel sharp nicks on any bare skin as shattered tile rained down on them. He tried to look around to gauge what was happening, but his head wasn't going anywhere, Alec had it securely held beneath him. The *pop* and *crack* continued, but the sound was almost drowned out now by screaming and the pounding of running feet. He was devastated to realize he actually recognized the noises of a shooting. But it wasn't a single lonely shot this time. There were many—too many.

He had no idea how much time was passing as he lay there under Alec's body, but eventually, the pop of the gun stopped and was replaced by the sounds of screams and sirens. He began to wriggle under Alec, hoping he'd move off him now the shooting had stopped. Asher needed to check on Kane and Maddy. They hadn't been far away when Alec threw him to the ground.

"Alec, I need to get up," he grunted. "Alec?"

There was no reply from Alec, and no movement either. Panic looped its insidious way throughout his body. He thrashed beneath the heavier man, desperate to get out and help Alec because something had to be terribly wrong.

"Alec," he screamed as his anxiety spiked.

"Asher?" his brother called from nearby.

"Kane. Kane, what's wrong with Alec?"

Suddenly his brother's feet came into his field of vision, but he could only awkwardly peer up at him from where Alec had him trapped. "Kane."

"Stay calm, Asher. Alec's hurt. I'm gonna ease him off you so you can get out."

Alec was hurt—so badly he couldn't move off Asher. Asher's heart was thumping manically. He knew Kane was all right, and Maddy had to be; otherwise there was no way his brother would be here, calmly helping him.

"What happened? What happened?" he babbled as Alec's weight finally eased, and Asher was able to slide away and get to his knees.

He was surrounded by a wasteland of tile shards, shredded plants and blood. Asher blanched at the blood soaking through the sleeve of Alec's shirt as Alec lay still beside him. But the obvious gunshot wound to his arm didn't cause fear to race up Asher's spine; it was the giant lump on Alec's head and the fact they couldn't wake him that left him terrified.

"Alec? Alec, can you hear me?" Asher prodded him gently as he spoke, too afraid of the head wound to shake him. People were starting to come out from wherever they'd hidden during the shooting, but Alec wasn't responding at all. "Alec?"

"Asher, paramedics are here," Maddy said quietly in his ear. Asher had no idea where she'd come from. He didn't remember seeing her since before the shooting. But she was there, kneeling right beside him, with Kane standing over them both. Asher quickly glanced up and noticed his brother looked as though he was ready to throw himself over all of them if the gunman came back.

As he glanced around, he was blinded by a sea of flashing lights as emergency vehicles of all kinds descended on the scene. Looking down the pathway he noticed several other huddles of people, a few desperately waving over the arriving paramedics.

Asher didn't know much about guns at all, but he knew what had been used wasn't a simple handgun. It had been some kind of automatic weapon, and from the looks of things, the gunman had sprayed bullets randomly throughout the crowd. The tiled fence wall of Café Coyote was in ruins, evidence of the bedlam of the shooting. He couldn't bring himself to think too hard about the human evidence of the chaos.

"Ash, we need to move back, honey; the paramedics need to get to him," Maddy cajoled.

If Alec would open his eyes. If only he could hear his voice, even if it was to tell him he was a fool for coming here. Because he had been a fool. He'd endangered everyone because he needed to say goodbye to his brother. Kane could have been killed—Maddy. His selfishness could have cost Jack his parents. And Alec, oh, Alec.

Asher stood away from Alec as two paramedics knelt beside him. Kane and Maddy flanked him. His body was shaking as the adrenaline from the moment leached from his body.

"You're both okay?" he murmured without looking away from Alec.

"Fine, we're fine. The bullets came nowhere near us," Kane answered.

"What should I do now?" Asher asked, thinking out loud. The situation was finally clear to him: he had to get far away from everyone he cared about, including Alec. It couldn't be coincidence that he was here and so was a gunman. This shooting had to be about him. He was a danger to his loved ones and he needed to get away—but how?

"Let's get you to the hospital so you can be with Alec, and we'll go from there," Maddy suggested.

There was no way Maddy or Kane would let him walk away now, but he couldn't risk their lives. He hated what he was about to do, but he'd take any action necessary to keep them safe.

"Is he going to be okay?" he asked the closest paramedic.

"He's got a gunshot wound to his upper arm, but it's non-life-threatening. He has a serious concussion, though. We're ready to transport him now."

"Which hospital?" Kane asked.

"Sharp Memorial," one of the paramedics called as they stood and wheeled Alec away.

"I'm gonna get my car and meet you there," Asher said with as much authority as he could manage, trying to leave no room for argument.

"No. We should stay together," Kane countered.

"Kane, my car's right there, and nothing's gonna happen with all these cops around."

Kane's gaze swung between where he was pointing to the side street across the road where his car was parked and him as he assessed the danger. Kane had to believe him and let him go because every second he stood here with his family was another chance for them to be hurt.

"Okay, all right, but don't mess around, Asher. Drive straight there, and park in emergency so you don't have to walk far. Promise me."

"I promise, Kane." He hugged his brother, holding him tightly for probably too long. He hoped Kane didn't think him dragging out the hug was anything more than a reaction to surviving a near-death experience. Maddy was next, his guilt building as he whispered he'd see her soon. It was the only goodbye he could give them.

Asher raced across the street without looking back on the scene. The cops were busy getting names and rounding people up for questioning, but in the confusion, Asher managed to slip away. He got behind the wheel, not dawdling as he peeled away from the scene with no real clue where he was heading, except away.

He drove aimlessly for half an hour, taking as many twists and turns as he could manage. He, perhaps naïvely, hoped by driving erratically, he'd lose any tail he might have. Maybe he'd watched too many cop shows, but he didn't know what else to do. He'd never felt more lost and alone.

Eventually, he pulled to the side of the road in a deserted industrial area, unwilling to risk another heavily populated area because, yeah, it didn't seem as though the gunman cared at all about collateral damage. Asher was determined nobody else would be hurt because of him.

He pulled out his phone and ignored the nine missed calls—he knew who'd made them, but he couldn't talk to Kane right now. Maybe when he was farther away, the temptation to turn back would lessen, and then he'd be able to risk talking to his brother. He wasn't cruel though, so he sent a quick text explaining how he'd fled but was safe.

Then he called Ben, thanking god he'd kept his number after Jack's kidnapping. He didn't want to involve anyone else in his mess, but he knew he couldn't do this alone—he had no idea where to start.

"Hello?" Ben's voice was laced with curiosity.

"Ben, it's Asher Winsome."

"Hey, Asher. Anything wrong?"

Asher's panic stealthily crawled its way through his body again, cruelly doing its best to hinder him, but he pushed it down. "There was a shooting," he gasped as the words tumbled out of him. "Alec was shot, but I think the gunshot wound is okay. They were more worried about his head. Shit, Ben, I need your help."

There was a momentary silence before Ben spoke. "Okay. Slow down. Where was the shooting?"

"Old Town. We'd just left the restaurant where we met my brother and sister-in-law, and someone...shot up the place." Asher's body tensed so tightly his muscles ached with it. He was coiled and ready for more bullets to come flying at him at any second.

"Are you hurt?"

"No. Alec got me down, but he was shot in the arm, and he must have hit his head. He's got a massive bump." Asher swallowed past the lump in his throat. "He wouldn't wake up," he whispered.

"Okay." Ben's tone was so soothingly calm that Asher knew he'd called the right person. "And they've taken him to the hospital?"

"Yeah, Sharp Memorial."

"Is that where you are, Asher?"

"No. No, I left. I can't let anyone else be hurt because of me." His words drained him, leaving him exhausted from their weight.

"Okay, so where are you?"

"I'm not a hundred percent sure. I'm in an industrial area, and I know I'm not too far from the naval base."

"Naval base? Mm...hold on a minute, Asher."

Nothing but muffled voices came across the line as Ben pulled the phone from his ear and presumably pressed it against his body. He hoped to god Ben knew what to do because he was floundering.

Some minutes later, Ben came back on the line. "Okay, listen to me, Asher. I want you to go to the naval base and ask to see Lieutenant Harmer. He'll bring you on base until I get there."

"Why?" Asher didn't really mean to question Ben but was curious why a naval officer, who was a stranger, would help him out.

"Ethan and I helped him out with his missing kid. Ethan's on the phone with him now, so he's expecting you. He'll keep you safe. I'll be there as soon as I can."

"You have to promise me to keep Alec away. Promise me you won't tell him where I am. I can't risk him getting hurt again," Asher begged.

"Asher, it's okay—"

"No. Promise me, Ben. Or I'll run, and I'll do this on my own."

"Fuck. Banner wasn't kidding, you are a mule. All right, I promise. I won't tell Alec where you are."

"Thanks, Ben."

"Yeah, no problem, Asher, but hurry up and get your ass to the naval base."

Ben quickly hung up, leaving Asher to follow his instructions. He longed to call Kane to find out how Alec was, but he wouldn't risk it. He started his car, barely hearing the beep of a message over the roar of his engine.

The text was from Kane. Asher's hands shook as he read it.

Ash, don't do this. Come back. We can help. They've taken Alec in for surgery. He needs you. We need you.

He read the message over and over, feeling Kane's concern in every word. But Asher was more than simply concerned—he was dead terrified someone he loved might be hurt. What if they went after Jack again? He couldn't bear it. He had to get away. His reply was simple.

I'm sorry. Tell Alec I'm sorry.

Chapter Nineteen

ALEC

He wished to god whoever was pounding on his head with a fucking hammer would cut it out. He desperately wanted to do something to stop them, but for some unfathomable reason, Alec had no control of himself. Where the hell was he?

The monotonous beeping he'd been listening to for a while was really starting to piss him off, but at a slightly louder level, he could hear his name being repeated. Somebody was telling him to open his eyes. Maybe he should do what they said, and then maybe they'd stop hitting him with the fucking hammer.

Alec concentrated on what should be the simple and instinctive task of opening his eyes. The voice kept calling his name, encouraging him, and Alec finally managed to open them a sliver. Ben's smiling face filled his vision.

"Welcome back, buddy."

"Ben," he croaked. He recognized immediately he was in a hospital, and the awareness brought foggy memories of the shooting rushing back. "Asher?"

There was a momentary flinch from Ben, and Alec's stomach dropped. Where was Asher?

"He's fine. He's safe," Ben finally answered.

"Where?"

"Alec, let's get you taken care of first, and then we'll talk about Asher. But trust me, he's fine."

Alec nodded and tried to relax. There was no way Ben would lie to him about something like that. His head was still screaming at him, and he'd do anything to make it stop. Releasing his tension would help.

Ben called for a nurse, and suddenly two doctors, a nurse, and another mystery guest were surrounding him. Alec was poked and prodded and repeatedly told how lucky he was. His gunshot was little more than a flesh wound, the bullet skating along the top of his skin, leaving a nice little trail, requiring minor surgery. His head wound was more serious, so he'd be there for a few more days while they ran tests to make sure there was no permanent damage. It had been a near miss.

As soon as the medical team left, with rather ominous promises to return soon, Alec turned to Ben.

"What happened?" Alec had memories of the shooting, but they were like jumbled pieces of a jigsaw puzzle and he wasn't able to put them together clearly enough to form a coherent picture.

"From what we can gather, somebody shot up San Diego Avenue all to hell. You and fourteen other people were shot. No deaths, but one of the victims is still listed as critical—"

"Kane and Maddy?" He knew they were there but couldn't place exactly where they'd been when the shooting started.

"Completely unharmed. They went home a while ago. They're not very happy with me." Ben pouted, though Alec suspected he didn't really care. Ben would do what was right even if it pissed people off.

There was a soft chuckle, and for the first time, it registered to Alec that Ethan was there in the room too. When he looked around, he spotted him casually leaning against the far wall, smiling as he looked fondly at Ben.

"That's not unusual, Cronin. You do have a knack for pissing folks off," Ethan drawled.

"Yeah, yeah. I do what I must. As long as you and the pixies still like me, I can live with it," Ben shot back.

"Eh...you have your moments."

Ben turned and glared at his partner. "Some people simply don't appreciate perfection," he sniffed.

"I appreciate your perfection all right." Ethan winked.

"Oh my god. Really?" Alec sighed.

"You should have heard his dirty talk when we first got together, Banner. It was shameful." Ben tsked and shook his head.

"Am I still under or maybe high on painkillers? This conversation can't be real," bemoaned Alec. "Tell me why Maddy and Kane are pissed, and where the hell Asher is."

"Asher called Ben after the shooting," Ethan answered. "We came straight down and got him out, but he made us promise not to tell anyone, including his family and you, where he is. But he's safe, Alec. A couple of the Krispin's Security guys are with him."

"Where is he?"

"I'm sorry, Alec. I had to promise him. It was the only way he'd come with me," Ben murmured. "He's terrified of getting someone hurt."

"What about him, though?"

Ethan stepped forward, finally joining Ben at the side of his bed. Such a handsome man, but the tiny crush he'd once had on him had completely disappeared. He had his heart firmly set on Asher now.

"He couldn't be anywhere safer, Alec. I know this is hard, but trust us," Ethan said.

Alec knew Asher was safe because he did have faith in Ben and Ethan, but it was still hard not knowing where he was, not being able to contact him. Perhaps being torn from Asher, left in the dark about him was his punishment.

"Jesus, I fucked this up," he murmured.

"How so?" Ben asked.

"I shouldn't have let him come back to meet with Kane. I should have known his family was being watched. It's my fault."

"Bullshit," Ben snapped. "I've negotiated with his stubborn ass, and I'm telling you nobody tells Asher Winsome what to do once his mind is set on something. You did the best you could, and he's still breathing, with hardly a mark on him, and that's thanks to you."

"What marks?"

"Jesus, Banner, don't get your panties in a twist. He's got a couple of scratches from tile shrapnel and a nice gravel burn on his cheek from you smashing him into the ground. But, Alec, he's fine."

Alec let out the breath he'd been holding since he'd woken. As long as Asher was safe and well he could deal with everything else.

Three weeks later...

Alec wasn't sure he was up for a party. It had been weeks since the shooting in San Diego. Three long weeks without hearing a word from Asher or seeing his beautiful face. Ben contacted him every day to let him know Asher was fine, but those calls and brief mentions of Asher weren't enough.

Alec's arms ached to hold him, hear his voice, touch his perfect skin.

Ryan hadn't let him work much either while he recovered from his head knock. The lack of something constructive to do with his time wasn't helping him to keep his mind off his fears for Asher. To keep busy, Alec had been doing what he could from the periphery to try to figure out who was after Asher.

Morgan Fincher had miraculously woken from his injuries, though he was still in a serious condition. From what Alec understood, he'd told the police he knew nothing about the threats to Asher or who could have made them.

Kane had told him the Fincher's grandfather had a mild heart attack, and everyone was blaming it on his grandson's troubles. Alec would do anything to get his hands on the Fincher family. They were wealthy—the kind of wealth that could pay for someone to, say, take out a person they wanted revenge on. The San Diego police were looking into it, so if there was a money trail, hopefully, they'd find it. But he'd asked Jacey to investigate it as well, and she hadn't found anything yet.

He sat in his car out the front of Cameron and Zach's home trying to talk himself into going in. He'd been invited to celebrate the end of Zach's father's trial and the conviction and lengthy sentence he'd received. Last time he'd been here, he'd fled because he'd been jealous of all the love he'd seen and saddened because he had none for himself.

There was no question it was way too soon to whip out the big L word where Asher was concerned, but from where Alec stood, if they had the chance to really explore a relationship, then they were on the right path. Alec enjoyed every second he spent with Asher, even if the man frustrated the hell out of him half the time.

With his background, Alec knew a lot of brave men and women, but there was something special about Asher. The way he lived his life on his terms, the forgiveness he had for an animal that had almost killed him, the love he had for his family. Asher Winsome was an innately good person. Alec missed the hell out of him.

Taking a deep breath, he stepped out of the car and made his way through the open front door. The party was in full swing in Cameron's enormous backyard. Children were running and screaming with laughter as they chased each other or were chased by Ben—of course. There was an enormous amount of people. Alec suspected most of them were Zach's newly reunited family. Ryan and Lucas were there, too, with their son, Charlie. This was the most family-looking scene he'd ever witnessed, and it made his heart fucking ache.

He only made it two steps outside when Cameron halted him.

"Hey, Alec. How're you doing?"

Alec knew Cameron would know all about what went down in San Diego. Ben didn't keep secrets from his brother.

"Almost back to full strength. You guys must be feeling pretty good today," he answered, trying to deflect attention from himself.

"It's a huge relief. Zach can move on now without looking over his shoulder for his father." Cameron looked at him seriously. "You sure you're okay? You look tired."

"I'm good. Still feeling what happened a bit, I guess."

"Ben told us about San Diego. I'm glad you're okay... He, um, also told me about Asher. He hates not being able to tell you where he is, you know."

"I know." Alec fought not to let Asher too far into his thoughts right now. He wanted to relax a little and be there for his friends. He gave Cameron a little half smile. "At least

I know Asher's safe. He won't let Ben tell me where he is, but knowing he's safe helps." Alec's voice broke a little.

Cameron's gaze flicked to Zach, who was approaching them, before returning to Alec. "I'm so sorry about what happened. You must know it wasn't your fault."

"I fucked up, Cameron. I fucked it all up. I deserve what I'm getting." Alec turned to face Zach.

"Hey, Alec. Good to see you," the young man greeted him.

"You too, Zach. I'm glad to hear about your father's sentence." Alec cast his gaze around. He felt so lost. "Anyway, I should let you two get back to your guests."

"You let us know if there's anything we can do, Alec. Anything at all," Cameron offered.

"Thank you. I...ah...guess I should get going." The familiar itch to turn tail and run prickled beneath his skin, even though this right here was what he wanted for himself. Family and love. He had his parents still, but he wanted more. He wanted to be *in* love.

"Stay, Alec. Please stay," Zach urged. "You're family, and you should be here today. Cameron and I have a lot to be grateful to you for."

Alec gave him a weak smile and nodded.

"Get yourself a drink and join us, Alec," Cameron added. "Zach and I have some more good news to share, and we want all of our family here to celebrate."

"Mm, intriguing. Of course, I'll stick around for a while. Thank you both for including me."

"Always," Cameron replied. Then he took Zach's hand and led him away.

Alec made his way to the bar and grabbed himself a corona. He chose a spot near one of the beams supporting Cameron's massive outdoor awning and leaned against it as he watched this huge family just...be.

Without even noticing their approach, Ben and Ethan were suddenly standing beside him.

"You snuck in here quietly, Banner," Ben whispered.

"You know me. I don't like those grand entrances you're so fond of."

Alec watched as Cameron and Zach walked hand in hand to the center of the yard, and Cameron let out a huge whistle, which stopped everyone in their tracks. "All right, everyone, if I could have your attention for a moment," Cameron called out. People all over the yard stopped what they were doing and turned to the two men.

"First of all," Cameron continued. "Zach and I would like to thank everybody for being here. Not only today but being here for us every day. It's been a long hard road for us, but today sees a new beginning. And Zach and I would like our new beginning to really be something special. So, with that in mind, I couldn't be prouder to let you all know this wonderful man has graciously agreed to be my husband."

Alec was sure Cameron had more to say, but whatever words he had were cut off by cheering and congratulations as people rushed to hug them both.

"Son of a bitch," Ben cursed. "Bastard never breathed a word to me." Ben's smile was enormous despite his disgruntled tone.

"Don't be like that, Ben. Maybe he'll ask you to walk him down the aisle," Ethan consoled.

"Well, of course, he will." Ben sniffed. "I just like to be told things before everyone else is all. I mean, he's my brother, and that should come with some perks, that's all—ooh, do you think they'll want the pixies to be flower girls? Imagine how adorable they'll look."

Ethan threw Alec a long-suffering look and whispered, "And we're off." Then he returned his attention to his increasingly excitable boyfriend, who, astoundingly, was saying something about tulle.

Alec laughed as he watched them walk toward the crowd surrounding Zach and Cameron. In his pocket, his phone vibrated, so he pulled it out. The caller was Jacey. Alec answered immediately. Jacey rarely made social calls.

"What's up?" he answered.

"It's the security at Chasing Hope. I keep it tight, Alec, but if someone wants in badly enough…"

"Yeah, yeah I know. So someone breached the server?"

"Yeah, and they searched one specific thing."

"And…"

"They were searching for Asher Winsome."

Fuck. "Stay on the line, Jacey," he ordered and ran to Ben.

He found him in the crowd beside his brother chatting animatedly while those around him looked on. "Ben," he called. "Ben."

Heads turned to him, but he didn't care. Ben immediately began moving toward him. As soon as he was within reach, Alec grabbed him and towed him to a quiet corner.

"What's wrong?" Ben asked.

"It's Jacey," he said and held up his phone as though it offered all the answers. "Someone hacked the servers at Chasing Hope and the only files they went after were Asher's. What info is in there?"

"His location isn't in there," Ben said, and Alec felt a whoosh of relief, which was short-lived, given Ben's troubled expression.

"What?"

"His location isn't in there, but it is noted that we've brought in Krispin's Security and if they could hack our stuff with Jacey in charge then they can damn well hack Krispin's. There'll be information for them there to find."

"Jacey—"

"Yeah, I'm on it. I'll call the Krispins and check out their server." She hung up before he could answer. Alec pocketed his phone.

Alec grabbed Ben's upper arms and shook him. He hadn't meant to be so rough. He let go of Ben as soon as he noticed Ethan coming forward. "Where is he?" he demanded, contrite, but not willing to back down when Asher could be in trouble.

Ben looked at Ethan quickly and then back to him. "Shit. Okay. They're at a safe house up in Canmore, not far out of Banff. You get going and I'll text you details. I'll call Krispin's Security, too, and get the guys with Asher some warning."

"Okay, good. Okay."

"Alec. He'll be okay. Jacey got on top of this."

"Okay. Thanks. Listen, tell the people watching him that if they feel they have to move him, they should do it, but keep me in the loop."

"You got it," Ben replied as he gave Alec a quick hug. Alec thumped Ethan on the arm and left with no goodbyes or apologies to his hosts. He knew Ben would explain, and he knew they would understand. Nothing was more important than getting to Asher.

Chapter Twenty

ASHER

There was no question the scenery was extremely beautiful here at the base of the mountains, but Asher still desperately missed his ocean. He couldn't remember the last time he'd been away from the water for this long.

Justin and Terri were great company, and even though none of them really wanted to be out here in the middle of nowhere, they were making the best of the situation. After the second week, Asher got the impression the two bodyguards wouldn't mind being here alone. He might not be the most observant person, but not even he could miss the looks the two regularly shared.

Ben called, often with updates on his family and Alec. He felt bad because Ben was copping so much heat from his family for keeping Asher's location secret. But worst of all, this whole thing had to be putting a strain on Ben's friendship with Alec.

He sat back on his Adirondack chair and sipped at his coffee, allowing the crisp mountain air to surround him. He'd had one of these chairs at home. An old friend of his had carved the back of it into a shark head complete with gaping jaw in honor of the shark that almost got him. He didn't know if the chair survived the fire. Thinking about it now reminded Asher of what he'd already lost and the seriousness of his situation.

From where he was sitting on the back porch, he saw nothing but mountains, each peak with a smattering of snow. The weather was really starting to cool down now, and the nearby park ranger had told Justin to expect heavy snows within weeks. With luck, none of them would still be here by then.

The cabin was about as isolated as Asher would want it to be. He could survive on the ocean, but he wasn't so confident of his survival skills out in the mountains. Fortunately, the only danger they'd encountered so far was a black bear sighting, their first week here.

The cabin was in a beautiful spot, but despite the scenery and the constant company of his two protectors, Asher was lonely. He'd give anything to hear Kane's voice, or Maddy's, or Jack's. Hell, at this point, he'd be happy to hear from his parents. He tried not to think about how much he missed Alec.

"Justin? Asher?" Terri called. She was one of the most competent people Asher had ever met and being in her presence was enough to put Asher at ease. She had a friendly face, but there was steel beneath the surface. Her calm composure had guided them through the bear encounter, when he and Justin had both been ready to run, screaming.

"Back porch, Terri," Justin called back. There'd be about four hours where they'd all be together before Justin would go get some sleep for his watch tonight.

Terri came storming out the back door, walking with purpose to stand before them. "Ben just called. We might have a problem," she said in her no-nonsense way.

Justin was immediately on his feet, and Asher quickly joined him, the beauty of their surroundings long forgotten. "What's going on?" Justin calmly asked.

"Server at Chasing Hope was hacked. They were searching for anything on Asher. There's nothing on there with our location, but there is mention of Krispin's Security. Ben's got his IT whiz checking to see if Krispin's system has been hacked," Terri explained with a composure Asher was insanely jealous of. His own heart was thumping madly, and despite the coolness of the weather, he could feel sweat beading on his forehead.

"What do we do?" Asher asked.

"Sit tight for now. Ben will get back to us when he hears from Jacey." Terri looked at him, and her expression told him there was more. "Alec's on his way, Asher."

"What?" Was it possible to be elated and devastated at the same time? God, he was thrilled because Alec was coming but terrified he'd be in the line of fire again.

"Alec got the call from Jacey, and he was frantic. Ben couldn't keep it from him anymore. It'll be good to have another man here, too, Asher. I know it's not what you want, but it's better to have too much manpower than not enough." They'd talked a lot over the long boring days they'd been here together, so both Terri and Justin knew about Alec. They knew Asher cared about him but not the depths of Asher's feelings.

Asher understood it would be good to have another person here; he really did, but why did it have to be Alec? He'd never get over the loss if someone was killed protecting him, but if Alec died... He couldn't even think about it.

"No, Asher."

He turned to look at Justin, not really sure what he was talking about.

"I can see what you're thinking, and you're not taking off. We know you're worried about Alec—we get it," Justin said, flicking a glance at Terri. How hard must it be for them to work in such a dangerous field together if there was something between them? "Banner is ex-military and ex-FBI. He knows what he's doing. And I can tell you, when someone you care about is in trouble, it's easier to be there than being made to sit on the sideline with no clue what's going on."

How did everyone read him so well?

"It's all over your face," Terri said.

"Huh?"

"It's all over your face, whenever Alec is mentioned, that you care about him more than you're willing to admit." She smiled.

"Oh. I was wondering."

Terri shrugged her shoulders. "Some people are easy to read."

"How far away is he?"

"He'll be at least six hours, closer to seven. He's gotta catch a flight to Calgary and then there's the hour and a half drive here."

"Should we be hanging around so long?" Asher wasn't sure if he was still worried about Alec now or himself. He wasn't stupid, and he certainly didn't want to die; he definitely had a sense of self-preservation.

"We'll make that call once we hear back from Ben. For now, let's get you inside, then Terri and I will do our job," Justin said with the same calmness both he and Terri had possessed from day one. "Asher, trust us. We know what we're doing. Okay?"

Asher nodded because he did trust them. "Okay."

Ben called an hour later to tell them there'd been no breach of Krispin's Security's servers; at least none that Jacey had been able to detect, but she'd set up a program to alert her the second someone managed to hack it. So for now, they were all on alert but taking no further action.

Asher tried to relax, but there was a hard line of tension all through his rigid shoulders and back. As much as he wanted Alec far away from any danger, he also ached to feel his arms around him.

Time passed agonizingly slowly as they waited for news from Ben, and Alec's arrival. Asher tried to distract himself with solitaire, using a deck of cards Terri had bought during one of her trips into town for supplies. He longed to go for a walk, but there was no way his protectors would be allowing him out of their sight any time soon. They had both been rigidly alert for hours now, and though Terri had tried to convince Justin to take his downtime, he'd refused. Asher didn't know much about bodyguards or being protected, but he did know they couldn't sustain this heightened awareness and lack of sleep for long. At some point, they'd need to rest.

Late into the night, sensors at the gate into the property finally picked up an approaching vehicle. Terri and Justin's only backup here was the technology Krispin's had installed, but it was enough to give them a head start, if nothing else.

Asher watched with Justin and Terri as a dark-colored sedan approached the gate. The darkened driver's side window rolled down as the car pulled up to the security camera. All three of them let out a breath of relief as Alec's face filled the screen, lit up by the small light from the camera. Justin allowed him entrance and the big car rolled on. Within moments, Asher could hear the crunch of tires on the gravel drive outside.

Terri went out to greet Alec, refusing to allow Asher to move from the inside of the house. He wasn't even allowed near the windows at the moment.

Asher forced himself to stop pacing now he'd heard Alec's voice talking with Terri outside. His body twitched in anticipation though he had no idea what kind of welcome to expect from Alec. Understandably, Alec would be pissed off with him for running as he had, but how badly?

Terri led Alec into the living area, and for the first time in weeks, Asher laid eyes on the man he was beginning to care very much about. His heart thumped and butterflies fluttered in his stomach. He wanted to jump into his arms like in some kind of ridiculous romance movie but contented himself with looking him over. He looked healthy, and too damn good.

"Ash?" Alec's beautiful hazel eyes raked over him, as though looking for any sign of injury, much as he'd just done. Then Alec was striding toward him. Asher melted into his arms, like in those damn movies. Alec's hands were everywhere but not in a sexual way. He was making sure Asher was whole and okay. He understood this because he was doing the same thing to Alec.

He tentatively stroked his fingertips over where the giant egg had been on Alec's head. The lump was gone now, but slight bruising was still visible on the right side of Alec's face. "You're all right?" he murmured.

"Yeah. I'm all right. No permanent damage."

"And your arm?" Asher couldn't see the wound through Alec's clothes, but he knew it was there.

"It's healed up fine. It'll be a nice scar to brag about." Alec smiled, but his expression was strained. There would be things Alec wanted to say to him, some angry words he'd want to exchange, but there'd be time for that later. For now, Asher only wanted to revel in having Alec in his arms again.

A slight clearing of a throat behind him reminded Asher they weren't exactly alone. He stepped away from Alec and turned. "Alec, this is Justin. Justin, Alec Banner. And I guess you met Terri outside."

The two men shook hands and exchanged pleasantries. Then it was Terri's turn to take charge as she demanded Justin get his overdue sleep. Once they'd sorted out their watch duties, which now included Alec, apparently, Justin went to bed while Terri took the first watch.

Asher made coffee while Alec and Terri talked quietly. He offered a cup to Terri and then he and Alec sat on the sofa, mirroring each other with one knee bent up as they faced each other. Terri stayed in the kitchen allowing them some privacy.

"You know, I don't know whether to kiss you or yell at you," Alec began. "I know why you did it, Ash, but don't leave me out again. Not me. I can look after myself."

"I know you can. But you were hurt—because of me—and I was terrified that, if I didn't get away from everyone, the next time we might not be so lucky." He tentatively stroked his fingertips down the side of Alec's face and leaned in to press a gentle kiss against Alec's lips.

"I'm scared, too, Ash, but not for me. Whoever's after you either knows how to hack or has enough money behind them to pay someone to do it for them. That shows resolve. They're not gonna back off any time soon."

"So we have to catch them?"

"Yeah. We have to figure out who it is."

"Have the police gotten anywhere?" Asher asked, though he knew the answer. Ben kept him informed.

"Not really. Usually we'd follow a money trail, but even Jacey hasn't found anything, and we've had her checking the accounts of all of Morgan's known associates."

Morgan's known associates. Asher could think of one unknown associate. "What about the mystery player in Jack's kidnapping? The one who got away with a million bucks? Could they have something to do with it?"

Alec looked thoughtful as he sipped at his coffee. "We've considered it, but we still haven't figured out who that was or how it played into Morgan's scheme. The money disappeared before we could get it back, but it never made any sense. I mean Morgan could have been a decoy, so this guy could get his money while we were all focused on Morgan and Jack at the zoo, but if so, why would they care if Morgan was beaten in prison?"

"Maybe Morgan wasn't supposed to get caught. Maybe they thought they had it all figured out and they'd both walk away with their money?" Asher suggested, but Alec was already shaking his head.

"They had to know Morgan's part was a big risk. It was extremely likely he'd get caught—exactly as he did."

"But he only got caught because I recognized him. Maybe they thought it was worth the risk. Maybe they didn't think I'd spot him."

"We had access to security camera footage of everyone at the zoo, though, and the FBI would have made your family watch it for recognizable faces. He would have been recognized eventually. No, none of it makes any sense. We're missing something."

Asher's head ached as it always did whenever he tried to untangle the mess of Jack's kidnapping. He was tired, but Alec looked dead on his feet. The time was close to midnight, and he had no idea how long Alec had been awake.

"Alec?"

"Yeah?"

"Come to bed. You look exhausted, and I know I'm tired." Asher stood and held his hand out to Alec.

As Alec's hand slid into his, he closed his fingers around it, enjoying the warmth and strength. Alec stood, giving him a gentle kiss as he got to his feet. "Okay," he agreed simply, and Asher led him toward his bedroom.

Chapter Twenty-One

ALEC

Alec had a quick shower as soon as Asher finished in the bathroom. He'd have liked to join Asher in his shower, but he was still nervous about how he'd be received. Once he was done, he dried himself, threw on some boxers to sleep in, and went in search of Asher.

Alec was confident he'd be welcome in Asher's bed tonight, but whether only to sleep or more he was less certain. There was no question what he wanted, but he'd already fucked up once with Asher, so he was determined to let him set the pace, just as he'd done on the *August Moon*.

He found Asher sitting up in bed, resting against the headboard. He was shirtless but had the blankets pulled up to his waist. His eyes were closed, but he wasn't sleeping because he leaned over and pulled the blankets back, patting the mattress in invitation for Alec to join him. Alec didn't hesitate.

The sheets were cool, but it wouldn't take long for him to heat them up. He leaned back on the headboard beside Asher and waited. Asher would need to make the first move here.

"I missed you," Asher whispered.

"I missed you too."

"I'd have given anything to be there for you while you were recovering." Asher reached across and threaded their fingers together as he spoke.

"It wasn't too bad. I swear. The bullet wound was nothing, and there was no permanent harm from the head knock," Alec reassured.

"You're sure?"

"Positive."

Alec shuffled down a little and turned on his side. Asher copied his movements so they lay facing each other. Alec kept their hands joined, but with his other, he carded his fingers through Asher's long mane, tangling them through the wisps. He loved Asher's hair, the carefree length and way he wore it, the smell of apples from his shampoo, the way the sun caught on his highlights, making the darker brown appear almost caramel.

"Alec?"

"Yeah," he whispered.

"I really wanna fuck you right now."

Alec burst into laughter. Their first encounter had been a desperate one, spurred on by the nightmare they'd been caught up in, but since they'd reunited, their time together had been all about romance. And Alec had loved every second. He'd expected Asher to maybe ask him to make love to him or something along those lines, but Asher had once again surprised him.

"You're laughing at me," Asher said affronted, though his smile suggested otherwise.

"Sorry. I guess I was expecting something a little more...romantic."

Asher leaned forward and kissed him hard on the mouth, pressing his body along Alec's length. "Oh, I can do that too." He smirked and cleared his throat. "Alec, would you do me the honor of sharing your body with me in a night of sweet, sweet lurve," he drawled.

"Okay, that is not romantic. I don't even know what that is." Alec laughed.

"Alec?"

"Yeah?"

"I want you." Asher's voice was low and husky, laced with a tinge of desperation, which sent a shiver up his spine.

Alec slammed his mouth down on Asher's and wiggled his body until there wasn't an inch between them. He threw one of his legs over Asher's and pulled him in even tighter. It was impossible to get close enough.

Asher's body was pliant beneath Alec's hands as he explored every inch of skin he could reach, their lips busy with an exploration of their own. The soft moaning coming from Asher was one of the most erotic sounds Alec had ever heard.

Alec kicked off the blankets. His fingers dipped into the waistband of Asher's boxers, edging them down enough to expose his perfect ass. Alec gave one of his cheeks a little pinch, laughing as Asher squirmed in his arms.

"God, you're perfect, Ash." His gaze tracked down Asher's body. A comment was on the tip of his tongue about the Wonder Woman boxers he was wearing, but Asher's scent and the feel of his breath ghosting over his heated skin threw him off.

"Get these off," Asher said while snapping the waistband of Alec's boxers against his stomach. They both wriggled out of their boxers before coming together again in another kiss.

This time Asher's hard cock rubbed against his as their bodies came together. Alec reluctantly pulled away from the kiss and rolled Asher on to his back before straddling his body. He gently gripped either side of Asher's waist and then leaned down to trail kisses down his bared throat all the way to a dusky brown nipple. He licked and nipped at one before giving the other equal attention.

Asher's hands were in his hair, gripping tightly as he whimpered under Alec's ministrations. Alec licked a path down Asher's taut stomach, wriggling back so he was sitting, almost hovering, over Asher's knees. He circled Asher's belly button with his tongue before nipping the skin at the top of his left thigh. Then he did the same to the skin on Asher's right side.

Alec sat up and looked down at the man beneath him. His skin was losing the tan he'd had from being shirtless much of the time on the boat. His breath was heaving out, and there was the slightest tremble working its way through his body. He was fucking perfect.

Alec took the time to really look at the scarring on Asher's right thigh. The jagged crescent shape of the shiny purple scar left no doubt a big animal had bit into him. It went from the top of his thigh and curled almost down to his knee. There was a slight indentation where flesh had been torn away, but despite the horror of the wound, Alec counted his lucky stars that Asher was alive.

He'd seen those jaws in action tearing and ripping at their prey. For Asher not to have lost his leg, not to mention his life, was a miracle. He traced the jagged line downward with his finger, gently rubbing over the marks that clearly showed where the serrated teeth had pierced Asher's flesh.

"It was just a nibble, a taste test," Asher whispered.

"Thank Christ, she didn't like the taste of you," Alec replied.

Alec leaned over and pressed kisses along the scarring until he was right at the junction of Asher's thigh and torso. He shifted his focus to the thick, hard cock proudly reaching toward Asher's navel. He gently gripped the base and swirled his tongue along the head. Then he wrapped his lips around and sucked. Asher's hips bucked and his body squirmed.

Alec could have tasted Asher all day, but what he really wanted was Asher inside him. He quickly slid a couple of fingers in his mouth and got them dripping wet. Then he put his lips back to work on Asher's cock. He reached behind and played with his hole, gently preparing himself for Asher.

"Alec…" Asher begged, his desperation perfect.

He quickly pulled off Asher's cock and gently licked around his balls, sucking each one into his mouth. He was ready, Asher was ready. They both needed more.

Alec slid over and lay facedown beside Asher, tilting his ass up a little in invitation. Asher wasted no time straddling him this time. Asher kissed behind his ear and then all along his spine. His skin was hypersensitive, tingling with each touch, and Alec fought not to wriggle too much under the sensation.

Asher nipped at his ass cheeks before spreading them. He felt Asher's fingers lightly tracing around his hole. "Hang on," Asher gasped and then disappeared.

"Shit," Asher mumbled. "I don't have anything."

"My bag, side pocket," Alec threw over his shoulder. He listened as Asher rummaged around before eventually returning to him. He dribbled some lube on his fingers and immediately returned to Alec's ass. He continued playing with him, dipping one finger, then another inside, stretching him farther in preparation for something infinitely bigger.

"I'm ready, Ash. Ready, baby," he whimpered. He needed Asher and he needed him now.

Behind him, Asher shuffled around while Alec grabbed a pillow, awkwardly shoving it under his hips. He spread his legs, waiting for that perfect moment when Asher would enter him. In moments, Asher's hands were back on his ass, and the blunt head of his cock was pushing against his hole.

With tenderness Alec had never experienced before while getting fucked, Asher pushed inside, slowly, gently. The sensual way Asher moved was such an erotic experience—one unlike anything he'd ever felt before.

"Ash, fuck. Oh, god," he rambled. Words were spilling out without thought.

Asher rested against him and held still for only a moment before pulling out and pushing back in. His arms caged Alec against him as he pumped his hips, his cock sliding perfectly in and out.

The sensation of being fucked by Asher was so overwhelming, so good. The thick hardness of Asher's cock inside and the warm strength of his body blanketing him collided, eliciting irrepressible pleasure. Asher's lips were at his ear, licking and nibbling.

Suddenly, Asher pulled out and got to his knees. He grabbed Alec's hips and pulled him up onto his hands and knees before quickly pushing back inside. Alec's eyes rolled as Asher manhandled his body, forcing pleasure onto him. A hand reached around and grabbed his cock, pumping him in time to Asher's thrusts.

Asher leaned in again and licked along his spine, causing the same shudders as earlier. Asher was a flurry of motion as he thrust, stroked, and licked. Alec braced himself as a familiar tingle built in the base of his spine.

"Come for me, Alec. Come on. Do it," Asher ordered.

A handful of thrusts later, Alec was coming like a fucking geyser all over the bed. Asher kept moving, slamming into him over and over. Alec's mind was swimming with his orgasm, and he was unable to focus on anything other than the last spasms of pleasure.

Then Asher wrapped him in his arms again, laid his cheek on Alec's back, thrust a few more times, and growled—

fucking growled—in his ear. Asher's dick pumped deep inside as he shot his load.

They were both covered in sweat, panting hard when Asher eventually pulled out and they collapsed onto the mattress.

"Fuck," Alec gasped.

"Oh yeah, fuck," Asher agreed.

"That was…"

"Yeah. It was."

Asher jumped up and shuffled into the bathroom. He came back in seconds with a wet washcloth and wiped Alec thoroughly. Alec wanted to help, but his muscles weren't cooperating with him at all.

With the cleanup done, Asher slid in beside him and dragged the blankets up. Alec held him tight, terrified to let go because he realized he never wanted to. This relationship with Asher brought up emotions unlike any he'd ever had before, and god, he wanted it so fucking badly.

"You okay?" Asher whispered.

"Perfect," Alec replied.

They were quiet for a while longer before Asher eventually spoke again. "I want this, Alec. Whatever it is between us, I want it." He tilted his head up, pressing a kiss to Alec's lips. "Can I have it? Can I have you?"

There was only one answer he could give. "You already have me, Ash."

Chapter Twenty-Two

ASHER

He'd have been happy to stand there all day watching Alec. His handsome features were slack with sleep, making him appear much younger than his almost forty years.

Asher's body tingled pleasantly as he remembered last night. While he stood there watching Alec, he fantasized about a time when maybe they could be together like this without the threat of danger hanging over their heads. Asher knew the dangerous situation was one of the reasons Alec had—and maybe still—hesitated over their relationship.

Asher was determined to give a relationship with Alec a try. There was something there between them, and he didn't believe it was the high-intensity situations pushing them together.

He took one last look and quietly slipped from the room. He was an early riser, and Alec's shift on watch would begin in a few hours, so he wanted to give him as much time to sleep as possible.

The house was dark, apart for the light coming from the kitchen. Asher opened the drapes of the living room and looked out into the predawn hours. The sky was beginning to lighten, and it wouldn't be long before the sun would peek over the mountaintop.

Terri was sitting at the kitchen table with a coffee in hand when he entered. "Up to see the sunrise again?" she asked.

"Yeah. I still love the ocean, but these mountain sunrises are beautiful. Refill?" he asked as he set about making his own coffee.

"Nah. I'll be off duty soon, and if I have any more coffee, I'll never sleep."

It occurred to Asher then that Terri—and maybe Justin—had been awake when he'd fucked Alec last night. His cheeks heated with realization. He didn't consider himself a prude, but he wasn't really an exhibitionist either. He didn't know whether or not to apologize to Terri for having to sit through their sex show. How had he not thought of this at the time? And then he flashed to a memory of him and Alec together, and he knew he'd had no room in his mind for thoughts of anything except Alec.

"I'm guessing you didn't hear any more from Ben or your bosses?"

"Not a peep," she answered. Perhaps she saw the fear he knew he wore like a mask these days because she continued on. "Even if they get into the server, though, you'll be okay. The IT expert will warn us and besides the three of us are here. We won't let anything happen to you."

"Yeah I know, but I don't want any of you hurt either."

"Especially Alec?" She raised her brow questioningly.

Asher laughed. Over the three weeks they'd been stuck together they'd become friends, so he didn't mind the teasing at all. "Yeah. Especially Alec."

"Can't say I blame you. The man is damn hot," Terri stated.

"Careful, Terri, Justin might get jealous." He smirked.

"Touché, Asher. Touché." She clinked her mug against his as he took his seat.

They drank their coffee in companionable silence for a while. Through the window, Asher watched as the sky lightened, the dusky pink of dawn just beginning to show.

"Looks like it's going to be another beautiful sunrise. We can still take our walk?" he asked, unsure if it would be deemed unsafe.

"I don't see why not. Motion sensors have been quiet, so unless someone is hiking in over the mountains—which is really unlikely—then there's nobody around who shouldn't be."

Asher stood and put his mug in the sink. "Great. Let's go then." Asher was an active person used to being constantly on the move, so he needed these morning walks. They never went far anyway. About half a mile away, a stream flowed down from the mountain, all the way into Goat Pond. The spot was right where two mountains met, and the valley created was the best place to view the sunrise.

They slipped into their coats and boots and set out, the crisp morning air refreshing Asher. They'd walked more than halfway before Asher suddenly thought he should have left a note for Alec. Justin would know where they were because it was either Terri or him—sometimes both—who walked here with him each day. But if Alec woke up first, he'd have no idea.

He contemplated going back but figured Alec would know he was with Terri, and he'd wake Justin if he got worried enough.

The golds and pinks of the rising sun were in full bloom in the sky now, and as they reached the creek, the sun poked up in the valley between the mountains. As always, he stood in awe of Mother Nature.

"Never gets old, does it?" Terri said beside him.

"I should have woken Alec. Dragged his sorry ass out here." Tomorrow he would definitely make sure it was just him and Alec who came.

"It's certainly something worth sharing with someone special," Terri said with a smile that made her look especially beautiful. It wasn't hard to guess who she was thinking about sharing this view with.

"I hope this is done soon, Terri, and I hope you and Justin can get a break together." He really liked these two and was pulling for them to get together. "I can't thank you both enough for what you're doing for me."

Terri gripped his forearm and gave it a little squeeze. "You know I've guarded some absolute toolbags before; a few of them made me think long and hard about throwing myself in front of a bullet for them. But you, Asher Winsome, are one of the sweetest and most genuine people I've ever met. I'll be here until the end...until they've caught whoever's after you and you're safe."

Perhaps the one good thing out of this mess was meeting some of the most selfless people he'd ever encountered. In a world teeming with selfishness, it restored his faith in humanity to realize there were still people who cared and sacrificed for others.

They stood and watched the new day dawn for a while longer, occasionally exchanging comments, but mostly they were content in comfortable silence. Eventually, they began the walk back to the cabin, still each holding their own counsel.

As soon as they stepped into the clearing around the cabin, Asher knew he was in big trouble. Alec was pacing the outside of the cabin with a face like thunder. He looked up at Asher as he and Terri approached. Asher could actually see him trying to school his features into a mask of calm.

Alec stalked toward him—the only word Asher could use to describe his movements. He didn't know what to expect when he finally reached him, but Asher was hauled into Alec's arms and crushed against his hard body.

"You scared me," Alec whispered in his ear.

"I'm sorry," he replied because he was. He should have been more considerate.

When Alec finally released him, he turned to Terri who'd hung back from them a little. She smiled and then turned to Alec. "Sorry, Alec. I should have thought to leave you a note."

"No. It's my fault," Asher interrupted. "I wanted to go out there, and I should have left a note."

"Well, you both should apologize to Justin. He's the one who was woken by a crazed man practically ripping him off the mattress." Alec laughed.

God, he's so damn gorgeous.

"Terri, Banner," Justin called from somewhere inside. "We've gotta move. They're coming."

And immediately everything changed. Asher was half dragged inside by Alec with Terri—gun pulled—following close behind.

"What happened?" Alec asked as soon as they were inside. "Did they hack Krispin's Security's servers?"

"Yeah, but not how we thought," Justin answered. "Jacey—thank god—thought she'd do a bit of digging around and watch the other servers Krispin's has. She found someone had hacked into their private server—where all their property ownership files are. They got all the addresses of the properties the Krispins own—including their safe houses. Jacey was lucky to find it when she did, but they've had the addresses for over eight hours now. They won't know which one Asher's being kept at, but who knows? They might get lucky and be on our doorstep any second."

"Asher, grab your gear," Alec ordered, but he needn't have bothered because Asher was already moving.

Behind him, organized chaos ensued as Justin and Terri got their own things together. "Justin, check the cameras." Terri's voice trailed off in the distance as he entered his room.

Alec was right beside him, his own bag hardly needing to be touched, having not been unpacked. Asher flicked a glance at him. Alec's worried eyes were following his movements intently. Asher was trying so hard to appear calm and unconcerned, but in the face of Alec's obvious anxiety, he failed dismally.

Alec grabbed him hard by his arms. "You'll be okay. We'll get you out."

Asher only nodded and returned his attention to his bag. Sure, he might be okay, but what about Alec—and Justin and Terri? Would one of them lose their lives protecting him? It didn't bear thinking about.

He was ready to go in minutes. They met Justin and Terri in the living room, both with guns in their hand. He was kind of surprised Alec hadn't pulled one out of somewhere yet.

"Nothing on the cameras," Justin said. "But we should be cautious. I'm thinking standard decoy. Terri and I in plain view in our car. You in the other." He addressed Alec and Asher wondered where he was in all this.

"Yeah, you could pass at a glance with a ball cap pulled low," Alec replied. "But it'll be close."

"I'll call the Krispins to make sure there's been no breaches at the Montana safe house. If they're here and they take the bait, they should follow us. We might get lucky and be able to set a trap in Montana for them," Terri added.

"Wait. Wait a minute. Bait? What bait and where will I be?" Asher asked, unable to stay quiet any longer while these people he cared about seemed to be planning to put themselves in danger for him.

"You'll be with me, Ash," Alec answered. "You'll be in the trunk as we leave town, so hopefully if they're around, they'll think Justin is you."

"No. No way. I'm not letting anyone do that for me." He put his foot down.

"Asher, it's our job, and we're good at it. We'll be fine." Justin's voice was calm and reassuring, but this plan still seemed so wrong.

"I've got a place I can take him, and it's not linked to anyone, at least not closely, so they won't find it easily. Hopefully we'll have them by then," Alec said.

Asher didn't like this one little bit, but he knew he'd have a fight on his hands trying to talk one of these people out of their plan, let alone all three.

"Please. Couldn't we go to the cops?" Asher begged.

"There's nothing they can do, Ash. Not until somebody's actually killed you, so no, we're not going to the cops."

"Asher," Terri said, "We appreciate your concern for us, but everything will work out, and right now we all need to get out of here." She squeezed his shoulder, and he lost the battle, exactly like he knew he would.

"Okay." He walked over and embraced first Terri, and then Justin, not caring if either of them wanted the show of affection. In a way, they were his now, and he cared what happened to them.

"All right, well, I'm gonna pull the car up close. I can't see how they could be watching us because no alarms have been triggered and it's heavily wooded here but let's assume they are." Alec walked out the door while Asher was finishing up his goodbyes. He forced himself to memorize as much as he could about his two bodyguards, because if something did happen, he never wanted to forget their faces.

"Alec's got the car backed up and the trunk popped. You'll be able to get right in and the lid will block anyone who may be looking. Justin and I will walk out first as a distraction, and then you go. Okay?"

"Sure." He couldn't quite believe his life had come to this. He watched as Justin pulled a cap over his head. They were a similar build, but Justin had at least fifteen years on him and a buzz cut. Asher nodded his head and took a deep breath. He could do this.

He stood a little way back from the doorway as Justin and Terri exited. As soon as they reached the rear of the car, Asher walked out and eased himself into the trunk. He didn't hate being in small tight spaces like plenty of other people, but he didn't enjoy it either. It was something he'd have to grit his teeth about and endure. He tried to get comfortable and curl up as best he could, and he sure hoped the trip wouldn't be a long one.

Alec was suddenly at the rear of the car, reaching to grab the trunk lid. He gave Asher a half smile, half grimace and then mouthed what Asher took to be "I've got you" before slamming the trunk closed.

The trunk was exceptionally dark and quiet. Asher's heart thumped against his chest and he had an irrational fear there was something in the dark with him. Something horrible and terrifying. He concentrated on breathing slowly and deeply in an effort to relax. He was starting to panic, but he couldn't afford to. Not in here. He had the disposable cell Justin had given him weeks ago, but it suddenly occurred to him Alec's number wasn't in it. He had his own phone, but he hadn't been allowed to turn it on since he'd fled with Justin and Terri.

He pulled the burner from his pocket and pressed a key. The light it gave off was welcome, and Asher quickly assured himself he was alone in the dark trunk. Needing some light was childish, sure, but his nerves were frayed so he figured he could be excused. He had Justin and Terri's numbers, so at least he could call someone if he freaked out too much.

Suddenly, the car rumbled to life and drove off. He was on his way—to where he didn't know, but Alec was with him and the thought comforted him. He turned off his phone and thought over all the memories he had of Alec. Though he'd known Alec for months, he'd really only spent a fraction over a week in his company. It had been enough to learn the measure of the man, though, and Asher really liked what he'd seen.

He tried to put his current predicament from his mind and concentrate on Alec. The look in his eyes when he'd seen his first great white, his excitement mixed with terror at the big girl they'd encountered. The way his fair skin pinked in the sun and how little strands of gold were highlighted in his red hair in the sunlight. How damn good he looked in nothing but shorts. The sound of his laughter, the feel of his body, how tight his ass had gripped Asher's cock.

Asher closed his eyes and let himself float away with his memories of Alec.

Chapter Twenty-Three

ALEC

Alec pulled into the Inns of Banff, making sure to find a lot where nobody could see him from the road. He was 99 percent sure he hadn't been followed out of Canmore, but Alec wasn't taking any chances. Asher had been in the trunk for close to half an hour now, and the thought of him curled up alone in the dark was almost more than he could bear.

The trunk creaked on its hinges as he opened it and peered down at Asher. For a moment, he thought he was asleep, but then his gray eyes opened, and he stared up at Alec.

"Are we okay?" Asher whispered.

"We're okay. I think it's safe for you to come join me in the front seat," Alec answered and held out his hand for Asher.

He helped him out of the trunk, and they got back into the car. Alec started the engine and drove out of the parking lot, turning back onto the road heading out of Banff.

It'd be about six hours to Kamloops and then another three at least to Vancouver. Alec planned to stay there tonight, hopefully hidden in the large concrete jungle. Tomorrow he'd head to his parents' place. He needed to get his hands on weapons, and he had a nice stash stored on their property.

Not far from his parents' home was a cabin owned by a cousin, which was normally empty. Alec had stayed there before—with permission, but this time he needed to make sure nobody knew where he was.

"Have you heard from Justin or Terri?" Asher asked.

"Nothing yet, but I'm sure they're okay." Alec admired Asher's concern for others and desperately wished he could put his mind at ease.

"I can't live like this, Alec."

"They'll be okay, Ash."

"No. I mean the whole thing. Running, hiding, being cooped up and constantly afraid. I don't want to live like this."

Alec took one hand off the wheel and gripped Asher's. "I understand and we're gonna do everything we can to catch whoever is after you. But for now, you have to stay out of sight." He squeezed Asher's hand.

"But what if I don't? What if *I* was the bait? We could set up something so they'd know where I'd be, but the police or whoever could be there waiting for them and then—"

"You've watched too many movies, Ash. This is real life, and that kind of thing doesn't work."

"Sure it could—"

"No. I won't allow it," Alec fumed. There was no way he was letting Asher put himself at risk.

Asher dropped his hand and turned in his seat. Alec flashed him a quick look and knew he'd made a bad misstep when he caught a glimpse of Asher's furious eyes glaring at him.

"*You* won't allow it? I'm sorry, but I'm not exactly sure when you became my boss."

"I don't think—"

"Because if that's the way you see things between us, let me out right here, Alec."

Alec theatrically banged his head on the steering wheel. He wasn't one for drama and usually had control of his temper, thoughts and words, but when Asher had suggested he go out there and be bait for a killer, Alec had lost his control.

"It's not—"

"I'm not a damsel in distress."

Wait. What? "I never said—"

"I can save myself, and I will if you see me as some kind of weak—"

"You are one of the strongest people I know, Asher Winsome, and I've never for a moment thought of you as weak or incompetent. But, you can't wander around exposed. We can't—"

"I'm not going to just wander about. I'm talking about making a plan. Drawing them out and catching them." Asher's voice was calm again. *Thank god.* His thoughtless words had almost blown it.

He supposed the half hour stuck in the trunk had given Asher plenty of time to think about this because he didn't appear to be letting go of his crazy idea any time soon. But Alec needed time to think the notion through himself before he committed to anything.

"Ash...okay. First, I'm sorry. Of course I don't think I'm the boss of you... It's because you scared me when you started talking about being bait." Alec huffed in a breath, still having trouble even thinking about the idea of Asher vulnerable to a killer. "Second, I need time to think about it...if it can be done. I'm heading for my parents' place to pick up weapons, and then we're heading for a cousin's cabin. We'll need to stay in Vancouver tonight. So can we talk about it more when we get to our destination? Please?"

Asher was quiet a moment before responding. "Deal. But, Alec, think hard about how using me as bait can be done because we have to do something. This can't go on."

Alec nodded and concentrated on the road—and thought. It was pretty much all he did between there and Vancouver.

THEY STAYED THE night in a big hotel in the center of Vancouver, both of them falling asleep in each other's arms moments after they entered the room. Terri had woken them with a call a little after ten that night to give them an update. As tempting as it was to be with Asher again, when they'd been woken, he'd fallen right back to sleep after hearing the two bodyguards were safe with no sign of a tail.

A mutual blow job in the shower got them moving this morning, but already Alec was feeling weary. Close to fifteen hours on the road over the past two days was taxing.

His parents' home was only a couple of hours from Vancouver, so they should be arriving somewhere near lunchtime. Neither man spoke much during the trip, both lost to their own thoughts.

"Wow, this place is beautiful," Asher noted as they drove up to his parents' cabin.

His parents lived a little way outside of Maple Falls, a tiny speck of a town not too far from the border. The cabin and grounds were beautiful, and he knew the location brought peace to both his mom and dad while they dealt with his mom's dementia.

"Yeah, it is."

He'd called his father last night to let him know they were coming. He'd also told him they weren't coming for a social or long visit. If he didn't need his guns, he wouldn't be here at all. He believed he and Asher had made a clean getaway, but the thought of perhaps dragging danger behind him to his elderly parents was intolerable.

Four years ago, when his father had bought this place, Alec had made sure to hire them a live-in nurse to help his dad. He'd also selected a nurse with a military background, who could handle herself. It made him feel better about not being around so much and gave him something to spend his money on. Some wise investments over the years had left him with more than enough.

As they got closer, Alec spotted his father as soon as he stepped out the front door, heading toward them. This told Alec it wasn't a good time for a visit with his mom. If he was planning to be here for a while, he'd ramble about the property, doing odd jobs or repairs until she was up to visitors. But today, he'd only be able to see his dad, grab his guns, and be on his way.

"You look like your dad," Asher commented.

It wasn't the first time he'd heard that comparison, and when he was younger, the similarity had been even more striking. Now, they looked alike, but his father's ginger hair had faded to a silvery white giving him a more distinguished air.

"Except the hair," Alec added. His father stooped more now, and even from this distance, he noticed his father grinding his jaw the way elderly people tended to do. His body still looked strong, though, so Alec didn't think he was in danger of losing him any time soon.

They stepped out of the car once it came to a halt, and Alec walked straight into his father's arms. They hadn't always been a hugging family, but as soon as he'd moved out after he'd enlisted, his mother had insisted it would be a hug and a kiss for both parents every time Alec came or went. He didn't mind at all.

"Good to see you, Dad."

"You too, boy. Are you in trouble?" His father was never one to beat around the bush, and he demanded honesty of Alec.

"A little. Nothing I can't handle though."

They were still hugging, so Alec didn't think Asher would have heard when his father said, "Is this one your trouble? 'Cause something like that ain't no trouble."

Alec barked a laugh and stepped away from his father. "Dad, this is Asher. Asher, this is my dad, Phillip Banner."

Asher stepped forward and shook his hand. "Good to meet you, Mr. Banner."

"None of that. You call me Phillip."

"Thank you. Your place is stunning."

"It sure is. Kitty loves it up here. I think it brings her peace in the chaos of her disease." His father nodded and turned once again to him. "Your momma's not real good today, Alec. Best if you come back and see her when your trouble's dealt with."

"I'm so sorry we're bothering you," Asher blurted.

"Never a bother, Asher. And if my boy's in trouble, he knows I'll do what I can for him."

"I'll just grab my gear, Dad, and then we'll get out of here."

"All right. Let's get you boys loaded up then."

His father came with them as Alec led Asher to the shed, where he stored his weapons. He had a large industrial cabinet inside, where he locked away his guns. He'd offered a key to his father, but he'd declined because he was worried his mom might somehow get her hands on it and get into the guns. Alec promised himself that when this was over, he'd find somewhere else to store them.

"What is it you do, Asher?" his father asked as they unloaded the cabinet.

"I photograph sharks."

"Sharks?" Alec heard the shock in his father's voice, and he wondered how many times Asher had heard the same surprise when he told people what he did.

"Mm, yep. Especially great whites, but really I love doing any kind of underwater photography and filming." Asher heaved a bag out of the cabinet as he spoke. Alec had quite an arsenal, and he wondered what Asher would make of it because he knew Asher normally had nothing to do with guns.

"Well now, that's got to be...interesting." His father's eyebrows were practically up in the sky, rising so high with his shock. His parents were what he'd consider conservative, and things out of the ordinary had always tended to shock them. Yet, they were also incredibly loving and accepting. They may not understand something, but they didn't judge. Alec had felt confident enough in their love and acceptance that he'd been able to explain his bisexuality to them early on. There'd been stunned silence for a moment before his mother had hugged him, told him she'd always love him no matter what, and asked what kind of cake he wanted her to bake. If only more people were willing to accept something even though they didn't really understand it.

It didn't take them long to load the trunk with what they needed. And then he was back in his father's arms to say goodbye.

"You be careful, boy, and you look after each other," he said and then pulled away to look over at Asher. "And, Asher, I expect to see you back here when this is over, so my son can introduce you to his mother."

"It'd be an honor, Phillip," Asher said as he stepped forward to shake hands.

The cabin belonging to his cousin was about an hour away from his parents' place, so they should arrive in time for a late lunch. They'd stopped to buy food and other supplies, enough to last a few days, though Alec suspected they wouldn't be here long enough to consume all they'd bought. He felt certain Asher's stubbornness and determination to end this would have them out of there much sooner.

At exactly 1:00 p.m., Alec drove up the dirt drive leading to the wooden cabin in the middle of nowhere.

Smaller and more rustic than his parent's place, the cabin was still storybook beautiful. Alec's grand plan was to retire into the quiet of a place like this. He'd had nothing but noise, violence, and chaos in his life, and one day he wanted peace.

The rain started as they unloaded the car, a light drizzle, but the dark clouds suggested heavier was coming. Alec couldn't imagine a more perfect afternoon than curling up with Asher, watching a movie while the rain poured down outside. Maybe he'd go ridiculously romantic and grab a blanket and a couple of hot chocolates with marshmallows.

By the time he'd given Asher a brief tour of the cabin, the rain was teeming. But, the noise as it struck the roof was somehow soothing. All Alec wanted to do was forget the huge pile of shit they were in, forget the world, and *be* with Asher.

"Can I interest you in a movie?" Asher said, stealing his idea.

"I was about to ask you the same." He smiled. "What are you up for?"

There was poor reception out here, so he knew there was a well-stocked DVD collection plus a Chromecast, if something on Netflix took their fancy, not that the Internet always worked well. Asher knelt in front of the DVD's and in seconds, he had one in his hands. *Guardians of the Galaxy, Vol.2*. Alec could get on board with Asher's choice. Chris Pratt, Zoe Saldana...something for everyone, really, and plenty for him.

"You pop it in, and I'll make the snacks." He left Asher to it and went to make the hot chocolates because, damn it, there was something about Asher that brought out the ridiculous romantic in him.

An hour later, they were snuggled under the blanket as the rain continued. "Baby Groot is the most adorable character ever," Asher declared as they watched the little twig creature run screaming after a full-grown man and capture him with his roots.

"It's the eyes. They're so expressive."

Alec pulled Asher in tighter against him, inhaling his scent. He closed his eyes and allowed himself to relax into the serenity of the moment. He wasn't even really watching the movie; he was too busy enjoying the calm and the feel of Asher pressed against him. What if he could have this forever?

The peace didn't last long.

When Alec's cell trilled, he reached to pick it up from the side table. "Cronin? Any news, man?"

"Is Asher with you?" Ben's voice floated back to him.

"Yeah."

"Put me on speaker."

Alec eased Asher away from him and hit the button to pause the movie. He hit the speaker button and held the phone between them. "It's Ben," he advised Asher.

"Hey, Asher. I've got news."

"Okay..." Alec held his breath, hoping like mad Ben was about to tell them they'd caught the guy, and the nightmare was all over, and Asher was safe.

"A woman has come forward. She claims to be the mistress of Morgan Fincher's father, Gerald. And she had quite the tale to tell. We couldn't find a money trail because Gerald used her money to pay for the hit. She claims she didn't know what was going on when he asked for access to her bank account, but she put two and two together, and she wants no part of it. She's been very forthcoming, but Fincher has, of course, denied everything, including that she's even his mistress. The cops are questioning him now, but unless he confesses, they won't hold him because there's no evidence yet. Just the mistress's word."

"All right, so he used her cash to pay to put a hit on Asher so it couldn't be traced back to him. Where does that leave us?" Alec knew this was progress—at least they knew the who—but it wasn't over yet.

"She claims when she confronted Fincher, he told her the people he hired wouldn't stop until it's done. So we need him to talk. Jacey's already working on tracing the mistress's account, but...it's not safe for you guys to come back yet."

"Ben," Asher began, and Alec knew exactly what was coming. "I want to come back. I want to draw them out. I won't live like this."

Alec had his thoughts about Asher's plan—had already disastrously voiced those thoughts to no avail, but they hadn't had time for their big debate about it yet. He'd thought long and hard about using Asher as bait but still wasn't okay with the idea. He hoped Ben would agree with him and be able to talk Asher out of it.

"May not be such a bad idea—"

"Ben."

"Come on, Alec. We could control things. We'd keep him safe."

"Fuck. You know there's no way we can guarantee that." Alec was pleading for support now because the barest hint of approval from Ben would have Asher back in San Diego in the blink of an eye.

"Okay," Asher said, "so what I was thinking is we need to have a believable reason why I'm coming back and a well-publicized one so they're not suspicious. So what if we leak something about maybe someone in my family being hurt or sick and that's why I'm coming home. Then they won't wonder why I'm suddenly back. Then I thought maybe we could head out to my boat. I mean, it's got to be easier to defend than a house or building on land. There are very few people around to get in the way. It'd be perfect."

"Could work," Ben mused. "And I can feel you death staring me through the phone, Banner, but this is Asher's call. He's right when he said he can't live like he is forever—and you know it, man."

Alec let the silence sit as he thought. Of course, he'd happily stay hidden away with Asher forever, but that was no kind of life. Asher needed his ocean and his damn sharks. He needed to be free and wild and live his life. Running and hiding would slowly kill Asher—that was a certainty. He hated—absolutely hated—what he was about to do, but he'd have to put his own fear to the side and do what Asher needed.

"All right. I wish...I really wish there was another way, but okay. Let's figure something out."

Chapter Twenty-Four

ASHER

"I know how hard this is for you," he whispered as he lay with his head on Alec's lap.

Alec carded his fingers through his hair, his hazel eyes never looking away. "I've only just found you."

Asher's heart actually fluttered at Alec's words. "I don't plan on going anywhere, Alec."

"I know, but... Promise me you won't do anything to put yourself in extra danger. I mean you'll follow the plan won't you?"

They'd spent over an hour on the call with Ben working through a plan to draw out the person, or maybe persons, after him. To Asher, it all seemed surprisingly simple, but then all he had to do was stick his head up—and hope it didn't get shot off.

"I promise you I'll do whatever I'm told by you guys because, Alec—" He sat up and grabbed Alec's face, kissing him soundly. "—I've only just found you too."

Tomorrow they'd be heading back to San Diego so Asher could visit his brother who'd be having an "unfortunate accident" later tonight. For a few more hours, he'd be safe and alone here with Alec. Who knew what'd happen tomorrow, so he planned to make the most of tonight.

"Alec..."

"Mmm," Alec murmured and leaned forward to press kisses down his throat.

"Make love to me."

Alec pulled back and looked at him before he nodded and stood. Alec held out his hand, and Asher happily took it, allowing Alec to lead him into the bedroom. They stopped only to grab some supplies from Alec's bag.

Asher couldn't have picked a more romantic place if he'd spent months planning tonight. The bedroom was dimly lit by a stunning Tiffany-style lamp. The turquoise and purple hues were beautifully lit up by the dull bulb. The soft lighting it threw off loaned warmth to the king-sized bed covered by a luxurious comforter. Outside the rain still fell, and the forest was lit up by the occasional flash of lightning. It was perfect.

Alec led him to the bed where, ever so slowly, they undressed each other. Fingertips brushed gently over naked flesh, warm breath gusted against skin, raising tiny bumps of anticipation. Every nerve in Asher's body was pulled tight, ready for the pleasure he knew would come.

Asher stood proudly and completely naked before Alec. He'd never been ashamed of his scarring, but he'd never been exactly enthusiastic about showing it off either. He had no such hesitation in front of Alec. He knew Alec accepted him exactly as he was—scarred flesh, stubbornness, and all.

Alec wasn't happy about the plan, and if he was honest, he was terrified himself, but he also knew what kind of life he wanted, and it wasn't one where he had to hide and constantly look over his shoulder. He wanted a life of adventure and joy, a life where he was free to go where he pleased and be true to who he was. But most importantly, he'd come to realize, he wanted someone to share it with.

"You're so beautiful, Ash," Alec murmured.

Asher let the backs of his fingers glide down Alec's cheek, under his chin, and then cup around his neck. He drew him forward and tenderly kissed his lips. As natural as breathing, their arms came around to hold each other as though both were afraid to ever let go.

The tenderness of the kiss quickly fell into passionate desperation as Asher clutched Alec to him. Their bodies were slick with sweat as their desire grew. The rain had caused a drop in the temperature, but Asher felt nothing but hot as his and Alec's bodies moved together.

Needing more, Asher fell to his knees, grabbed Alec's ass and pressed kisses into the junction of groin and thigh. Alec's scent of cinnamon was potent here, the fragrance spurring Asher on. He swirled his tongue around Alec's balls and sucked each in turn. Then he licked his way up Alec's shaft, swirling his tongue around the crown before taking the length into his mouth. Alec's cock was long so there was no way Asher could take it all in. He held the base of the shaft to make up the difference and sucked. His movements were slow and languorous while he took Alec's cock as far down his throat as he could manage.

Alec's fingers were curled in his hair, gently guiding his movements. Moans and whimpers fell from his mouth as Asher continued his actions. He wanted nothing more than to drive Alec out of his fucking mind. He looked up at Alec whose head was tipped back in ecstasy. Alec's cock swelled in his mouth, so he gripped the base tighter to stave off his impending orgasm. He wanted Alec balls deep inside of him before there was any coming.

He pulled off Alec's cock with a delicious pop and stood. He put his hands on Alec's firm chest and gave him a little shove so that he fell back on the bed.

"Shuffle back," Asher demanded and Alec obliged. He looked fucking stunning sprawled out on the bed, eyes fixed on Asher, his legs slightly parted.

"Ash...c'mere," Alec whispered.

Asher crawled toward Alec, dropping kisses randomly along his body as he went: feet, knees, thighs, cock, stomach. Every inch of Alec was beautiful. He straddled Alec's body and leaned down to kiss him thoroughly. He searched around for the supplies Alec had tossed on the bed earlier, and his fingers curled around the bottle of lube.

He sat up and squeezed a dollop onto his fingers, swirling it around a bit with his thumb. They never looked away from each other as Asher reached behind himself and gently inserted his fingers. Asher writhed at the sensation, doing his best to put on a show for Alec. He watched as Alec's pupils blew even wider, his tongue poking out to lick at his lips. He appeared as mesmerized by Asher as he was with him.

With his other hand, Asher stroked Alec's cock, impatient to have the hard flesh inside him. He withdrew his fingers from his ass and reached for a condom. They'd yet to look away from each other. Without the benefit of watching what he was doing, Asher fumbled to get the condom on Alec's hard cock, but he wouldn't look away. Something was happening between them—something much deeper, much more significant than merely fucking.

"I've never felt...so much when I've been with anyone before," Asher admitted.

"It's...I don't even know how to explain it," Alec gasped as Asher finally rolled the condom down his length. "I want to fuck you so hard, but at the same time I want to ease into you and slowly, tenderly make love to you."

"That's it exactly," Asher whispered, "so how 'bout we do both." He smiled and raised himself onto his knees. He shuffled forward a fraction and reached behind himself to grasp Alec's cock. He tapped it a couple of times against his hole as he lowered himself, and then he allowed the head to press into him. Slowly and gently, he eased down onto Alec's long cock until his ass touched Alec's thighs.

He took a quiet minute to let the pain ease to a burn and enjoy the fullness. In this moment, Alec and he were joined together as intimately as they could get. They were like one. It was a thought he'd never had with previous partners, and it was a powerful one.

Leaning forward a little, he rested his hands on Alec's chest and rocked his hips. His groan sang with Alec's as pleasure sparked between them. He rocked and squeezed for a time, savoring the feeling of Alec so hard and long inside him. Then he raised himself up, not quite allowing Alec's cock to slip from his body, before lowering himself back down.

He closed his eyes at the intensity of the sensations sweeping through him. Alec's hands grabbed his hips, helping to raise and lower him over and over, faster and harder. Asher's head tipped back, and his lips parted as the pleasure grew.

One of Alec's hands moved to his stomach, his fingers spread wide before moving up to his chest. Asher tipped his head forward and looked down at Alec. He was watching closely where their bodies were joined. Asher leaned forward and kissed Alec senseless. Alec's arms wrapped tightly around him and halted his movements. And then in a blur of movement, Alec rolled them so he was now above Asher.

They wriggled a little to get into a comfortable position with Asher's legs wrapped around Alec's waist. Alec rolled his hips, grinding his pelvis against Asher's ass as he pushed back in.

"Jesus, Ash."

"I know. It's so good."

Alec kept his movements slow and sensual for an agonizing while and then he pulled back and began thrusting into Asher—powerful strokes that forced Asher's body farther up the bed. Asher squeezed his legs, holding Alec tighter to him, bracing for every thrust.

"I'm never," Alec panted and hit him with a hard thrust, "gonna let anything," pant and thrust, "happen to you."

The panting and thrusting went on and on until Asher came harder than he remembered ever coming before—with not even a hand on his dick. Come splashed between their bodies and Asher shook with his release, his toes actually curling.

"Jesus, fuck, Asher," Alec huffed and then Asher felt him tense and come as his own orgasm began.

Alec collapsed on him and Asher drew him in even tighter with one arm while he stroked his other hand through Alec's damp hair. He occasionally dropped a kiss to Alec's head while they both worked on calming down from their high.

"I trust you, Alec," Asher whispered, "I know you'll keep me safe."

Maybe Alec needed to hear those words as much as Asher needed to believe them. But he wanted to say them because he did believe Alec would keep him safe—he did trust him.

LESS THAN TWENTY-four hours later, Asher was standing in the terminal of San Diego International. His own phone was back on, and they'd made no secret of their plans, in the hope of giving Asher's hit man his scent. They were at the counter picking up the car paid for, like the flights and everything else, with Asher's credit card. Asher felt his phone vibrate in his pocket and pulled it out. The call was from an unknown number.

He flicked a glance to Alec, who was trying to look confident and untroubled as he nodded for Asher to answer the call. Alec was adorable.

"Hello."

"I'm assuming your bodyguard or someone is with you so let them know this is someone you trust," a voice said. Asher thought maybe he'd heard it before, but couldn't be sure. He smiled and nodded at Alec to let him know the call was okay. He had no idea if he was being watched. "Do it so I can hear," the voice said.

"It's only Kelly. Won't take long," Asher said to Alec and then walked a little distance from him so he could concentrate on the caller.

"I know you're back, and I know you've probably got something cooked up with the cops but, Asher, here's what's going to happen. You're going to ditch them all, and you're going to come meet me—alone, just the two of us."

"Why would I?"

"Because if I don't call the hit man in the next hour, his target will no longer be you; instead, it's going to be little Jack. And I'll only call him if you are standing here beside me, all by your lonesome."

A gasp of air whooshed out of him as the terror struck. At least he'd turned his back on Alec, giving him time to school his features. He couldn't fuck this up.

"Okay," he said. "Where do I meet you?"

"Fletcher Cove, at the viewing deck. I trust you remember the spot. I think it'll be rather poetic to finish you off where the shark started."

"I'll be there as soon as I can."

"An hour. Remember, Asher, or little Jack is the one who'll have to look over his shoulder." And then the line went dead.

Alec was still at the counter talking to the car rental assistant, so now may be the only time he'd be able to get away from him. His life for Jack's was a fair price, as far as Asher was concerned, so there was no question of him doing this.

"Alec, I need to use the restroom," he said as he sidled up next to Alec.

"What did Kelly want?"

"Nothing important. She said she'd been trying my phone for weeks on the off chance I'd answer and finally got lucky. I'll run to the restroom and be right back."

"I'd rather you wait," Alec said, completely ignoring the questioning look the car rental agent was giving him.

"It's safe here, Alec. Lots of people, and they probably haven't even picked me up yet. Come on, my last bit of freedom before you have me on lockdown again." He did his best to smile and wink, but he couldn't imagine it turned out at all convincing, given how violently his insides were churning.

As the rental agent called for his attention, Alec relented and gave him a small nod. Asher moved as quickly as he could to the nearest restroom. He turned and found Alec's gaze on him, so he entered. He waited maybe thirty seconds before he poked his head back out and looked at Alec. His back was turned as he finalized the car rental, so

Asher ran. He tried not to look panicked, tried to run like a traveler late for their charter bus so as not to raise attention.

The cab stand wasn't far from the doors and thankfully it was a quiet evening at the airport. Asher jumped in the first cab he came to and spat out directions to the driver. His heart was thumping and sweat streamed down his back. He'd have given anything for one last goodbye with Alec—one last kiss—but he guessed his memories of last night would be all he'd have to carry him through whatever came next.

Chapter Twenty-Five

ALEC

Alec was equal parts livid and terrified. His pulse was thrumming, and his nerves were frayed. Panic was already wrapping its sinister tendrils around his chest. Soon terror would start squeezing, and then he'd be no good to Asher.

He couldn't believe he'd been so stupid as to let Asher go off alone. The phone call should have sounded alarm bells to him. He knew, as he ran through the terminal, frantically searching, that if something had happened to Asher it would be the finish of him—Alec would never be able to forgive himself.

"Asher," he called, despite knowing his search was fruitless. Security were cautiously approaching him now because of the ruckus he was causing. He stopped running and held his hands up. He wasn't out of breath from his exertions, but his heart was pounding. Two security officers carefully approached him. This would be time wasted but not as much as it would be if he resisted. He was relieved he still had the presence of mind to realize his cooperation would get him out of here faster.

"My name is Alec Banner. I'm former FBI, currently working for a private investigations firm. I've been guarding a client who currently has a hit out on him, and he has gone missing from the terminal. You can call Agent Harry Doyle at the FBI for confirmation," Alec stated loudly and clearly.

The two security officers glanced at each other before turning back to him. "We need you to come with us, sir," one of the officers instructed.

Alec walked between them as they escorted him to their offices, away from the frightened, watchful eyes of the crowds. They lived in a time of mass shootings and terrorism, and any behavior out of the "norm" was viewed with suspicion and fear. He was led into a small interview room where they asked for him to repeat the name of the FBI agent they should call. Alec gave them Harry's name again and his number. One of the officers left to make the call.

"I need to call my partner," Alec said. He should have already called Ben. He'd fucked up again, his panic making him careless. The security officer nodded, and Alec pulled out his phone.

Ben answered quickly. "What's up, Banner?"

"I lost him."

"What?" He could hear the disbelief in Ben's voice. Alec didn't fuck up—usually.

"He got a call, said it was Kelly from his crew. Then he told me he needed to use the restrooms, and I fucking let him go alone. He never came back, and the restroom was empty. Fuck, Ben. I lost him." There was an audible hitch in his voice. This wasn't how this was supposed to go, and damn it, Asher had promised him he wouldn't risk himself, vowed he'd follow instructions.

"All right. His phone's on, right?"

"Yeah."

"I'll get Jacey to track him. He's got his credit cards like we planned, so if he uses one of those, we can track them too. We'll find him. Where are you now?"

"I'm being questioned by airport security...I caused a disturbance," he shamefully admitted.

"Jesus, Banner." Ben huffed. "Get your shit sorted out there. We'll head over to get you, and I'll call if Jacey has something." Ben clicked off. Alec hoped he'd be calling back real soon.

"Okay," the first guard said as he walked back into the room, "so Agent Doyle verified your story, though he did say if the situation wasn't so serious we should chuck your ass in the lockup. As it is, Mr. Banner, we'll ask you to calmly search for your charge and maybe consider calling in SDPD. You're scaring other travelers."

His charge. His fucking charge. Asher wasn't his charge; he was his... Well, he didn't know what he was yet, but he was much more than a job or a charge.

Alec stood and shook their hands. "Thank you. I'll have another walk through and call them if I have no luck."

He took his leave and returned to the main terminal. There was really no point searching here for Asher. If he was still in the airport, he'd be standing right beside Alec. Either someone was here waiting and took Asher, or whoever actually made that call convinced him to ditch Alec. What had they threatened him with? It could only be his family because Asher knew he was already in danger and was prepared to put himself in more to catch these guys. But if they threatened his family...

With nothing else to do until he heard from Ben, Alec walked the length of the terminal. He kept his eyes open, but he knew Asher wasn't here for him to find.

Ben called moments later. Alec almost dropped the phone as he frantically attempted to answer it. "Yeah," he practically screamed.

"Jacey's got him. Heading north approaching Del Mar on the coast. Ethan and I are about five minutes from the terminal. We'll pick you up and follow. I've called SDPD, and they're alerting their officers in the area. Jacey's gonna check airport cameras and see if she can pick up Asher leaving. If we know what vehicle he's in, it'll make trailing him easier."

"Thank you, Ben."

"Save it, man. Just get your ass out front so we can go after this guy, huh?" For the second time, Ben hung up without even a goodbye.

Alec was pacing the curb by the time Ethan and Ben pulled up. Every horrifying scenario of what could be happening to Asher right now had spun through his head while he waited, and it left him nauseous and barely standing. The worst wouldn't happen—it couldn't. Somehow, they'd get Asher back.

"Anything?" he asked as he threw himself into the back seat.

"They've hit heavy traffic on the five, haven't moved much in the last five minutes, at least. Gives us a bit of time to catch up—if we can avoid the jam," Ethan answered. He was driving and held himself in the same stiff manner he always did when he was working. Actually, it was only when Ben and their daughters were around that Ethan ever seemed to relax.

Ethan hit the gas as soon as Alec was in, and they were off. Alec had no idea where exactly, but he trusted Jacey and he trusted these two men, and he had to believe that, together, they'd get Asher back.

"Here," Ben said, reaching over the front seat and handing him a Glock. Ben had always liked Glocks, though Alec preferred a Smith and Wesson, but today he didn't care what weapon he had so long as it did the job of putting down whoever had Asher. He supposed it had been a waste going to get his weapons—there was no way he could have transported them on a flight. But then again, he wouldn't have missed last night with Asher for anything.

"Alec... You know we're gonna do everything we can, but you—"

"He's gonna be fine, Ben."

"Alec—"

"No, Ben. He's gonna be fine, because I can't imagine him any other way, and I can't... I won't be any good to him if I start thinking of him as anything but alive and well and happy." Alec had to hold on to that—he had to.

"I'm gonna turn off the five and head up the one-oh-one. Traffic is clearer and we may be able to get in front of them," Ethan said after a few minutes of silence. "Check the tracking, Ben, see where they are."

Ben ducked his head, the glow of a screen lighting his face. "They've started to turn west on Via De La Valle toward the one-oh-one. Either they're dodging traffic, too, or they're heading somewhere on the coast there."

"Keep your eyes on it, in case they stop," Alec said. "What about the dad, Gerald Fincher? Have we checked on him?"

"Jacey's working on him, too, and SDPD were gonna send a car to check where he's at, but we haven't heard anything yet." Ben's phone started ringing, so he put it to his ear. "Yeah?"

Alec listened to Ben's side of the call, which was mostly grunts and okays before he hung up.

"Okay. SDPD went by daddy Fincher's place, and there was no sign of him. Mother Fincher claims she doesn't know where he is."

So Gerald Fincher was in the wind and Asher was missing. It wasn't hard to figure out what was going on. Fincher had him and was determined to make sweet, innocent Asher pay for something that was his own monster of a son's fault.

"Okay. Looks like they've stopped. Fletcher Cove. Ethan, take a left up here on Plaza."

Complete darkness had fallen by the time they approached what looked to be a public park on the beach some five minutes later. This was about as close as they'd get to Asher's location—he was in this area somewhere, or at least his phone was.

When he opened the car door the sound of crashing waves and the smell of the salty seawater accosted him. It reminded him of the *August Moon* and his time on the boat with Asher. The sharp ache in his chest throbbed. If he lost Asher, he'd never survive the pain.

"Here." Ben handed him an earpiece. "We'll split up, call in if you see anything...and be careful."

Ben headed to the left, Ethan to the right, and Alec walked toward the beach. He did his best to stick to the shadows; he didn't want this to turn into a hostage situation if Fincher saw him coming.

There weren't many people around now that it was dark, which should make it easier to spot them. He made it to the sand and looked left and then right but couldn't see anyone at all. The beach was too open for Fincher to do whatever it was he wanted to do with Asher.

He walked a little way to the right, heading north up the beach. He didn't know how far he'd go before turning around and heading back. The area was a vast space for only three of them to cover.

"Got him," Ethan said softly through his earpiece. "There's a community center north of the parking lot with two small lagoons. They're on the south side of the building at the top lagoon."

It couldn't be far from where Alec was. In fact, he was pretty sure he could make out the community center a little way ahead. He resisted the urge to run because he didn't want to alert Fincher.

As Alec approached from the north of the building, hoping to surround Fincher, he was pleased to note the area was dimly lit. He couldn't see either Ben or Ethan, but he knew they'd be there, somewhere in the shadows.

Harsh voices sailed through the air to him. They weren't loud, just sounded angry, but if he got a little closer, he knew he'd be able to overhear what was being said and who was saying it.

Alec edged along the wall of the building, confident he'd be camouflaged in the shadows of the overhang. There were three figures visible now, and their voices were becoming clearer, the quiet of the night amplifying the sound, making them easily heard from a safe distance.

"Your son was trying to sell my nephew online. What did you expect me to do? Do you have any idea what he put my brother and his wife through? And for what? Money? And now, because he got caught for doing the wrong thing, you want to punish me?" Asher sounded angry and indignant, and Alec wanted to cheer his bravery as much as he wanted to scream at him to not poke the man with the gun.

"My son is an idiot. If he'd just stuck to the plan, we'd have all the money, and he never would have been caught," the deep, angry voice of Gerald Fincher said.

"You were in on it?" There was nothing but shock in Asher's voice, but so far there was little fear or panic.

"I planned it. I had the money and we'd have dropped the kid off safely, but Morgan had the idea of pretending to sell the kid to bump up the price. Human nature. Who wouldn't pay a fortune to keep their grandchild from being sold off to strangers to do god knows what with? But of course, stupidly, he went to the exchange, and you recognized him. This is what happens when you get greedy."

So Morgan Fincher had double-crossed his own father and gone off plan. It didn't seem as though they'd ever wanted to hurt Jack, but did that mean Gerald wouldn't hurt Asher now? There was a big difference between an innocent child and the man you erroneously blamed for your own child's predicament. Alec was fairly certain if someone had the balls to kidnap a child then they wouldn't have too much of a problem hurting someone.

"Alec, you getting this?" Ben's voice whispered in his ear.

"Every bit." So now they understood what was going on, but what were they going to do about it? How were they gonna get Asher out safely?

There were three men in total that Alec could see: Gerald, Asher, and a third man, who was probably Gerald's muscle—maybe even the trigger man. He couldn't see clearly enough to discern what, if any, weapons they had, but he doubted Asher would sit quietly if he didn't have some kind of gun trained on him.

"Yeah, your son got greedy, and he also got what was coming to him. I'm here like you asked, so call your man off. Tell him not to hurt Jack." Asher was pleading now but not for himself. That's how they'd gotten him here. They'd threatened Jack.

"No need to call. This here is the man I hired to kill you. It's amazing how easy it is to put a hit out on someone—and how cheap. Life doesn't mean much these days. I wanted to be here to explain why you have to die so I could watch your face when it happens. At least you'll only die once. My son will be locked up for a long time, and I'm sure this won't be the last time he's beaten for what he did." There was real fury in Gerald's voice, but as far as Alec was concerned, it was aimed at the wrong person.

"Why did you do it?" Asher asked. Alec wondered if Asher was genuinely curious or if he was trying to delay Fincher to give himself a chance to be rescued. "Your father is a partner with my father. I know the kind of money they make. Surely he could have helped you out if you needed it."

"My father cut me off. He said it was past time for me to earn my own keep, but at forty-four, it was too late for me. I was too used to a life of doing nothing. So I thought I'd scam it from your even richer father. After all, he was the one who convinced my father he needed to stop the handouts. My mistake was calling in my foolish, greedy son to help."

Alec could hear Asher's scoff, even from this distance. "Yeah, *that* was your mistake."

"Banner, this is gonna go south real quick if your boy keeps antagonizing this guy. I say we go in," Ben hissed in his ear. Alec knew Ben didn't have his sniper's rifle, but there was no guarantee in this light, and from this distance, a handgun would be accurate. They'd have to all go in, surrounding them and hoping Gerald Fincher wanted no part of a shootout.

"Okay, I've got north," he replied.

"I'm south," Ben said.

"I'll come in from the west," Ethan called in.

To the east was a hill of grass Fincher and his gunman would have to scramble up to escape. The setting gave them a good chance of getting these guys. He prayed, though, that Gerald wouldn't shoot Asher first and worry about getting caught later.

"Call in when you're in position. If shooting starts, watch for crossfire," Alec ordered as he crept farther along the wall of the building. The shadow should offer him plenty of cover until he was close enough to surprise the shit out of these guys.

"Ready," Ethan whispered.

"I'm ready. This is your rodeo, Alec, you say when," Ben responded.

He was close enough now to see Gerald had no weapon in his hand. His shooter did, but he should be easy enough to take out. He should be the only one doing any shooting, so there'd be less risk of friendly fire.

"On three," he whispered. He didn't even get to one when the shooter turned suddenly and opened fire. He was shooting toward the beach—west—where Ethan was. Alec would question why later, but right now he moved. He raised his gun and only then realized he'd been beaten to it. Ben's reflexes—always quicker than everybody else's—and probably his terror for Ethan—had propelled him forward, his own gun spitting fire at the gunman.

Alec ran the short distance to Asher, who'd already thrown himself on the ground. He'd been in enough combat situations with Ben to know he wouldn't miss and hit him with friendly fire from this distance. Gerald Fincher was frozen like a goddamn statue beside him, and the shooter was being propelled backward by the force of the gunshots hitting his body. As he got to Asher and covered his body with his own, Alec looked up and saw Ben striding forward, his gun still emptying bullets. Alec had seen a lot of people shoot before, but none did it with the same calm, ruthlessness of Ben Cronin. He was like a different person, his face a mask of twisted vengeance, in this case, because that asshole had shot at his lover.

Alec stood and trained his weapon on Gerald Fincher, who Alec noted with disgust, had pissed himself.

Alec didn't know why the shooter had started firing toward Ethan. He hadn't heard a sound coming from that direction. What had alerted him to Ethan?

"Ethan," Ben shouted, stealth no longer needed. "Ethan, answer me."

The silence twisted Alec's guts. Jesus, no.

Fincher was blubbering now, and Alec quickly patted him down, making sure there were no weapons he could surprise them with. Asher was slowly getting to his feet, his face turned in the direction of where Ethan should be. Alec turned a little more and saw Ben standing over his unmoving prey, his muscles coiled and straining to move.

"Go. I've got them." Alec barely got the sentence out before Ben was running toward the sand. There was a hedge of bushes separating the community center and the beach, and Ben disappeared in it—and Alec prayed. Not to god because he wasn't a believer, but he prayed to the universe to let Ethan be okay.

"Banner, Banner, Ethan's down. I need help—oh god, Ethan. No. No," Ben's strong voice trailed off in misery. Sirens blared in the distance, and in the black of night, the flashing red of the cherry lights lit up the dark. Somebody had already called in the gunshots.

"I'm already on with nine-one-one," Asher said beside him, closer than Alec thought he'd be. He hadn't even had a chance to connect with him and make sure he was all right. "I'll go and do what I can."

Alec watched Asher as he headed toward where Ben was pleading with Ethan to be okay and promising to kill him if he died. Alec was left alone with a dead hit man and the sniveling coward who'd caused this mess—not to mention his own heart—beating out of his fucking chest.

Chapter Twenty-Six

ASHER

"Get the fuck off me," Ben roared as two cops took him to the ground.

From about thirty yards away, Alec was also shouting, "Alec fucking Banner. I've told you my name at least five times. And if you don't let me go to check on my friends, I'm gonna put you on your ass."

Asher allowed a little chuckle to burst out because of Alec's words. It really wasn't funny at all, but Asher had always subscribed to the "if you don't laugh you'll cry" motto. And right now, he felt like crying. Ethan was hurt, badly from what Asher could tell, and the cops had arrived, adding to the chaos.

He supposed he couldn't blame them for wanting to round everyone up until they sorted out who were the good guys and who were the bad guys, but Ben was giving them no such latitude. At least they'd waited until the paramedics had arrived before they tried to drag Ben away, because Asher was pretty sure Ben had been holding Ethan's blood in with his bare hands.

Asher himself was remarkably calm, given he was sitting with his hands cuffed behind him, one man dead, Ethan—who he hadn't met before but knew was Ben's boyfriend—badly wounded, Ben in a scuffle with the cops trying to cuff him, and from the looks of it, Alec about to get into it with some other cops too. Gerald Fincher, the man responsible for all of this, was sitting a few yards away, pale and quiet and similarly cuffed. Asher would give anything to be able to exchange Ethan for Gerald—he was the bastard who should be lying on the ground full of holes.

He had no idea what had alerted the hit man to Ethan's presence. He hadn't been aware of a thing until the shooting started. And then he'd been completely focused on Alec as he'd run toward him—while the shooting was still going on. Asher's heart had stopped, completely and utterly stopped as he'd watched Alec approach. He'd expected, at any moment, to see a red starburst of blood spray from his chest or his head or somewhere else on his beautiful body.

"Ethan—"

Asher watched as Ben burst out from under the pile of cops and ran for his injured boyfriend.

"Ethan, I love you. I love you, and you better open your fucking eyes right this minute," Ben called as he ran toward where paramedics were still working on his lover. He skidded to a stop virtually on his knees. He was almost lost to Asher's sight, but he could hear Ben repeating over and over again that he loved Ethan, begging him to wake up.

The cops Ben had ditched were approaching again, more cautiously, in concern for the wounded man probably, but still determined to get to Ben.

"Ben," Alec called and Asher turned his wide eyes to his lover as he, too, approached where Ethan was lying. Alec was walking free and uncuffed, so Asher had to assume he'd won his battle with the cops. "Get those fucking cuffs off him," Alec hissed to a nearby officer and pointed at Asher as he walked past where he was sitting. "Ben, Palmer and Leyland are on their way. They've told these guys to stand down."

Ben either didn't hear or didn't care what Alec was saying, because he made no movement or sound at all, from what Asher could see, other than his continued soothing words for Ethan. Behind him, somebody was fiddling with his wrists and then he was free. He rubbed at his wrists to get the blood flowing, though he wasn't cuffed long enough for any real pain.

He slowly got to his feet and moved toward where Ethan was now being loaded onto a stretcher. Ben was at his head, his hands twitchy like they didn't know what to do. Alec was beside Ben now, talking quietly in his ear. Ben was nodding at whatever Alec was saying. Asher stood back, doing his best not to get in the way.

The police had formed their own little group and were talking among themselves, gesturing and pointing at different people or spots. Soon he imagined there'd be crime scene personnel and a multitude of others all over the area.

The paramedics slowly wheeled Ethan away, and naturally, Ben followed, Alec still beside him.

"Asher?" Alec suddenly stopped and called. He sounded a little frantic.

"Yeah?"

Alec patted Ben's shoulder and then walked away from him, toward where Asher stood waiting. He barely broke his stride as he scooped Asher into his arms. Both of them were trembling as they held on to each other. Not a word spoken between them. Alec pulled back and put his hands on Asher's cheeks, looking him over.

"C'mon. Let's go with Ben," Alec murmured and pulled him into his side. Alec left his arm around Asher's waist as they followed the procession heading toward the ambulance. "And, Asher, we're going to be talking about you taking off on me, later."

Asher actually shivered at Alec's tone. Alec was concerned for him and angry because he'd taken off, but Asher knew he'd understand once he explained. Asher hadn't had a choice; he'd had to do whatever he could to save Jack. Though with Ethan the one paying the price, shot and taken away on a stretcher, he felt guilt gnawing on his bones. He should have been the one hurt—the only one.

When they caught up to Ben, they managed to hear the tail end of Ben telling Detectives Palmer and Leyland which hospital he'd be at with Ethan, and he'd be happy to talk to them as soon as his partner was out of danger.

"Asher, good to see you safe and sound. We'll catch up with you all at Sharp Memorial," Detective Palmer said as she turned away from Ben. "Banner, we need you to stay on scene. We'll take you to them once we're done."

Asher wanted to argue with the detectives so badly, and he suspected Alec would, too, but a man had been killed and another seriously injured. Somebody had to explain to the police what had happened. He'd stay and do it, but Alec would get it done quicker. He'd know what information the cops would need, and he'd share it calmly and succinctly.

"I'll stay with Ben, Alec. You should stay and get this done," he urged. There was conflict in Alec's eyes. Alec would want to be there for his friend and for him, but unfortunately, Alec also needed to be here.

Asher was torn too. He really wanted to stay with Alec—in fact, he didn't think he ever wanted to let him out of his sight again—but Ben needed someone now. Ben was Alec's best friend, so he wanted to be there for him if Alec couldn't.

"I'll look after him for you. I won't leave him," he added when Alec remained silent.

Alec took a step closer so they were almost nose to nose, and then he carded his fingers through Asher's hair. "Are you okay?" he whispered.

"I'm okay. I promise. I'm okay," Asher answered. He gently pressed his lips to Alec's, savoring the warmth and the peace the simple kiss gave him.

"All right," Alec said when the kiss broke off. "I'll be there as quickly as I can. Tell Ben..." He faltered, but Asher knew.

"I'll tell him." He gave Alec a last kiss and ran to Ben, who was watching closely as they loaded Ethan into the ambulance.

"Ben..." he said quietly, not wanting to spook him.

Ben didn't even turn in his direction. "Banner has to stay?"

"Yeah, but I'll stay with you." Asher knew he wasn't an adequate replacement for Alec, but he hoped he'd do for now.

Ben remained quiet as they shut the back doors of the ambulance. He stood still, his face lit by the flashing lights, until the ambulance was out of sight.

"Come on, Ben. Let's go." He tried to get Ben moving when he remained motionless.

Perhaps it was his words or maybe the careful touch to his arm, but Ben finally seemed to snap out of it. "Thanks, Asher. Thank you," Ben said, but Asher had no idea what he was thanking him for. After all, he was the one who'd gotten his boyfriend shot. "Car's over here."

"Do you want me to drive?"

"No. I need to be doing something with my hands, or I'm gonna—" Ben sucked in a deep breath, and Asher wondered how he was so calm. If it had been Alec...

"Can I do anything else? Call someone maybe?" Asher asked as they approached a dark sedan.

"Yeah," Ben said, tossing him a phone. "Call Ryan—he's in there under Hot Aussie—and let him know what's happened."

"Ryan's your boss?" Asher asked as he settled in the passenger seat.

"Of sorts. He's also—ah, Jesus." He took another deep breath. "He's also got our kids."

"He's gonna be okay, Ben." Asher almost hated saying the words because how did he know? But what else should he say?

"Damn right, he is. He knows better than to leave me."

Asher smiled at Ben's snarky comeback. Whatever got him through this, Asher was okay with.

He scrolled through Ben's contacts as they peeled out of the parking lot and found Hot Aussie. He hit send and waited for someone to answer.

"Hey, Ben, it's Lucas. Ryan's wrangling the kids. What's up, bud?"

"Um, sorry, Lucas. This is Asher Winsome. I'm calling for Ben. There's been a—" A what? Accident? Incident? Shooting? God, he was no good at being the messenger. For the first time, he felt bad for his old friend Josh who'd been the one who had to call his parents the day the shark nearly got him. "Um...sorry, but I need to let you know Ethan has been shot."

"Fuck. How bad? And where's Ben?"

"We're not sure how bad. Ben and I are on the way to the hospital."

"I'll call from the hospital, Evers," Ben shouted, "once I know more."

"Tell him anything he needs we've got it. Okay, Asher. And tell him the girls are fine, and we're gonna keep them fine until their daddies are back."

"I'll tell him," Asher replied. There'd been a hitch in Lucas's voice, and hearing his sadness only thickened the lump in his throat.

As he was ending the call, he heard Lucas calling out to Ryan. Asher understood relationships—had seen how a good and stable one worked with Kane and Maddy. And now he was seeing it all around him, with Ben's desperation where Ethan was concerned, and Lucas's need for his partner as soon as he'd gotten bad news. All of it screamed to Asher that he was either already in or close to having a relationship with Alec. He desperately wanted him near and he needed to talk to Alec about all that had happened. But did Alec feel the same?

"Lucas said anything you need they'll help you and not to worry about the girls because they are fine."

"The pixies. Ethan's gotta hang around for them, if not for me," Ben muttered.

"The pixies?"

"Our daughters. They lost their mom a while back—cancer. She was Ethan's sister. We adopted them last year." Ben went quiet and then suddenly banged the steering wheel with his open palm. "Fuck. They're not gonna lose one of their daddies too."

Asher reached over and squeezed Ben's arm, offering the little comfort he could. The light touch was enough though, and Ben settled to focus on the road. Asher wanted to call his family, but he'd wait. Right now he needed to concentrate on helping Ben get through this.

The hospital lights brightened the night sky as they reached the end of the block. Ben didn't fuss with looking for a parking spot. He threw the sedan into a spin and parked on the sidewalk in front of a printing business.

"Keep up, Asher," he called as he leaped from the car and took off in the direction of the big red emergency room sign. Asher did keep up; he'd always been a fast runner. In fact, he was right on Ben's heels as they ran into the emergency department.

"Ethan, Ethan?" Ben called. Asher gripped his hand and led him to the desk where a rather harried-looking lady met them.

"Hey. We're looking for Ethan...ah..."

"Stone," Ben interjected.

"He would have been brought in with gunshot wounds a short time ago." Asher finished off.

"Are you family?"

"I'm Ben Cronin, his boyfriend, and don't even think about keeping me out because of some bullshit rules, lady, because I'm listed as his next of kin."

"I wouldn't dream of it, sir." She smiled, not unkindly, and ushered them to a small room with a handful of seats. "He's only just arrived, so he's still being assessed. Please have a seat, and I'll send the doctors in as soon as they can. Drink machine is down the hall and to the left. Cafeteria will be shut now, but the coffee there tastes like dirt anyway so stick with the vending machine."

"Thank you," Asher managed as she left the room. Ben immediately began pacing the room.

"Can I get you anything, Ben?" he asked. Ben shook his head and resumed his pacing. "I'm so sorry about Ethan."

"Not your fault. They threatened Jack. I heard and I'd have done the same thing. I don't know what tipped him off. Ethan didn't make a sound..."

Asher didn't have an answer for Ben and wasn't anywhere near experienced enough in these things to take a guess, so he left it alone. They'd likely never find out because the shooter was dead. What words would be of comfort now anyway?

"I'm going to call my family; they'll be worried." At least Kane and Maddy would. He hadn't really kept his parents in the loop much about what was going on, though he knew Kane had.

Maddy answered Kane's phone on the second ring. "Asher?"

"Yeah. It's me and I'm fine."

"What happened? We were expecting to hear from you, and then Ben called to tell us there'd been a change of plan. Scared the hell out of us." Kane was in the background talking softly, probably telling Maddy to ask him a barrage of questions he really wasn't up to answering.

"I'll explain it all when I see you, but it's over. They got Fincher and the shooter's dead—"

"Dead?"

"Yep. Like I said, long story. I'm at the hospital—I'm fine, but Ethan, Ben's partner, is hurt. He was shot, too, but everyone else is fine." He didn't want to go into detail with Ben standing close by. He wouldn't want to hear the story rehashed right now.

"Oh no. Poor Ben must be frantic. Please let him know we're thinking of them. When will you be here?"

"Not sure, Mads, but I really am fine, so go to bed, and I'll be round sometime tomorrow." They probably wouldn't sleep well until they'd actually seen him for themselves, but he'd promised Alec he'd stay with Ben and he wasn't breaking that.

"We love you, Asher. And we're so grateful for everything you've done for Jack. I'm sorry this has been such a mess for you."

"I'd do anything for him; you know that. I love you guys too." Asher's throat ached where he was getting choked up. They weren't huge on expressing their feelings in his family, but if ever there was a time...

When he hung up from Maddy, Ben was regarding him in a way Asher hadn't seen before. His intent stare was almost like he was sizing him up. "You're good people,

Asher. Alec needs good people." His words quietly trailed off, so Asher barely caught them. Once again, Ben had left him speechless, so he merely smiled and took the seat opposite him.

It always amazed Asher how time slowed down in hospitals, whether you were a patient in one or a visitor. He hoped it didn't work the same way for the staff because what a long work day they'd have.

It felt like days had passed by the time the door finally opened again. Days that had been spent soothing Ben when tears threatened and staying out of his way when the anger came.

"Mr. Cronin?"

"Yes." Ben was already on his feet when the doctor called his name.

"Doctor Milton," he offered and shook Ben's hand then Asher's after Ben introduced them. "Ethan's on his way to surgery. He's sustained three gunshot wounds. Two are not serious—flesh wounds. But the third went through the chest wall and into his lung. The trauma surgeon will most likely insert a chest tube to—"

"I know what a chest tube is. Just...does it look good for him?" Ben's face was pale and drawn, and Asher's heart ached for him.

"It looks very good. Someone will come out and talk to you once the surgery's complete, but he's fit and strong and very lucky. I expect everything to go smoothly. Hang in there."

"Thank you," Ben murmured and resumed his pacing. Asher nodded to the doctor as he left the room and then got back to the business of watching over Ben.

Sometime later, the door pushed open again. "Anything?" Alec asked as soon as he stepped over the threshold. Asher practically leaped into his arms. Alec pulled him against his body, and they held each other tight. Asher reveled in the warmth and strength of the embrace.

"Got his lung," Ben began, his voice quiet and shaky. "They're putting in a chest tube, but the doc seemed confident."

"Jesus, Ben. I'm so sorry," Alec replied.

"No one's fault but the asshole who shot him—and I took care of that fucker." Ben's face twisted into a snarl as he spoke, probably remembering killing the man who'd almost killed Ethan. That man had been a true predator and, unlike Asher's sharks, he hadn't been killing for food or to protect. He'd been killing innocent people for money. People often called sharks monsters, but Asher knew the real monsters.

"Leyland and Palmer have got everything in hand at the scene. Gerald's talking—he's confessed to everything, to anyone who'll listen. I think the reality of what he's done finally caught up to him."

"I hope he rots in hell," Asher blurted. He was still being held loosely in Alec's arms, neither of them seeming to want to put much distance between them.

"Whoa, he's got some bite, Banner." Ben smirked.

"I told you, Cronin. Toughest man I've ever met—yourself included." Alec pressed a kiss into his hair. Asher wasn't fooled by their banter at all.

"Yeah, yeah. I know you've got something to say to me about taking off, so let's get it done, because really, all I want to do is be wrapped up in your arms for—" Oh hell, he'd almost said forever and he wasn't sure they were there yet. It felt right; it felt as though he wanted it forever, but was the admission of his strong feelings too soon?

"Well, this could be awkward, and, oh yeah, I don't have to stay for it," Ben said as he walked to the door. "I'm gonna grab a coffee. Anyone else? No? Okay, well, I'll be back in five—be done by then." And then he was out the door. Leaving him and Alec with five minutes to hash out what he knew would be an ear bashing from Alec.

Alec waited until Ben was out the door and had closed it before turning to Asher. "I know why you did it, Ash. I heard you talking to Fincher. He threatened Jack—"

"He told me he'd send the hit man after Jack instead of me, Alec. I couldn't let anything happen to him. He's just a baby."

Alec put his finger under his chin and tipped his head up. His hazel eyes bored into his, and Asher was entirely captured in this man's thrall. Then when Alec gently kissed him, he happily returned the kiss.

"I understand, Ash. I really do. I wish you'd have told me because we could have worked together, but I know why you did it."

"Next time, I promise I'll tell you," Asher vowed.

"Next time? Are you planning on getting yourself into this kind of mess often then?" Alec smirked.

"God I hope not. I'm not sure I've got the nerve for it."

"Like I said, you're the bravest man I know, Asher Winsome, and I think I'm falling in love with you." Alec held his gaze while Asher attempted to parse his words.

Alec had spoken his thoughts because Asher knew he was falling for Alec too. What he couldn't believe was that his feelings were apparently returned.

"You're falling in love with me?"

"I am. And I'm not sure what happens next, how this will work, but I want to try. I want to keep you...oh god, it sounded better in my head."

"That all sounded fine...perfect." Asher smiled and kissed Alec again because how could he not? They were really going to do this. Asher had no idea how a relationship between them was going to work, but he didn't even care one little bit.

"I don't even know where you live," he blurted and was rewarded with his favorite sound ever—Alec's laughter.

"I've got a place up in McCall on Payette Lake." Alec's voice dropped into the flirty, needy tone he sometimes got—the one that sent shivers up Asher's spine and blood to his cock. "I think I'm ready for a change though...maybe somewhere nearer the ocean." Alec was so close now, close enough he managed to suck Asher's earlobe into his mouth. Was he the most awful person because he was fucking hard in a hospital waiting room? Well he could justifiably blame Alec for his state. He was the one pushing all of Asher's buttons so relentlessly.

"Oh yeah," he drawled, hoping for a bit of payback, though god knew he wasn't much of a flirt. "I will be living *on* the ocean now my house is gone. Will that be near enough for you to maybe test it out...see how you like it?"

"Mm hmm." Alec didn't ease up on him, sucking, kissing and nipping along his throat and at his ear. "I think I'm gonna like it very much."

Alec's hard cock pressed against his thigh told Asher how turned on he was. But Ben would be back any minute, and it was really beyond inappropriate for them to be caught this way, with their raging erections and desperate need for each other on full display.

"Don't scare me like that again, okay?" Alec murmured.

"I really am sorry I scared you." Alec nodded against his neck as he pulled him tighter and then released him.

Almost as though he'd been waiting for their moment to end, Ben suddenly came through the door, coffee in hand.

"All done?" he asked.

"Don't be an asshole, Cronin," Alec huffed.

"Hey, I don't want to interrupt anything."

"Yeah, well we're done—for now." Alec winked at him. He was so damn sexy when he did that, and fortunately for Asher, he winked a lot.

"Why'd he pick Fletcher Cove?" Ben asked out of the blue. "I was thinking about it while I was getting my coffee." He shrugged.

"That's where the shark got me." Asher almost—almost—laughed at the way two heads whipped around to face him so fast with twin looks of horror on Alec and Ben's faces. "Guess Fletcher Cove is definitely a no-go spot for me now."

"Jesus, Ash." Alec pulled him into his arms again, and Asher felt a slight tremble in his body.

"I really need to hear about this shark story. I went toe-to-toe with a rampaging squirrel one time, barely got away with my life, so I can appreciate what it's like when one of nature's fierce predators comes at you. Luckily I was on land. I don't know how I'd go in the water, though...phew."

Asher and Alec both burst out laughing, but Ben's face remained serious.

"What?"

"A squirrel?"

"Yeah. It was a twitchy little fucker. I think he was after the wrong kind of nuts that day." Ben seemed completely serious, refusing to even crack a grin when Asher and Alec kept laughing.

Several hours later, the door opened again, and this time admitted a fairly young woman wearing scrubs. She also wore a smile that Asher took to be a good sign for Ethan's recovery.

"Mr. Cronin?"

"Yes," Ben called and walked to her.

"I'm Doctor Patel. I'm Ethan's trauma surgeon."

Ben shook the doctor's hand before gesturing to him and Alec. "This is Asher and Alec, our good friends. You can speak about Ethan in front of them."

Doctor Patel quickly shook their hands before continuing. "He's out of surgery. We were able to repair his lung without removing any lobes, which is great. His chest tube will remain in situ for a few days at least, possibly a week, until his lung can stay inflated on its own. He'll be on a ventilator overnight, but though it looks scary, it's not, so don't be alarmed when you see him. On the whole, he's a very lucky man, and I expect he'll make a full recovery."

"Can I see him?"

"Right now, if you like." The doctor smiled as Ben shot to the door. "And I see that you do. You gentleman can wait here. Only one visitor at a time for now."

"Thanks," Alec said, "Ben's the one he's going to want there. We can wait. Stay as long as you like Ben."

Ben nodded and followed the doctor out the door. Asher suspected they wouldn't see him again tonight. In fact, they'd very likely need a crowbar to pry him from Ethan's side any time soon.

Chapter Twenty-Seven

ALEC

After Ben left the room, he and Asher settled in for what Alec suspected would be a wait that would at least feel like hours. He needed to call Ryan. He'd already spoken to him when he was still out at Fletcher Cove with the detectives, but he'd promised he'd call back with news on Ethan as soon as he had some. He might as well ease Ryan's mind a little.

"Hey, any news?" Ryan answered. Despite the lateness of the hour, he sounded wide awake. Alec knew Ryan wouldn't let himself rest until he was convinced Ethan was out of danger.

"Yeah, bullet got his lung, but the doctors said he'll be fine. He'll probably be in about a week because of the need for a chest tube, but he should make a full recovery. Ben's with him now."

"Tell Ben we'll be down with the kids tomorrow, and we'll be staying until Ethan's out."

Ryan sounded adamant, but Alec checked anyway. "Are you sure?"

"They need their daddies and their daddies need them. Besides, we can take them to the zoo and SeaWorld. Charlie's really into dolphins right now, so it'll be perfect."

"What about work and Lucas?"

Ryan let out a laugh. "You know I can work from anywhere, and Lucas is between projects. He's not due on his new film set for another month. It'll be fine, Alec."

"Okay. I'll tell Ben. I'm sure he'll be happy to have you all here."

"I bet he's like a lion with a thorn in his paw right about now," Ryan mused, not far off the mark.

"Three cops tried to take him down and cuff him while the paramedics were still working on Ethan. I'd bet money they'll all be walking funny tomorrow." Alec laughed. Ben was...well, he was unique, and Alec was glad he was on his side. Ben Cronin wasn't an enemy you'd want to have.

"Oh, Jesus. He really should come with a warning label. Tell him I'll see him tomorrow, and you and Asher take it easy too."

"Sure thing, boss." He smirked as he ended the call. Ryan didn't like to be called boss at all; he thought of himself as more of an administrative assistant in the company. Ben, on the other hand, well, he'd bought himself anything he could find to remind everyone of his position: Best Boss mugs, a fake-gold statuette proclaiming him Boss of the Year, and one unfortunate bear-cross-lion-cross-cow stuffed toy with a World's Greatest Boss T-shirt on it.

"Was Ryan okay?" Asher asked, bringing his mind back into the little waiting room.

"Yeah. He'll be down with Lucas and the kids tomorrow. I should probably give Cameron a call too. He might want to be here for Ben and Ethan...and Ben does enjoy a fuss being made about him."

"Cameron?"

"Ben's brother. His twin actually, though you'd never guess it. I mean physically they look nothing alike, and their personalities are like apples and oranges."

Footsteps thumped along the hallway before Ben suddenly burst into the room. He was shouting at someone down the hall about going back in when the horror movie was over.

"What happened?" Alec asked, unsure whether or not to be concerned.

"Oh man, they're gonna do something with Ethan's catheter, and I just think—" Ben shuddered. "—well, if I ever wanna touch his dick again, I probably shouldn't be in there to see that."

Alec bit his lip to stop from laughing, but Asher had no such qualms. He let out a full-bodied snort; his laughter was the best sound Alec had heard in a long time.

"Oh, god," Asher gasped. "You're as bad as Kane. He refused to go 'down that end' when Jack was born because he thought he might never want to touch Maddy again if he saw what was happening there."

"Right," Ben agreed. "I mean there should be some boundaries, a few mysteries left in our relationship."

Asher continued laughing and Alec was glad because he knew it'd help him feel a bit better after the night they'd had. He looked at Ben and smiled.

"Goddamn nurse laughed at me, Banner," Ben mumbled. "Told me not to be a pussy. Me? A fucking pussy. She's the one the size of a fucking doll, and she—"

"Probably not a good idea to get into it with Ethan's nurses, Ben. Especially not the ones having anything to do with his catheter," Alec said and all three men winced at his words. "How was he, anyway?"

Ben sobered and turned serious eyes to Alec. "Tube down his fucking throat, one in his chest, one in his fun bit. Hardest thing I ever did was walk in that room and not burst into fucking tears." Ben swallowed down a sob. Alec noticed he was still fighting those tears.

"Ryan and Lucas will be down tomorrow with the kids. And I was about to give Cameron a call. Is that okay?"

"Yeah," Ben sniffed. "I could use some pampering, and butterfly kisses from the pixies wouldn't go astray right about now either."

"Well don't look at me, Cronin. I neither pamper nor butterfly kiss—whatever the hell that is."

"Jesus, Banner. A hug wouldn't go astray though," Ben said with apparently all the effrontery he could muster.

Alec didn't hesitate. He scooped his friend into his arms and held on.

"I thought I'd lost him," Ben mumbled into his chest. Alec dropped a kiss to the top of his head. "Never been so fucking scared."

"I know. I'm so sorry, Ben."

Ben pulled away because apparently cuddle time was over. He glanced at the door, and Alec knew he was itching to get back to Ethan.

"Go on. I'm sure they're done, but make sure you knock first, just in case." He gave Ben the tiniest shove toward the door.

"Thanks, man, both of you. You guys should take off. I'm gonna be in with him all night, so go home. Get some sleep...or get some whatever." He winked. "I'll call Cam. Need to hear his voice anyway."

"Okay. All right. But you call if you need anything," Alec instructed.

"Sure, sure. Go on now."

Asher walked over and pulled Ben to him. Ben flailed about and then relaxed into the hug. "Thank you, Ben. Thank you."

"You got it, shark bait." Ben gave Asher an awkward little punch-shove move. "Go on. See you both tomorrow."

The corridors were probably as quiet as hospitals ever got as he and Asher made their way back to the car. They found it exactly where Ben had left it, half up the curb. Alec chuckled when he saw it.

They belted themselves in, Alec in the driver seat, and looked at each other. "Where to?" Alec asked.

"Let's go to my boat, please. Let's go there for a while, away from all this."

Alec leaned in and kissed Asher's soft lips, savoring the taste. After what had happened, he didn't think he'd ever take it for granted again he'd always have Asher. He knew that, of course. You didn't have the career he did and not know anyone could be lost at any time. Fate was cruel and cared nothing for age or innocence or how much a person was loved. If fate wanted someone, it plucked them straight out of the arms of those who loved them most.

Asher had seemed too good, too wonderful, right from the start. He'd been one of those people Alec could never imagine as being anything but full of life, wild, free, and happy. Gerald Fincher had almost stolen him from this world, though, and Alec wouldn't forget how close it had been, ever. He'd treasure the time they had.

"The *NautiBuoy* sounds pretty wonderful about now." Alec started laughing when a thought occurred to him.

"What's so funny?" Asher asked, watching him curiously.

"I'm just picturing Ben when he hears the name of your boat. He's going to love it." Alec thought again how Asher was so like Ben but without the military past and the streak of danger.

"Ben's um..." Asher trailed off.

"Yeah, he is." Alec supplied, knowing how hard it could be finding the right words to describe Ben.

"Ethan must be a very...patient man."

"Like a fucking saint. But they're perfect for each other. They both had bad experiences they went through, but they found each other, and somehow it works. If you watch Ethan closely, you can see he only ever really smiles when Ben's around. Or their daughters now."

Alec threw the car in gear and drove away from the hospital. He hated leaving Ben behind, but he really needed time alone with Asher. He was still a little shell-shocked that he'd admitted he was falling in love with the younger man. Admitting to strong feelings wasn't his way at all, but then he'd never felt like this before.

"So, how did you and Ben meet?"

"Army. He transferred into my unit. I've never seen someone take to military life as easily as he did. Saved my ass a few times." Alec huffed. He tried not to let those memories infiltrate his mind. They weren't pleasant.

"Something else I have to be grateful to him for because I happen to really like your ass." Asher leered when he looked over at him.

"So this boat of yours? What are we talking here? Tell me I'm not gonna have to squish into one of those tiny fucking bunks like on the *August Moon*." He groaned, remembering trying to get comfortable on that thing.

"Wow, you really are a little precious aren't you?"

"Not precious, but when I lay you out and taste every fucking inch of you before I slowly sink inside your perfect ass, I want *you* to be comfortable." Alec smirked at his own teasing. "But, honestly, Asher, I'll have you wherever the hell I can get you. Just give me any flat surface." He happily gave himself points for his dirty talk.

"Flat surface? Where's your sense of adventure, Alec? Ever done it in the ocean? The waves pounding against you while my cock is pounding that sweet ass of yours. Sand rash on your cheeks—both sets. The sun on your back nowhere near as hot as the tight heat of—"

"Got it. I got it. You win...ocean sex." Alec shook his head. It looked like he'd met his match. "And you've done this?"

"Sure. Oh my sweet innocent, Alec. So much for you to learn." Asher winked...actually winked at him. Sweet? Innocent? Him? Jesus, he'd have to find out more about Asher's past. The thought popped into his head he'd have years to learn everything about his man.

Asher's hand covered his on the stick. "Alec?"

"Yeah," he grumbled.

"None of the wild sex I've ever had compares to sex with you. It might be clichéd, but it's so much better when there's real feelings involved."

Alec didn't think he could drive to the marina fast enough. And what was really shocking was that he realized it wasn't even the sex he was most looking forward to. Of course he wanted Asher desperately, but it would be enough to simply be with Asher alone—fully clothed if needed.

He linked their fingers and drove the rest of the way to the marina with Asher's hand firmly held in his.

Asher's boat was—in a word—stunning. The vessel was at least fifty feet long, maybe closer to fifty-five, and had an elegance and sense of luxury Alec would expect to find in the waters off the French Riviera. Its awesome name adorned the side in bold cursive. Sleek and modern, it looked as though it was designed to cut through the water with grace and style.

Alec was financially comfortable, but this boat was in a different monetary stratosphere entirely.

"Grandparents' trust fund," Asher said, interrupting his thoughts. "In case you're wondering how a marine photographer can afford something like this."

"I kinda was, yeah," Alec confessed.

"They were my mom's folks. Best people I've ever known. Pop was a submariner in the war, and he loved the water. Introduced me to the ocean, actually. When I was in the hospital after the shark attack, he told me a story from his time in the war. He was on leave in Australia, and he and a friend went swimming at the beach. They got chased to shore by a tiger shark. He never lost his nerve, though, and went right back in the next day. It inspired me, and the first time I went in the ocean after the attack, Pop was right there with me."

Asher's eyes were full of loss. Asher didn't exactly have a close relationship with his parents, so it was nice to know he'd at least had a good one with his grandfather. He'd had someone there for him when he was growing up.

"He sounds terrific."

"He was. We lost him a week after Jack was born, and Gran went a month later. Always together those two."

"Happens a lot. One partner following the other soon after, especially if they've been together a long time. It's kinda like they know they can't live without each other."

Asher linked his fingers through his again and squeezed. "Come on. Let me show you around my home."

Asher led him across the gangplank and onto the main deck. There was a table surrounded on one side by built-in chairs. The space was big enough to add sun loungers and hold at least half a dozen people. Asher opened a glass sliding door and Alec walked into a living area more luxurious than he could ever have imagined.

A large mirrored cocktail table was surrounded on three sides by plush white sofas. Two patterned armchairs were on the fourth side allowing a pathway into the area. One side of the sofa backed onto a console table, separating the living area from a six-seater dining table. The chairs matched the pattern of the armchairs. Past the dining area was a well-appointed kitchen and bar area. Everything was of the finest quality, and Alec felt completely out of his depth.

"Asher, this is..."

"Don't let it bother you, Alec. This was a gift from my grandparents, really. I didn't earn it, and it doesn't define me. If I hadn't dreamed of one day living on the ocean permanently, the money would be rotting away in a bank, and I'd be living in my modest little house at Coronado Cays. Well...if it hadn't burned down."

Alec still couldn't stop his amazement at what he saw. He was sure he must have looked a fool with his mouth gaping open.

"The point is, Alec, I don't need luxury or fancy, and I don't want you to think you need to compete with all this, because there's no way I could if it wasn't for Pop and Gran."

Alec had seen how Asher lived on the *August Moon*—and it wasn't in luxury. The boat was intimidating, sure, but Asher wasn't. Alec knew the kind of man Asher was, and he was definitely one he wanted to get to know a whole lot better.

"Can you drive this by yourself?" Alec asked walking further into the cabin.

"I can *sail* it alone if I have to, but I don't. I usually take her out with friends—you've met some of them already." Asher smiled.

"Oh...your crew."

Asher fully laughed then. Alec had liked Asher's crew very much, even if they had scared him a little to start with. He was still looking forward to a Ben and Kelly meet up.

But, he quickly forgot about Asher's crew as he looked over at him and was struck by how beautiful he looked caught in the moonlight. Alec needed to touch him. He knew he was safe, the danger had passed and Asher had been unharmed, but it had been too close.

"C'mere," he whispered. Asher moved willingly into his arms, and Alec let himself relax into their kiss. He'd never felt so at ease with someone physically before, like he didn't need to *think* while he was with Asher but instead could relax and enjoy the intimacy. Asher's arms snaked around him, one hand dipping to cup his ass, and Alec moaned at the sensation.

He wanted to get Asher to a bed; he really did, but the kitchen countertop looked damn good, and it was nice and close. As he deepened the kiss, he walked Asher backward until his back was flush against the fridge. He reached down, circled Asher's wrists, and lifted his arms above his head, pinning them to the fridge.

"Don't move them," he instructed and then released Asher's wrists and sank to his knees. He stretched his arms up Asher's body under his shirt, as high as he could reach, and slowly scraped his fingertips back down, enjoying the feel of Asher's hard body squirming.

When he reached the waistband of Asher's jeans, he popped the button and slowly dragged the zipper open.

"Alec..."

Alec looked up into Asher's gray eyes—eyes that drove him fucking crazy—as he peered back. He looked so needy, so beautiful, and so fucking perfect. He winked and bent his head back to his task. He slid his hands into Asher's jeans and wrapped them around his ass, giving his cheeks a squeeze before slowly dragging the denim down over his perfect ass.

Asher's hard cock popped free and bounced against his stomach. Alec could smell his arousal, so potent right there, and he hardened even more. He dipped his head lower and sucked Asher's balls, one at a time into his mouth, relishing the heavy feel of them on his tongue. He heard Asher's soft moans above him and feel his body writhing beneath his hands where they were gripping Asher's hips so tightly. Alec was quickly losing his control.

He was acutely aware there wasn't going to be soft, sweet lovemaking—this time. He'd nearly lost Asher, and Asher's need for connection felt as strong and urgent as his own. Alec closed his lips around Asher's cock and pushed down his length, touching the back of his throat with the tip until he gagged. Didn't matter. He needed. He needed so badly to be in Asher, for Asher to be in him, for them to be joined in some way so he knew he was still here, still alive. He had to know he hadn't lost his chance with this beautiful man. He dragged his lips back up and then down again.

Neither was going to last if he kept this up. He let Asher's cock slip from between his lips, dropping a gentle kiss to the tip before he stood.

"Supplies?" he asked.

"Top drawer, bathroom to the right. I'll go."

"No." Alec pressed his lips to Asher's in a hard and fast kiss. "I want you naked and bent over that countertop when I get back." He smiled at Asher's shocked—and wanting—expression as he walked away.

He found the bathroom easily enough. Condoms and lube were exactly where Asher had said. He caught a brief glimpse of himself in the mirror and was stunned by his reflection. He'd never seen himself look so happy, so...what was it...? So alive.

It took only moments, but by the time he got back to the main cabin, Asher was exactly where Alec had told him to be. He didn't have a stitch of clothing on, and he was lying with his torso flat to the granite surface of the kitchen counter. He was watching Alec from over his shoulder.

"Jesus, Ash. You're so...so fucking gorgeous." Alec didn't think he'd seen anything more erotic or enticing than the way Asher looked right then. He almost wished he could take a photo. He watched him for a moment, committing the perfect image to memory.

Alec tossed the lube and condom on the counter and fumbled to get himself as naked as Asher. As soon as he was, he stepped behind him, pressing kisses along his spine, all the way down to his ass. He nipped at Asher's fleshy cheeks and reached for the lube. He blindly drizzled some on his fingers and pressed them to Asher's hole.

Asher wriggled back against his fingers and moaned as Alec sank them inside. God, he was so responsive; everything about Asher was so perfect for him. He worked his fingers inside and then leaned over him to nibble at his ear. His body was pressed flush along Asher's back so he could feel him trembling.

Alec's own need was bordering on desperation. "Asher, I..."

"I'm ready, Alec. Please. Fuck me."

How the hell could he say no? He gently pulled his fingers from Asher's body and then rolled on a condom. He grabbed Asher's hips and eased his aching cock inside. He may be desperate to fuck Asher, but he'd never hurt him.

Asher moaned and wriggled back, taking the rest of Alec inside. Alec rested over his body and waited, giving him time to acclimate. He kissed the familiar trail down his spine as he waited for Asher to adjust. Those knots of bone down Asher's back might be his new favorite place to kiss.

Alec gave a tentative thrust, and when Asher moaned in response, he did it again and again and again. He gripped Asher's hips for leverage and pumped into him. Every movement made better by the tight squeeze of Asher's ass around him and the desperate little moans falling from his mouth.

Lost to the pleasure, but unable to get enough purchase in this position, Alec spun them and pushed them both to the floor before shoving back in. Their knees would ache later, but he needed—they needed more.

"Oh, god, yes," Asher moaned and Alec relaxed, knowing Asher wanted this as much as he did.

Asher was on all fours, with Alec leaning over his back, one hand on the floor by Asher's shoulder. His other arm was looped around Asher's chest, giving the purchase needed. He was humping into Asher as he lost control. This was an animalistic coupling born of desperate need, and Alec had never felt urgency like it.

"Fuck, fuck, fuck. Oh, god, Alec."

Asher had taken one hand off the ground so Alec knew he'd be stroking his cock.

"I'm gonna come so hard in you, Ash." He groaned, the sound pulling his orgasm from him. His entire body shook and throbbed as he came. The sensation was overwhelming, brutal in the pleasure it gave him. Beneath him, Asher was grunting and shaking as he found his release too.

Asher went to his elbows, and Alec followed him down, breathing hard. His entire body felt wrung out but incredibly sated. With a last burst of energy, he pressed a kiss to Asher's head, gently pulled out, and stood. He went to the bathroom to get rid of the condom. He grabbed a towel, wetting the corner so he could clean them both off. On his way back, he grabbed a throw rug and pillows from the sofa, knowing once he was on the floor again he wouldn't be moving for a while.

When he returned to the kitchen, Asher was on his knees, reaching up to hold onto the counter. He tossed the pillows on the ground and encouraged Asher to sit back. He cleaned him as tenderly as he could manage, knowing he'd been rough with him.

"I'm sorry if I was too rough, Ash," he whispered.

Asher put his hands on Alec's face and drew him down so he could press his lips to his. "It was awesome—you were awesome. Alec, I loved it," he said with complete earnestness.

Alec tossed the towel when he was done and sat beside him. He pulled Asher to him and threw the rug over them. He pressed a kiss to the top of Asher's head and allowed himself to relax.

"Comfortable?" he asked.

"Yeah."

"Thank god, because I don't think I'll be able to move for a while."

Asher laughed. "Me neither... Alec that was... Do you think it'll always be like that between us?"

Oh, lordy, he hoped so. "Maybe. Though if it is, I'm not sure how we'll get anything done." They both giggled—and at almost forty, Alec didn't think he'd be capable of giggling, but there it was.

They were quiet for a while, so long Alec thought Asher might have drifted off until he softly asked, "We can make this work, can't we? You and me. Because I want that, Alec. I want it so bad."

"Yeah, we can. I think you and I can do anything together, Ash. Anything."

Asher nodded against his chest, and he pressed another kiss into his hair. Asher's manbun he was so fond of wearing had come loose, and his hair cascaded around his shoulders, occasionally tickling at Alec's nose. He knew he was so close to being in love with his wild and free man, but something held him back—maybe fear. Fear he would love Asher and lose him.

Chapter Twenty-Eight

ASHER

Somehow they'd found their way to bed last night, though Asher's memories of getting there were murky. Asher had never experienced the kind of blissed out feeling he'd felt last night. After he'd come so hard, he'd felt relaxed and peaceful. Asher had enjoyed good sex before but being with Alec was something else entirely.

Despite the ridiculously early hour, they were already on the move. Neither of them, apparently, was the type to sleep in. Alec was itching to get to the hospital to be with Ben and check on Ethan if his constant movement and glances at his watch were any indicator. One day he'd love to spend a lazy morning in bed with Alec, but today he settled for a shared shower and hand jobs.

Visiting hours weren't until ten, so Asher was driving them to Kane and Maddy's. Beside him, Alec was stoically silent—and Asher had already had enough of it.

"Hey, something wrong?" he asked without taking his eyes off the road.

Alec seemed to startle at the question. "Huh... Oh, no. No, nothing at all."

Asher rolled his eyes, wishing Alec would see it. "Come on, Alec. You've hardly spoken all morning. Do you... I mean, do you have regrets about us?" God, it hurt even to ask the question; he couldn't imagine the slice of pain that'd rip through him if Alec actually admitted to having regrets.

"What? No. Oh, god, no. Ash, I'm so sorry. I didn't mean to give you that idea. Last night was wonderful. We, the two of us together, are wonderful."

"Then what's wrong?" If they were going to do this relationship thing, then Alec had to be prepared to be open and honest with him because he couldn't see how it'd work otherwise.

"It's stupid, really. But I... I can't stop worrying about losing you. I'm terrified I'll love you, and then somehow I'll lose you," Alec muttered.

Asher understood where Alec was coming from. He'd thought about losing someone so close since Jack's kidnapping. The scenario was something that had kept him lying awake night after night. "I've thought the same way, especially about having kids after what had happened to Jack. I don't know if I'm strong enough to survive if I had kids and then lost them. Or if I love you and somehow lose you."

Asher kept his eyes fixed on the road. As much as he wanted to look at Alec now so he'd understand the truth of his words, sometimes it was easier to say what needed to be said without looking, especially if it was a depth of feeling you weren't used to acknowledging.

"Alec, I am falling so desperately in love with you—and yes, that scares the hell out of me. But everything in this life is a risk, particularly the things that mean the most. We can't let fear keep us from doing the things we love or being with the people we love." Asher gripped the wheel tighter and took a steadying breath. "Do you think I'm not afraid whenever I get in the ocean with the sharks?"

"You sure seem unafraid," Alec answered, and Asher allowed himself a little laugh at his pouty tone.

"Well, I am scared, terrified some days. But I love doing what I do. I love being in the water, and I love the sharks. So, yes maybe for a few moments I'm frightened, but then I look around me, and I know there's nowhere else I'd rather be. No other job I'd rather be doing. And then it's all so worth that momentary fear."

Alec sat quietly for the remainder of the trip and Asher allowed him the time to consider what he'd said. Besides, he had his own fear to deal with. Alec had admitted he was afraid. There were no guarantees he wouldn't run and then it would be Asher left without him, only a broken heart for company.

"Asher Charles Philip Arthur George Winsome. About time you got your ass here," Maddy called from her front yard when they eventually pulled up at their house.

"What the hell?" Alec asked.

"Don't start. Mom was obsessed with Prince fucking Charles when I was born. At least I got Asher for a first name." He laughed because, ugh, he'd always hated his other names, but Maddy had always loved pulling all of them out when she was mock angry with him.

She was marching toward them now, hands on hips in pretend outrage, with a giant smile on her face. Kane was several feet behind her with Jack and Maxy trailing alongside.

Asher met her halfway and scooped her into his arms. She felt good, like warmth and family. "Glad you're safe," she whispered into his ear. He held her a little tighter.

Maddy released him and turned to Alec. "It's over?"

"It's over," Alec agreed.

"And your friend who got shot?" Maddy stepped the short distance to Alec as she spoke.

"Ethan will be fine."

"Thank god." She pulled Alec into one of her hugs, and Asher was pleased to see he went willingly. "Thank you." Asher heard her whisper the two words to Alec.

"I'll never let anyone hurt him." Alec's voice hitched a little with his promise.

Kane and Jack had joined them by now, and Asher hugged his brother, the feeling he'd come close to losing all this suddenly swamping him, weakening his knees. Kane held him tight, held him up.

"Come on. We're all here, all safe, and Jack and Kane have been whipping up a delicious breakfast. Let's go in and enjoy," Maddy said from beside them.

The little group walked together into the house with Jack excitedly explaining how he'd helped flip the bacon and scramble the eggs. Asher noticed he kept a wary eye on Alec, which was reasonable. The little boy would probably always be wary around strangers.

"Granny said I made the best eggs," Jack finished and Asher registered what he was saying.

"Mom and Dad are here?" he asked anyone who'd answer.

"Yeah. They're trying, Ash." Kane replied.

His parents were trying. They hadn't tried too hard in the days and weeks following Jack's kidnapping. In fact, their relationship had gotten back to the status quo pretty quickly, but now maybe they were changing.

Regardless of whether or not they really were trying, Asher was in no mood to fight with his family. He was still so fucking blissed out and he only wanted peace and love. He sniggered as he imagined himself as some sort of Woodstock-going hippy.

Asher made sure to link hands with Alec before they walked inside. He wanted to be honest from the get-go that he and Alec were together.

Phyllis and Edmund Winsome were sitting like a couple of austere statues at the dining table when they all walked back inside. The façade crumbled a little when their gaze landed on Asher, and for the first time in a very long time, Asher entertained hope for his parents; maybe they'd be able to change.

"Asher, thank god," his mother said as she stood and pulled him into her arms. It was the first hug Asher could remember, and he realized, in a small way, even Alec was in on the embrace with their hands still joined. The hug felt family-like—and good.

There was no hug from his father, but there was a brief handshake and acknowledgement he was happy Asher was still alive. This civility was a good start.

Neither of his parents acknowledged Alec, but rather than jumping down their throats, Asher took hold of Alec's hand that he'd dropped to shake his father's and decided to try to make an effort too. "Mom, Dad, you remember Alec, of course…"

"Yes. Of course we do. Thank you, Alec. Maddy and Kane have explained everything that happened…and I'm sorry, Asher, we didn't make ourselves approachable so you could come to us with what's been happening. Your father and I…well, we're trying." His mother was watching Alec as she spoke, her gaze drifting to their joined hands, her eyes flaring a little as comprehension settled in.

"You should both know he and I are together now. We're a couple." Asher stood tall and proud and suddenly realized he hadn't even had to think about it—he was proud of being with Alec.

"He's a good man, Asher," his father said. "You're both lucky to have each other. I know I've been harsh on you because of your choices but when I look at the Finchers and what they've done, what they're putting Piers through... Well, you may not have wanted the career I would have picked for you, but you worked hard to make a success out of the one you chose, Asher. And I was wrong not to be proud of that—of you."

"Um, thanks, Dad," he muttered. "That means a lot." He was admittedly a little stunned by the unexpected words coming from his father.

Six adults and a four-year-old boy stood around looking at each other, each waiting for someone to, hopefully, break the silence, but it was such an unusual scene that nobody seemed to know what to do or say. Even his mother, who usually took the lead in social settings, seemed to be fumbling for something to say.

"Alec, has he told you about the tiger shark and the tongs yet?" Kane blurted out and then shrugged his shoulders when Maddy slapped his arm.

"Thanks, Kane," he laughed. It wasn't exactly how he would have wanted to get the conversation flowing as they sat down to breakfast together, but it worked.

THEY DIDN'T MAKE it to the hospital until after eleven. Alec had called Ben, who'd told him Ethan was taken off the ventilator early this morning and was breathing on his own. From Alec's whispered words, Asher got the impression Ben had been crying as they spoke—not that Asher could blame him. He got teary from imagining it was Alec in there.

Ben met them in the lobby. He looked haggard and drawn, as though he hadn't slept at all, which was likely, but there was a spark behind his eyes that told Asher Ethan was improving every second.

"Hey, come on through. We've appropriated one of the waiting rooms back near ICU. Everybody arrived this morning, and Ethan still can't have more than one visitor at a time in with him. Cam's in there now giving him hell for scaring the bejesus out of me." Ben turned and winked.

"Ryan and Lucas were here early this morning with the kids, but they're gonna head out soon and take them back to the hotel—they're staying at the Del Coronado. Pools and beaches and kids club and all that. Far more interesting for the kids than being here," Ben continued.

Asher watched as Alec reached out and squeezed Ben's upper arm. "Are you all right?"

Ben stopped to face him. "I will be now. He's awake and talking and knows who I am. That's all I need."

Ben turned to keep walking, and he and Alec followed quietly behind. Alec reached for his hand again, and Asher willing surrendered to his firm grip.

The waiting room was only small, even smaller with all of the large men assembled in there. Three little kids were running around the men's legs, with happy smiles on their little faces. They weren't exactly being quiet and when the noise increased, one of the men turned and called out, "Maya, Riley, enough now. Come and do some coloring." He was an extremely good-looking man, and Asher knew he recognized his face from somewhere, but at the moment couldn't place him. The two little girls came over to him immediately, the younger boy following close behind them. The man squatted and faced the little boy dead on. He tenderly stroked his cheek and then began moving his hands in front of the child's face. He was signing to him, so Asher recognized the child was deaf.

Despite their rambunctiousness when they'd first walked in, the man had no trouble quieting the children and settling them on the floor with their colors. A younger man, maybe in his early twenties, came and joined them. He sat on the floor, and the little girls immediately climbed as close to him as they could get before they began coloring.

"Alec," the third man in the room said and approached them. "So glad you...and Asher are both okay." He hugged Alec briefly and then held his hand out to Asher. "I'm Ryan Lowe."

"Asher Winsome. You're Alec's boss?"

"I wouldn't call him that, Asher. Ry hates being called the boss." The gorgeous man who'd wrangled the kids said as he approached. "Think of him as the guy who pays the wages and tries to tell these clowns what to do," he added fondly.

"That's my partner, Lucas Evers. Ignore his smart mouth—and no, Luke, we're in a hospital, so don't turn it into something dirty." Ryan pressed his lips to Lucas's as though he might need further encouragement not to say anything inappropriate.

"Over there, sensibly staying out of things is Zach. He's my brother's fiancé," Ben continued. Asher looked across at Zach who gave him a shy smile and a wave before turning his attention back to the children sprawled around him. "Those little pixies are my girls, Maya and Riley, and the little champ with them is Charlie. He's Ryan and Lucas's son."

Asher felt a little overwhelmed in the group. He could tell they were close and he made a note to himself to ask Alec how they'd all made their way to each other.

"I'm sorry about Ethan," Asher said to the room in general. He knew Ethan was important to them all because they'd dropped their lives to be here for him. Apologizing for Ethan's shooting seemed the right thing to do.

"No need for you to apologize, Asher," Ryan said. "We know where to lay blame, and it isn't with you. Hopefully Gerald Fincher will get the justice he deserves."

"I'm gonna pop in and see how things are going with Ethan and Cam. Don't go anywhere till I get back," Ben said before he quickly left the room.

Asher wandered over toward where Zach was on the ground with the children, while Alec drifted closer to Ryan and Lucas. The only experience he had with children was Jack, but he felt it was a good start.

"Hey, that's Moana, right?" he asked as he slid down to sit on the floor with Zach and his following of little ones.

One of the twin girls turned toward him, looked him up and down, but clearly found him wanting as she turned her head back to her coloring without answering him. It's always humiliating to be brushed off in social situations even if it's a four– or five-year-old doing the brushing. Asher felt his cheeks heating and considered getting back up and moving away but running away seemed even more humiliating.

"Yeah. Moana's the best," a small voice answered, but it came from the other twin.

You only had moments to establish rapport with kids before you lost their interest, so Asher thought hard. He'd seen the movie with Jack, and he wracked his brain for something to say—some comment which would make him acceptable in the young eyes of these twin girls.

"I kind of liked the rooster...can't think of his name, but he was funny."

"Heihei was funny."

Asher let out a sigh of relief because he hadn't totally fucked it up. "My name's Asher. It's real good to meet you."

"Our daddy got shot." The first twin turned to him again, her enormous blue eyes watching him with the kind of truthfulness only children possessed. "He's not our real daddy, but we think he's real and we love him lots."

"I'm very sorry about your daddy. I think he's going to be okay, though."

"Oh, we know he is because Benben told us he would be."

Asher flicked a glance at Zach, who was quietly watching the interaction. "Benben?"

"That's Ben," Zach answered. "It's leftover from when they were very little. It's good to meet you, Asher."

"And you."

The girls turned back to their coloring, quickly losing interest in Asher. Zach was still watching him though.

"Cameron told me you film sharks, and you were almost eaten by one. That must be... I don't know? Scary? To get back in the water with them, I mean. Obviously when you were almost eaten would have been terrifying."

Asher laughed. Had he ever meet someone who didn't have that reaction to his chosen career? "Can be. They're beautiful creatures, really. Ask Alec. I think I've converted him."

"I've only been to the beach once, but it was beautiful. Cameron and I are getting married soon, and we're going to honeymoon in Australia. I plan to visit lots of beaches there."

"Oh, yeah? Australia's a gorgeous country. I've been a few times to film their great whites. They've got some good cage diving off the coast of South Australia."

"Cage diving?"

"Yeah. So ah, you basically hop in a cage in the water so you can see the sharks. But you're safe in the cage." Asher had a vague memory of Alec telling him Zach had grown up in some kind of fanatical cult, and he was pretty naïve about the world.

Zach sat up a little and turned to face Asher more straight on. "So you can be in the water with the sharks? That sounds amazing."

"It is. Maybe you and Cameron could fit it into your honeymoon plans. I can suggest some places, if you like."

"Really? That would be awesome. Cameron's going to kill me for this," Zach answered with a wink.

"You're not causing trouble over here, Asher, are you?" Alec's smooth voice caused funny flipping and flopping in his stomach as it usually did.

"Just trying to convert another shark lover."

"I'm going to take Cam cage diving on our honeymoon," Zach proudly announced.

"Oh, Jesus," Alec groaned.

"Can you watch the children for a second while I go to the bathroom?" Zach asked, standing as he did.

"Sure," Asher replied. It would only be for a few minutes. He could do that. Especially now that Alec sat beside him and twined their fingers together.

Asher looked around the little waiting room, his gaze briefly stopping on every man and child in there. "Quite a family you've got, Alec," he murmured.

"I'm a lucky man."

Asher lifted their joined hands to his mouth and pressed a gentle kiss to Alec's knuckles. "I think we're both pretty damn lucky. And I plan on keeping that luck forever if I can."

He looked into Alec's beautiful hazel eyes, the green in them so noticeable today. He squeezed Alec's hand because he couldn't lose this.

"So do I," Alec whispered.

Epilogue

THE FLICKERING LIGHTS of the sparklers lit up the night sky as the guests waved them through the air. Some created patterns with theirs while most waved them randomly as they cheered the two men walking hand in hand through the pathway the crowd had formed. It made the night seem as beautiful and magical as it deserved to be.

Asher was beside him, madly swirling his sparkler. His man was laughing and cheering as loudly as anyone, even though he'd only known the grooms for several weeks. Ben was to his right babbling to an almost fully recovered Ethan about how adorable their twins looked. Lucas and Ryan were across from them, with Charlie perched on Lucas's shoulders waving and smiling.

Alec watched Zach and Cameron as they went by. Their gazes flickered around their guests, but more often than not, they came to rest on each other. Alec understood. It was difficult for him to look anywhere but at Asher most of the time.

In the weeks since the events at Fletcher Cove, Alec's life had changed completely. He'd rented a little place in Chula Vista so he could be close to Asher, but he was seriously considering giving up the lease. He didn't think he'd spent more than five nights there. The majority of his days and nights were spent with Asher on the *NautiBuoy*. And Alec was learning to love it.

They had both taken time off work but were both due back in the coming week. Alec wasn't quite sure how he'd manage going from being near Asher practically twenty-four seven to days, maybe even weeks, apart. Just the thought of the separation made him sick. He wondered if he'd go through some kind of withdrawal.

"Hey, you with me?" Asher asked. He was speaking close to Alec's ear so he could hear him over the noise. Alec shivered as Asher's breath tickled the fine hairs on his skin.

"Sorry, I wandered off for a second." Zach and Cameron were well past them now, and many of the guests were slowly filling in the pathway and following them toward their waiting car. It left him and Asher standing alone.

"I know. Your sparkler drooped, and I could tell you were gone."

Alec had forgotten about the sparkler in his hand and looked down to see he held nothing but the burned remnants of the sparkler stick in his hand. Asher was watching him, his gray eyes almost black in the darkness left behind now the sparklers had fizzled out.

Asher's warm hand gently touched his cheek. "Where'd you go?"

"I love you, Ash." He was sure it wasn't the answer Asher was expecting, but he hoped it might be one he wanted. They hadn't quite gotten to these words yet, though they both knew it to be true.

"I love you too. And, god, that feels good to say. I love you, Alec Banner, more than anything." Asher's smile was beaming and genuine, the kind of smile that couldn't be repressed. Even without his words, Asher's smile would have been enough for Alec.

"I love you so much, and I've been thinking about us and our living arrangements and going back to work.

Everything's going to change. We won't see each other as often, and I need you to know I love you. I need you to remember how much while you're away from me." He pulled Asher to him and folded him into his arms. God, he'd miss this.

"I've been thinking about it too. And you know it seems pretty silly to me that you're paying so much money for a little apartment you're hardly ever at anyway. So I was kinda hoping you'd maybe want to move onto the boat with me?" Asher's voice was muffled against his throat, but Alec heard him.

His heart was thrumming. He was getting everything he'd ever wanted; he wasn't sure that was fair, but he sure as hell wasn't turning it down. He pulled away from Asher and looked into his gorgeous face. "You mean I could be your live-in cabin boy?" He winked and tried to look sexy.

"Oh, god. Okay, if that's your kink, I can go with it. Yes, Alec, I want you to be my live-in cabin boy." Asher laughed and, as always, it was the best sound ever.

"I'll move in as soon as we get back. McCall's a lovely place to live, and Chula Vista is okay, but I can't wait to get back to the ocean. Seems you've converted me."

"They always say there's no place like home, wherever that may be."

About the Author

Karrie lives in Australia's sunshine state with her husband and two sons, though she hates the sun with a passion. She dreams of one day living in the wettest and coldest habitable place she can find. She's been writing stories in her head for years but has finally managed to pull the words out of her head and share them with others. She spends her days trying to type her stories on the computer without disturbing her beloved cat, Lu, curled up on the keyboard. She probably reads far too much.

Email: author@karrieroman.com

Twitter: @karrie_roman

Website: www.karrieroman.com

Other books by this author

Saved
Advent Adventure
Shipped
New Year's Shippin' Eve
Sentinel
Trusted

Also Available from NineStar Press

Connect with NineStar Press

Website: NineStarPress.com

Facebook: NineStarPress

Facebook Reader Group: NineStarNiche

Twitter: @ninestarpress

Tumblr: NineStarPress